I0773560

Firefly

Firefly

by Suzannah Blattner

ISBN: 979-8-9863636-0-8 (Paperback)

ISBN: 979-8-9863636-1-5 (eBook)

Any references to historical events, real people, or real places are used fictitiously. Names, characters, and places are products of the author's imagination.

Front cover image by Angela Seo.

First printing edition 2022.

Psithurie Press

to Michelle —

my constant

ELEMENTARY SCHOOL

"You're already home

where you feel loved,"

The Head and The Heart

One

THE EVENING AFTER my world collapsed, my head brought me back to the day we met. And the look in his eyes when they met mine.

The sun beat down on my shoulders. I remember wiping my brow and looking down at my sweat-soaked palm. That August day didn't promise us a thunderstorm like most did, so we were forced to spend our recess outside running around lethargically, playing tag, and avoiding getting near the sandbox that radiated heat. I tucked myself away in a corner to avoid the sun's glare and my classmates' screams.

Oda sat next to me, perched on the side of the garden box that sat at the edge of the yard. She begged me to go play tag with the others, pulling on my arms and whining. Her complete disregard for the heat made me want to slap her. I kept shaking my head and looking back at the clock at the front of the school building, counting down the minutes until I got to go back into the gloriously air-conditioned classroom. Oda finally gave up on me and ran off to go play tag with the rest of the kids in our class. I settled back in my chair,

switching my gaze between the clock and my classmates.

As I waited for lunch to end, a scene took place
about five yards away from me. A girl, who I knew as the
daughter of one of my mom's good friends and my dad's
boss, stood over a small boy who looked strangely
unfamiliar to me. The girl, Hally, sneered at the boy and
then turned to her friend behind her. Something about
her eyes held the poor boy down. He couldn't move
away and she hadn't even laid a finger on him. The boy
grimaced and his fingernails scraped desperately at the
asphalt as he tried to back away from her.

It was quite odd for there to be someone in school I
didn't recognize. The closeness of our small town didn't
allow for much anonymity. News traveled fast.
Although, I did know someone this boy could be. Over
the summer, I heard my mom mention that a woman
and her son had moved in just a couple of blocks away
but, for some reason, my town didn't treat them the
same way they treated other people that moved here.
Usually, the busybodies in the neighborhood organized
a large gathering and the new people in town would be
paraded around by their neighbors for everyone to
meet. No event had been organized for this boy.

I mulled it over as I watched them until the boy
turned his head and caught my eyes with his. They were
tired, unlike those of any kid my age, and full of fear and
forsaken optimism. That look in his eyes will forever be
engraved in my mind. Those vivid green eyes that would
become so familiar, but in that moment, stricken with
an emotion which, soon, I would no longer recognize in
him. Not after that day. Not for years after that day. Not

as long as his eyes were filled with hope. Not as long as we could be together.

As Hally skipped away with her friends, I peeled my damp thighs off the plastic of the chair and walked over to the boy. Something about his desperation made my heart ache and our town's disdain for him made me want to talk to him even more. I stuck out my hand to him, "I'm Tori."

He took my hand and shook it. "I'm Quentin."

ALMOST A YEAR AFTER we met, we took a bike ride. It was nearly dusk when we set out. The sun had just gone below the horizon, but if I squinted my eyes just right, the vibrant colors of the sunset didn't blind me, they faded into the greys and blues of the night. I pushed harder with every circle around the pedals to go faster up the hill. The wind blew across our faces, and we let out whoops as our bikes accelerated up the hill. My long brown hair, which my mom always tried to braid, and I refused to let her touch, flew out behind me and got in my eyes as I turned corners. The sky continued to change and the tiny lights on our handlebars became the only lights in our path.

"Hey wait up!" Quentin yelled from behind me.

"You have to catch me!" I laughed, my voice echoing back to him.

His strained breaths appeared next to me and, with a grin, I forced myself to pedal even faster. We slowed as we turned the corner, just enough to wave at our friend Oda, who sat on her porch swing with her parents.

"Hi Mr. and Mrs. Sullivan," Quentin yelled at our neighbors, an elderly couple sitting on their lawn, sipping drinks, and watching the sunset over the neighborhood.

We made our way to the hill that loomed above our houses. That night wasn't the first time that we climbed the hill on our bikes. We always went on the same loop, starting from my house and riding the two blocks past Quentin's, turning left on Linn, three blocks, right on Bell Street, left at Oda's, and right at the Christopherson's, up the hill, then round again back to my house. As we turned back into our neighborhood, we commenced our routine again, circling each other and our town like specks of dirt going down the drain.

At the bottom of the hill, I inhaled sharply and let it all out, readying myself for the incline, but as I did, Quentin took the opportunity to pass me. I yelled out behind him, "Hey, you can't have a head start!"

"I'm not starting ahead of you, you're the one that stopped!"

I couldn't waste any more breath yelling after him. I focused all my energy into my thighs and willed them to propel me up the hill faster than him. When we got to the top of the hill, we let go, speeding down the slow decline, heads tilted back with laughter, the wind billowing through our clothes. We lifted our arms in the air when we could find a moment to balance our weight perfectly and allow the bike to sweep us down the street on its own.

Around our loop again we went. The three Pfeiffer boys and their dad had taken out their football and were playing two versus two on their lawn. Oda's family, now deep in conversation, sucked on lime popsicles. When Oda saw us, she waved her popsicle around in her mom's face, her mom batting her hand out of the air. Mr. Sullivan picked up his hand and swung it back and forth at us in a wave. We made our way up the hill again, my bike passing Quentin as we went. He yelled from behind me, "Hey! No, you don't!"

He pedaled even harder, catching up with me, I could hear his strained breaths as he struggled to keep my pace. "Don't push yourself!" I laughed, "Your mom might get mad!"

"Shut up!" I heard him say before the car came barreling down the street. I didn't see it until Quentin yelled for me to stop, and it was already too late.

WE GOT MORE FREEDOM than we should have at the age of eight. Maybe because my parents cared more about how our family looked in society than what their kids were actually like or because of all Quentin's mom had to deal with, so young and alone. The bike ride we were on the evening of the accident wasn't unique to all the other ones we had taken in the year prior. When Quentin and I both got bikes for our birthdays, no one could stop us from riding all day if we wanted to.

That day began no differently than any of the others. I woke up early to my mom fussing with the dishes in the kitchen, had a breakfast of something I can't remember, probably scrambled eggs or cereal. I found my window of opportunity to escape my family's grasp, so I ran out to the garage to grab my bike and rode as fast as I could to Quentin's house.

We spent the morning in the park with Oda and her parents playing games and running around. Oda's parents brought us a basket of peaches which we devoured, the sticky juice dripping down our chins and arms as we ate.

Oda left with her parents around one in the afternoon, so we biked back to my house to collect some things to put in a time capsule. I explained to Quentin how I'd seen in a TV show a bunch of friends who put mementos in a box, buried it, and dug it up 10 years later. He shrugged when I told him my idea because he didn't like that we had to bury it in the ground. So, we made up our version of the time capsule. We would put objects and memories in it now, store it on top of Quentin's bookshelf, and throughout the years we would add things to the box without looking at its contents. Much to his chagrin, I made him agree not to look inside of it until we graduated high school, and then we could look inside whenever we came back home.

"It won't just be memories from now, but from our whole lives, as long as we are friends."

"Okay! Like a friendship box," he agreed.

"Yes," I nodded, "our friendship box."

From my house, Quentin tore my soccer ball keychain off my backpack, and I grabbed Quentin's favorite Lego man out of my little brother's Lego sets. I would just pretend I thought he lost it if Cole asked me. I pulled out a baseball cap that Quentin had splattered paint all over when we were making signs for a project at the end of the school year. The stains on the fabric didn't show any signs of coming out.

I gathered the few things we found in my shirt and put the baseball cap on my head. As we walked out the door my mom yelled after us, "Where are you going?"

"We're just going to go to Quentin's house!"

My mom walked into the entryway and tapped my hat. "Oh, don't wear that," she scolded. "You have plenty of other hats."

"I'm just taking it for a project. I didn't want my other hats to get dirty."

She frowned, "Alright. Be at the park by four-thirty to help set up for the barbeque."

We escaped out the front door and walked our bikes the two blocks to Quentin's house. As we walked, Quentin picked up a rock from our neighbors' yard and put it in his pocket.

"You know that's stealing right?" I asked him.

"It's just a rock."

"It's still stealing, it was on their property."

He looked back at me, "But I want to put it in the box."

"Why, it's just a rock."

He shrugged, "I just want to." He leaned down and picked a dry twig off the sidewalk. "This too."

I laughed at him and continued to walk down the block, swaying in the heat with each step. "Why does it have to be so hot?" I sighed.

"Because it's summer."

"The heat is only good because summer means we don't have to be in school."

"I like winter better. The snow is so much more fun."

I shook my head, "But we can't ride our bikes in the winter."

"We could if we wanted to!"

I jogged down the street, careful that the swinging pedals of my bike wouldn't scrape my ankles and calves. Quentin ran after me the rest of the way to his house.

When we got there, we placed more tokens of our friendship at the bottom of the box. I went into their kitchen and twisted the top off the bottle of pills Quentin had to take, ignoring the fact that I wasn't exactly supposed to be able to get into it considering the childproof top. I rifled through the drawers in their kitchen until I found a roll of plastic wrap, tore off a small piece, and placed it on top of his pill bottle.

I handed the cap of the bottle to Quentin, "Here, put it in the box."

"Why?" he asked.

"Because it reminds me of you."

He shrugged, knowing that if he didn't let me put this in, he wouldn't be allowed to put his rock in. I picked up the cardboard shipping box we found and swished the objects around in the bottom. There weren't even enough to cover it, and my hat took up most of the space.

"It's okay," he told me, "We'll put more things in it later."

I nodded, "Yeah."

For the rest of the afternoon, we took refuge from the heat in Quentin's house. His mom made us a plate of fruits and vegetables that we ate while talking about a book we both had just read. Quentin spent what felt like hours drawing the characters from the book while I finished mine in 10 minutes. The hairs on my forearm prickled when he showed me the finished product and

I forced myself to tell him I liked them while grimacing at the pictures I was proud of only moments before. At four, Ms. Flasch made us get up and walk our bikes to the park with her for the neighborhood's annual summer barbeque.

Oda's family never came to the barbeque which meant that most years Quentin and I just sat with the adults and tried to understand what they were saying. Most of the time, they talked about politics, but my parents were never willing to explain to me what it meant afterward. The other kids ran around in the park and played catch, but we never joined in. Not because we didn't know how to play; I made sure they all knew that I knew how to play by pulling my brother out of their games and playing catch with just him. I would throw the ball way too hard at his chest so he would drop it and then catch every single one of his throws.

Once the adult's conversations got too unbearable, Quentin and I went to our parents and begged for them to let us leave to ride our bikes. It didn't take much to get their consent, so we gleefully hopped on our bikes and rode away from the barbeque.

That's how we ended up riding in our circle that night and how we ended up in the hospital nearly an hour after leaving the party. That's how Quentin and I became inseparable, or at least we thought we were.

WAKING UP IN THE HOSPITAL, my mind immediately jumped to Quentin. The possibilities of what might have happened to him filled my head. Was he able to stop his bike in time? Of course, my mind spun to my bike, my precious bike, my freedom. On my birthday, my dad put his hands over my eyes and led me onto our front lawn where, when he lifted his hands, my eyes were greeted with the sight of my brand-new bike. I grinned at the purple lines streaking down the pastel blue color that covered the rest of the bike. I ran my hand along the slick frame, its metal pinching my skin in the frigid air. When the snow finally melted a few weeks after my birthday and the streets were finally dry, I wrapped my face up in a scarf and brought my bike over to Quentin's house, where we took turns riding it around his block. He got a bike of his own for his birthday in May.

The doctors told me that I had a broken leg, elbow, and a concussion. The skin on my right shoulder had suffered serious damage and they were going to have to graft skin to close the wound. Quentin only had a broken wrist from falling off his bike after I got hit. His mom scolded us because it should have been worse considering Quentin's health. We were lucky that time, but she couldn't bring herself to imagine something like this happening again.

That summer is not one I like to remember, especially the time I had to spend in the hospital. Even when I got home, I had a constant watch by my mother and felt her resentment that she had to tolerate my pain and frustration. Relief came in the afternoons when Quentin would come over to my house and tell me about the camps he went to. One day he brought me a card signed by most of the kids in our grade, which I forcefully handed back to him. They didn't actually care about me; they just were forced to sign it by their parents.

The urge to jump out of that bed and run away buzzed under my skin. Quentin telling me all those stories and trying to make me feel a part of everything only succeeded in making me more jealous and upset that I didn't get to participate in all the fun. On the day I went home, Quentin rushed over to my house and into my room with a soggy box of popsicles. While we ate them, he played with my toys as I bossed him around and told him which one to put where and exactly which direction it should be facing and scolded him for doing the wrong thing.

"But shouldn't the dog be playing with the other stuffed animals?" he whined while waving a stuffed dog in the air.

I shook my head firmly, "Quentin, you know *that* dog is way smarter than all the other dogs and she should obviously be with the Lego men; in fact, she should be the king of the Lego men."

"She can't be the king of the Lego men! She's a girl. Girls can't be king!" he fought back.

"Girls can do whatever they want," I retorted, then winced in pain after trying to cross my arms.

He reached into the box of popsicles and pulled one out, "Here, you can have the last one," he smiled.

I reached out my arm, "Why thank you."

He pulled it away, "But only if the dog plays with the other stuffed animals."

"Fine," I said with chagrin at his smile, "you can have the popsicle."

Before he could respond we both heard my mom yelling at my brother in the room next door. "I think she is mad that she can't yell at me anymore because I'm injured."

"She yells so loud," Quentin said, as we heard my mother scream at my brother.

A muffled, "Pick that up," came through the wall, along with a very loud cry from my brother.

"This is my fault," I said and turned my head away.

I heard Quentin sigh and looked back to see him placing the dog in front of our mini army of Lego men. He turned to me with a fake concerned smile on his face. "Shut up!" I yelled and threw the stuffed elephant next to me at his head.

"Hey, hey," he said jokingly, "the bones in this skull are very fragile!"

"Shut up," I said again and threw my pillow at his head.

His goofy smile softened the corners of my frown and soon we were in uncontrollable fits of laughter. Quentin rolled on the ground, and I held my shoulder in bed.

Most of our days that summer went the same way. Quentin came over after whatever day camp he had and kept me company until dinner when he would walk back to his house. Before the summer ended, the day came when the skin healed enough that I could crutch to our car so my mom could drive me the two blocks to Quentin's house.

I jumped out of the car and crutched as fast as I could up the steps to the front door of his house.

The first time I came over to Quentin's house, my mom stood behind me, waiting for them to respond to the doorbell. After a couple minutes, she decided that the doorbell didn't work and pinched the handle of the screen door with two fingers to knock on the front door whose white paint didn't peel like the paint of the rest of the house. When Ms. Flasch answered the door, my mom told her the house was "cute," which we all knew meant she thought their one-story, two-bedroom house had nothing on our two-story, plus a basement, five-bedroom house, whose paint would never even imagine peeling.

I rang the fading yellow doorbell that Ms. Flasch got fixed a few months earlier and waited until the front door swung open. Quentin looked at me with a huge smile across his face. He pushed open the screen door. "Who might you be?" he said in his fake proper voice.

I stuck out my hand while still leaning my arm on my crutches, "My name is Victoria Lucas Bowen, but you can call me Tori if you're nice."

He grabbed my casted hand and shook it vigorously up and down, "I am Quentin Isaac Flasch, but you must call me Quentin."

"Okay, Quentin, are you going to let me in?"

"Well, the only Tori Bowen I know isn't able to walk around like you, so I'm not sure about that."

"Well, I am clearly not her. Now let me in, kind sir."

"Okay Madam," he said and made a sweeping welcome gesture with his broken arm.

I walked into the house that opened into their living room, where drawing paper was scattered all over the floor. Trying my best not to step on Quentin's drawings, I hobbled over to the couch and flopped down on its brown cushions.

"Hey, Tori!" Ms. Flasch said from the other side of the house where I could hear clacking sounds of dishes. "Your mom called to tell me to make sure you sit down immediately and put your leg up. You two can watch whatever you want on the TV!"

I sat down on the couch and put my leg up on the coffee table in front of me. Quentin plopped down on the couch next to me and flipped the TV on. The show we settled on featured a family who was very involved in each other's lives. In the first couple minutes, we met an older man and his younger Colombian wife who had a son from before they were married. In the next scene, we met the man's daughter who worked at her dad's closet company and had three kids of her own.

During the first ad break, Quentin turned to me, "Woah, that was so good!" he almost yelled.

I nodded my head vigorously back at him.

"What are you watching?" Ms. Flasch said as she walked in drying her hands with a towel.

"I don't know," Quentin said, and picked up the remote controller, hit the guide button, and looked up at his mom. "*Modern Family*," read the TV.

"Oh, yes," she said knowingly, "you like this?"

"Yes," Quentin said and shushed us both because the show had turned back on. It opened with a scene that showed the brother of the woman from the closet company and his husband.

I had never seen two men together before, and neither had Quentin. When they got affectionate, both of us looked up at his mom with a questioning gaze. "What is this?" it seemed we were both asking.

She laughed a little at our inquisitiveness of this foreign concept, "Men can marry men, and women can marry women if they want," she explained, "I know here it seems a little strange." Ms. Flasch often had to explain modern topics like this to us, she often referenced the fact that she grew up in San Francisco as the reason she knew so much. "But it is actually quite normal," she continued. "Tori, I'd really like it if you didn't tell your parents I am letting you watch this."

"Why?" I asked.

"Some people don't believe kids your age should be exposed to these kinds of things. It's not my personal parenting style, but I don't think your mom would appreciate you knowing these things."

"Like men marrying men?" Quentin asked.

"That and other things," she sighed and left us to the TV.

We sat there, completely engrossed in the TV for the rest of the afternoon and spent many later afternoons that summer the same way.

ON THE FIRST DAY of third grade, I showed up at school only to find that Quentin was not there. We had already been informed that we would be in the same class that year. When we found out we both stood up and jumped around the room, laughing. On the first day, I left my mom at the steps of school to get to class early and ask my teacher if Quentin could sit next to me. She reluctantly agreed and I sat in our place expectantly waiting for him to get there. When the first bell rang, and all the rest of the kids filed in and sat in their assigned seats, Quentin never came in, and never sat down next to me.

I squirmed in my seat until we got out for our lunch break. I ran to the main office at our school and begged them to use the phone.

The secretary narrowed her eyes at me, "And why exactly must you use this phone?"

"I need to call my friend. I need to make sure he is okay," I whined at her.

She scowled at me, "Who is the friend you *must* call?"

"His name is Quentin, Quentin Flasch," I pleaded.

She typed something into the computer on the desk, each clickity clackity noise seeming to take forever. I sighed dramatically and laid my forehead on the cold desk. "It seems that Quentin's mother called him in sick this morning," the lady said coldly.

I picked up my head and squinted at her, "That's exactly why I need to call him, you don't understand." The truth is, she really didn't understand. Quentin had a genetic condition called thalassemia that gave him severe anemia. He had to be really careful about taking his medications and going to his regular doctor's appointments. It also made sickness much worse for him than it would be for other people, and it made his bones a lot weaker than most people's, which is why we were so lucky that I got hit by that car and not him; he might have died if he had been riding in my place.

He had been pretty healthy that summer besides the accident as far as I knew. A few years later, his mom took me with them to one of his appointments to get a blood transfusion. It seemed quite odd to see someone else's blood transferring into his body to keep him healthy.

He didn't always need the blood transfusions; his case being one of the more moderate cases of thalassemia, but I still worried about him every time he had to miss school.

The lady at the desk had said something to me, but my mind fluttered away from the sound of her voice and back to worrying. "Can I just call him, please?"

"You may not."

I ran out of the office and to my classroom, even though lunch had barely even begun. I leaned my back against the classroom door and stuck my feet out into the hallway. I pulled my sandwich out of my backpack and took a bite out of the dry wheat bread and turkey sandwich that my mom made for me every day of school.

I felt the door press against my back. It pushed me out further into the hallway until it swung all the way open, and I lay flat on my back, looking up at my teacher. "Victoria," she said, "what are you doing here?"

"Eating lunch," I replied, still lying flat on my back.

She wiggled her foot under my back and lifted my torso off the ground, "Why don't you come to eat with me?"

I got up and looked at her. "Okay," I agreed.

I walked into the classroom and pulled up a chair across from the teacher's desk, setting the container with my sandwich in front of me. She sat across from me and pulled out a salad. I wondered if she didn't know any other teachers yet because it was her first day teaching. They must have been intimidated by how smart she looked with her thick glasses and long dark hair. Even though she hadn't been a teacher for very long, it felt like she really knew how to be one. I liked her more than my second-grade teacher who was so old she could have taught my parents.

"So, why aren't you eating with the rest of the kids?"

"I always eat with Quentin."

"So, tell me about this Quentin," she smiled at me.

"Well, basically Quentin is my best friend. Well, Oda is too, but Oda says Jules is her best friend which means Quentin is mine. Jules is friends with Hally so I don't want to eat with them at lunch. And we like to ride bikes together and watch this show that we both think is really funny, but his mom says that I shouldn't tell my parents because they wouldn't like that I was exposed to those kinds of things. And he is really nice, he brought me popsicles sometimes when I couldn't get out of bed, because I got hit by a car when we were biking, look I have a scar." I pulled down the collar of my shirt to show her. "And what else? I can tell you what he looks like so you recognize him when you see him!"

"Okay," she laughed.

"He has these green eyes that my mom is always telling me are spectacular, she likes people with green eyes, she has brown ones, and so do I. And Quentin has brownish-blonde hair that's kind of curly and messy, my mom always says that we both need to be neater, she says that we look like wild children every time we come back from a bike ride. And he has very pale skin and is kind of short, except he has long legs, but that is because of his thalassemia, well not the long legs, but that's why he is not here probably, and that is why I needed to call him, to make sure he is okay, because he is my best friend and all," I finished.

She gave me a big smile, "Well I think he sounds great."

"Of course, he is."

"Well, do you still need to call him?"

"Yes, but the lady in the office wouldn't let me use the phone."

She reached into the bag next to her desk and retrieved her phone, and handed it to me, "Just this once."

I flipped open the shiny black phone and pressed Ms. Flasch's cell phone number into the keypad.

It rang twice, then I heard her tired voice, "Hello, this is Leah Flasch speaking."

"Hi, Ms. Flasch, this is Tori."

She tried to lighten the tone of her voice a little, "Hi! Tori, Quentin is okay. It's just a cold. He should be back at school tomorrow. We are just being cautious."

"Okay, will you tell him I called, and that our class is really great?"

She sighed, "Of course, I will, Tori."

"Thanks!" I said and handed the phone back to my teacher.

THE NEXT DAY, sure enough, Quentin returned to school, his skin paler than ever. I took this opportunity to show off to Quentin. I brought him into the classroom early and introduced him to the teacher because we had become friends, showed him our seats, all the art supplies, and how we each had an assigned coat hook and cubby for our things.

I asked the teacher if we could use one of the class's big red bouncy balls, and she agreed, so I took Quentin out to the yard that we got to use as third graders. I puffed my chest up with pride, I liked how mature I seemed, showing him everything. We got to share the yard with the fourth and fifth graders. It didn't have a play structure like the little kids did, which disappointed me, but when Quentin saw the freshly mown grass field and the tiny track, I noticed a little grin appear on his face.

Of course, my enemy Hally decided to come over to us and interrupt my tour. "Hey Quentin," she said, dragging out every word. "Whatcha doing back at school so early? I heard you were sick; you wouldn't want to infect us all with that disease of yours would ya?"

"That's impossible Hally," I growled.

"You just think it is because you probably have it too," she laughed. "It doesn't look like you have been out a single day this summer, you are so white. What were you doing? Playing nurse to your little dying boyfriend?"

If I didn't know I would get suspended, I would have punched her in the face right then. "You know Hally, number one: he is not dying, look at him. He is very much living and breathing at this moment and maybe he is even more alive than you are because he has a soul. Number two: he is not my boyfriend; he is my boy-space-friend. And number three: you are much whiter than me." She stood there and stared at me for a couple of seconds, then laughed. I grabbed Quentin's hand and led us back to our classroom, leaving her laughs alone in the yard.

Two

IN EARLY DECEMBER of third grade, I went to my first Chanukah party. According to Ms. Flasch, it was prime Chanukah time because you could still get some of the leftover Black Friday sales.

The fact that Quentin and Ms. Flasch were some of the only Jewish people in the area didn't stop Ms. Flasch from acting, how she put it, "Jewish, or 'loud and very opinionated.'" I personally had liked all the Jewish people that I had met; at that point my count added up to two. Of course, as soon as Ms. Flasch found out about this, she took it as an opportunity to throw a Chanukah party with every Jewish person she knew.

On the day of the Chanukah party, Quentin told me to be at his house by four because he had to teach me all the traditions before everyone got there. He opened the door for me when I arrived at 3:57 and shook his head solemnly, "No, no, no," he said. "You already have it wrong, in order to practice Judaism, you must be at least one minute late. Try again." And he shut the door in my face.

I sat on the stone steps of his house and stared at the snow-covered grass on their lawn until I checked my little purple watch and it said 4:01. I stood up and knocked on the door again.

He opened the door with a huge smile. "Why hello again!" he exclaimed.

"Hello?" I replied.

"More enthusiasm," he said and brought his arms up and down, up and down. "Now the next step is to touch that prayer on the door before you walk into the house." He pointed at this tiny box in the door frame that I had never noticed. I touched my hand to an engraving on its front, which looked like a sideways E, and followed him into the house.

As I stepped over the threshold, my nose filled with the scent of fried potatoes wafting in from the kitchen. "Come with me," he said, and led me through the house to the kitchen.

Most of the foods in the kitchen were things you could find at the parties I had been to before, like cheese and crackers, salads, and loads of desserts and other dinner items. The rest of the food was a dish I didn't recognize: piles and piles of something that smelled strangely like french fries.

I let myself drift over to the smell and soon saw that Ms. Flasch stood over the stove frying more of them. They looked like disks of hashbrowns. "Ahhh, you like the latkes," I heard her say from behind me.

"What are they called?"

"Latkes!" Quentin said, popping up behind me. "Some people call them laht-KEES," he said, stressing the last syllable of the word, "but, it is definitely more correct to say LAHT-kuhs."

"LAHT-kuhs," I murmured, repeating him. "Are these special for Chanukah?"

"Yes, but you have gotta stop saying 'Hanukah,' in order to act like a Jew you gotta say Chanukah," he said, hacking at his throat as he spoke.

"Chanukah," I said, trying to imitate the noise he made, but only succeeding in coughing up mucus that arose in the back of my throat.

He laughed, "Nice try," and grabbed my hand, pulling me into the living room. "C'mon, I'll teach you how to play dreidel."

He dumped out a bunch of chocolate coins onto the coffee table and pulled out a top-like thing that had some symbols on each of its four sides. He flipped the top around in his hand, explaining how each of the symbols made up an acronym. You were supposed to spin the dreidel and when it landed, the letter told you how many coins you were allowed to take.

We played this game until we got bored, then we sat on the couch and tried to take the chocolate coins when Quentin's mom wasn't looking. We watched our favorite TV show until the guests were supposed to show up at five-thirty.

At five-thirty Quentin's mom yelled at us to come help her set up the food in the kitchen. Quentin began shoving all the food and plates into one corner of the counter space, and not using any of the space on the kitchen table. "Why are you doing that?" I asked. "You should probably spread it out, so it looks prettier." I learned this one from my mom and I swelled up my chest with pride, glad to know something better than Quentin did for once. I reached over to move one of the salads onto the kitchen table.

Quentin grabbed it from me and placed it back in the corner with the other food. "Oh no, you'll see. We're gonna want all the food over here."

"But why?"

"Oh, you'll see," he said, and the doorbell rang. "Go get it!" he told me.

I looked at the clock on the stove - 5:46, it read. I walked to the door and opened it, only to be bombarded with the loudest people I had ever met, shaking my hand and swarming around me like flies to a light. They all asked me questions like "where should I put this?" and "who are you?" and "you must be Quentin's girlfriend" and "it's so nice to meet you." I just stared at them and tried to force answers out of my mouth.

"Oh! It's the Silvermans!" I heard Ms. Flasch say from behind me, "Put the food in the kitchen and let Tori get her feet under her, this is her first Chanukah party!"

All four of them followed Ms. Flasch into the kitchen and the doorbell rang again. Quentin came up next to me, "You want me to get this one?"

I nodded my head at him vigorously and stood right behind him, using him as a shield for the storm that might blow into the house. He opened the door to reveal an older woman with short curly white hair, red and brown cat eyeglasses, and the largest pastel sweater I have ever seen. She crowed, grabbed Quentin and pulled him into a big hug, crushing his face against her shoulder. She pushed him away from her and examined him, "You do look taller, but you look so pale, maybe you should eat some shrimp, I hear it makes flamingos pink!" I couldn't see the look on his face, but I'm sure he looked very confused. She laughed this big open laugh, "Oh, I'm just kidding!" Her gaze turned to me, "And who are you?"

"I'm Victoria," I said and stuck out my hand to her. "I'm Quentin's friend."

She pulled me into a hug, crushing my outstretched hand between us. "Victoria! That's a beautiful name, but it's too long! I'm going to call you Vic."

"Actually—" I started.

But she cut me off. "Now Quentin, where is your mother? I have food!" she said and pushed past me and into the kitchen.

Quentin turned to me and laughed, "Vic! That's very fitting, maybe I will use that from now on."

I punched him in the shoulder, "Shut up Quen! Or should it be Tin. Oh, maybe just Ent! Now that's good."

"Okay Icto," he laughed.

The party became loud very quickly, and every person who came brought with them food and a lot of it. I couldn't get enough of a sweet noodle dish with raisins called kugel. Quentin and I weaved our way through his house and at one point found ourselves lodged between two men in the middle of a heated political discussion, using big words I wanted to understand but couldn't for the life of me imagine what they meant.

At another point Quentin pulled me over to talk to the woman who had hugged us before, who he later explained to me was, "all Jewish things bundled into one person."

We stood there and listened to her tell us about her granddaughter who participated in "the arts," as she put it. She loved her granddaughter so much that she moved to this area to live with her. She loved her enough to move away from New York City, which she told us is where all the greatest Jews live. She told us about growing up Jewish in New York after the Holocaust; she herself had been born here, one year after the war ended, but her parents were in a concentration camp in Poland before they moved to New York City. I couldn't drag my attention from the animated way she moved her hands around and smiled as she talked.

We switched to playing dreidel with the other kids at the party who kept trying to trick me into thinking that I had to give up all my coins instead of taking all the ones in the center. Most of the kids were older than us, except one little girl who had dark curly hair all bunched up on the top of her head. Every time she spun the top and got to take something, she bounced up from her place on the ground and ran a victory lap around us all, waving her arms in the air.

After the sun set, we lit the candles on the chanukiah, and everyone stood around and watched as the little lights were born from the first one. As if someone had told them to do it, everyone started saying the same words that I couldn't understand, but they somehow connected these people in this moment, with this tradition and the little candles that we allowed to burn until the last drop of wax dripped down the chanukiah and the flame finally flickered out.

When the party came to an end and everyone had said their very long goodbyes and Ms. Flasch had begged the guests to take home the pounds of extra food that remained, I called my mom and pleaded with her to let me stay the night at Quentin's house where, I assured her, I would be polite and sleep on the couch. She agreed like she always did, glad to have me anywhere else but home.

As we were cleaning up the kitchen, Ms. Flasch asked me what I thought of the party.

"Well," I started, "it was actually very exciting. All the people are so interesting, and I hope I can have conversations like them when I am older, because it just all seemed very interesting. And that one woman we met, I loved listening to her talk. And when you all said the thing when you were lighting the candles, that was really cool."

"That's amazing Tori. That woman you were talking to, her name is Madeline Meyer. If you ever come to any more religious things with us, you will be sure to see her again."

I certainly did want to go to more religious things with them. I loved their version of Judaism, their community, and their joy. One day later that year, I even went up to my mother and asked her if I could become a Jew just like Quentin was and go to synagogue with them whenever they went.

When I told her, she scoffed. "Well, honey, your father and I are Christians, so I'm just not sure that would work out. We just don't know very much about it."

"But Mom! It wouldn't even affect you," I whined at her.

"I say let her try it!" my father said from the dining room table. He sat there reading the newspaper, and he had looked up just to help me.

"Cory," my mom said angrily, "I would really appreciate it if you backed me up on this one."

"Amelia," he said, mocking her tone. She huffed at him, she hated it when he called her Amelia; she had gone by Amy since before she could remember. "I would really appreciate it if you let our daughter make her own decisions." My mom huffed at him again. "Wouldn't you like that Tori?"

I shook my head up and down, "I mean it's not like you care very much about anything else I do."

"No, you can't *become a Jew*, you just want to do this because you want to be exactly like Quentin, and I don't want you to be exactly like Quentin." She slammed the plate she had in her hand on the kitchen counter. "They told me this wasn't supposed to come until you were a teenager," she muttered under her breath. "I really don't have the patience to deal with this Victoria. I already have to deal with Cole's outbursts and..." her voice trailed off. "For God's sake, you are only nine!"

I slammed my hand down on the table imitating her and ran out of the room. I heard her yell after me, but I ignored it and slammed the front door behind me, grabbed my bike, and rode away from my house as fast as I could. I got to Quentin's house, dropped my bike in the driveway, and ran up to his front door, repeatedly ringing the doorbell until he opened the door smiling.

"Let's go!" I said desperately to him.

And he knew not to ask any questions, and to just yell to his mom, "We're going for a ride!" He grabbed his bike and followed me as I rode as fast as I could away from our houses. This time, instead of staying in our same little routine, Quentin and I rode past our town's boundaries and to a little path that wandered through the woods and made our bikes bounce up and down over the roots and unevenness of the trail.

After riding a few miles, I stopped pedaling in the middle of a clearing and dropped my bike on the ground. I pushed my messy hair out of my face and smiled up at Quentin, who had just pressed on the breaks and slowed next to me. His blonde curls were straightened and pushed back with the wind. He looked bright and alive. His skin looked pinker, and his freckles seemed darker somehow. His electric green eyes looked wild; I felt like I could almost see into his soul. He took a deep breath in, taking in the life of the cool spring air. I watched as he allowed it to fill his body and let his body fall to the ground. He put his hands behind his head, crossed his feet over each other, and stared up at the bright blue sky. "C'mon, Tori!"

I laid myself down next to him and put my body in the same position as his. The world became quiet, except for our breathing and the occasional chirp of a bird in the woods. I listened to his breathing and changed mine, so our chests rose and fell at the same time. He breathed in and so did I; he breathed out, I breathed out too. I don't know how long we lay there, our chests rising and falling with the same rhythm of our friendship. I soaked in the sun that warmed our faces despite the cold of the almost spring air that nipped at our noses.

After a while I shifted my body and placed my head on his chest and my hand on his stomach so I could hear his heart beating and feel his life with every breath he took.

"Tori?" he asked, interrupting the peacefulness of my thoughts.

"Yeah?" I responded quietly.

"I wish it could always be like this."

I didn't respond to him even though I think that at the time, I still thought it could always be like that day.

Three

The summer we were nine years old split itself into two parts, the first part carefree and innocent and the second one tense and unsure. Nine is a good age. Nine is an age where you can understand just enough to be truly grateful, yet not enough to lose your optimism.

We spent the long summer days going on bike rides down the path we had found that day in the spring, parking our bikes in the clearing and eating the sandwiches we packed and discussing everything we knew and wanted to know.

One of those days, Quentin and I sat in the clearing, out of breath because we had just biked there in record time. Quentin grinned at me, reached into his backpack, and procured a bag full of slightly squashed watermelon. I grabbed the bag from him and pulled out one of the slices, and he did the same.

The cold juice hit our teeth and we both smiled at each other, momentarily relieved from the heat of the sun beating down on us. My mind paused on Quentin's cheeks stuffed full of watermelon and his pink lips pulled tight into laughter. A ray of sunlight burst through the tree branches above us and shone on his freckled nose.

"Let's go sit in the shade," Quentin said as he wiped drops of sweat from his forehead.

I followed him back into the shade and leaned up against the opposite side of a giant hemlock tree. I took a bite of my turkey sandwich and slowly chewed. Between bites, I said, "Q, I have a question."

"What is it?"

"Well, my mom told me the other day that if I didn't listen to her, I wouldn't get into heaven, but who says that heaven even exists? I mean, we couldn't ever ask anyone in heaven because they are all dead, and I don't know, I keep thinking about things like this, and keep going in circles all day long. I guess my question is: Do you believe in heaven and God and all that?"

He became silent for a moment, "Well as a Jewish person, my mom says we are supposed to question God in general. I'm not sure if that means to question if he exists or not, or just things about him. And I'm pretty sure we don't believe in heaven and hell in that way, that's a Christian thing."

"But what do you believe, not as a Jewish person, just as a *you* person?" I persisted.

"I guess I want to believe."

"Quentin!"

"I don't know, Tori! I can't tell! I love you and I love my mom and that feels like it's never gonna end, and I hope dying doesn't mean it will. But it's still hard to know because there is no proof. I mean, actually, now that I think about it, it's kind of ridiculous, how is it even possible."

It took me a while to comprehend what he had just said and to make sense of what it meant to me. After minutes of silence, I said, "I think I believe in it now. Except I don't believe what my mom said, because I am definitely going to see you there. Maybe we will just continue to exist separate from our bodies or something, maybe we don't have to go somewhere. Like ghosts. Maybe it's not possible, but everything was impossible at one point."

"That's definitely not true. Some things were definitely always possible. And if something ends up being possible that means that it was never impossible in the first place."

I waved my arm around in front of me, "Who cares?! I'll see you there if it is."

"Yes, you will, but you have to promise not to die first!"

I jumped up from my place on the tree and ran over to the other side to look at him, "No you! You have to promise not to die first!"

"Fine!" He laughed and stood up next to me. "We will die at the same time."

"Sounds like a plan!" I said. "And when I die first your soul will just die along with me."

"You mean when I die first your soul dies too."

I turned around for a second to put my sandwich bag in my backpack, and I felt a cold slosh of water on my neck and drops running down my forehead, "Ach!" I yelled and turned around to look at him, a sly smile showing his slightly crooked teeth and empty water bottle in hand.

"Did you do that on purpose?" I scolded him.

He laughed, "Accidentally on purpose."

"Shut up!" I said and bopped him on the side of the head with my hand.

AT THE END of the summer, Quentin's health started to deteriorate pretty quickly. Everything proved to be difficult for him and I soon realized biking would be completely out of the question until he got better. So, the days that we were able to spend together were spent at his house watching TV, which we would do until he fell asleep. As he slept, I would sit at the kitchen table and talk to Ms. Flasch about her life and mine.

She told me all kinds of stories about growing up in San Francisco and about its color and its vibrance. It all intrigued me; I had always been drawn to people who lived differently than the way my parents expected me to and Ms. Flasch's stories made me imagine a life separate from their expectations, living out a life surrounded by the most fascinating types of people. She told me about meeting Quentin's father, and she warned me to be careful with the partners that I chose, and to only have kids when I'm ready. "As much as I love Quentin, I wish I was able to provide him with more than I am now." Quentin's dad had become very successful by that point, but he didn't want to have anything to do with them, he didn't want his kid to compete with his success. So, he sent them enough money to pay for all Quentin's medical bills and to keep them out of his life.

"Ms. Flasch?" I asked one day.

"You can call me Leah," she said. "I know that people around here don't normally do that, but you are like another child to me, and I think it would be better if it didn't sound so formal."

"Okay, but I have a question."

"Yes?"

"Well, you said you always felt like you were meant to be a parent and even though you had Quentin young, you still love him because he is what you wanted?"

"I did say that."

"Well, what if my parents only had me because they felt like they were supposed to?"

She looked down at her hands; my question put her in danger. It forced her to break the silent rules that my mom had given her. The rules I knew she had broken many times before. "Well Tori, your parents and I are from very different worlds, and I don't know what it is like to be them, so I'm afraid I don't know the answer to your question. What I do know is that they love you very much."

"I don't think they love me, or Cole, like you love Quentin."

"And why is that?"

"I don't think they ever wanted to love us, and people don't usually like things that they are forced to do."

"Tori, you have very mature feelings for a kid your age." She took my hand and gave it a squeeze. "If you ever feel like you need to talk to someone, know I am always available."

SOME DAYS, WHEN QUENTIN started to improve, Leah would drive him over to my house and bring him inside. We would spend those days playing board games and trying to get Cole to leave us alone. Of course, when he wouldn't, and my mom scolded me for excluding him, we would allow him to play the board games.

One day in the middle of a huge thunderstorm, we were playing a sea battle board game. Cole built a block tower in the corner and we all were sharing a huge bowl of freshly made popcorn.

"B3," Quentin guessed.

"Nope!" I grinned and tilted my head up towards the ceiling.

"You are supposed to say miss." Cole walked up behind him and whispered something in Quentin's ear. "F7."

"First, it's not your turn! Second, Cole saw my side, so that's not even a fair guess. And third, miss!"

"Hey," Cole whined, "that's not fair! You moved your ship!"

"Did not!"

My mom walked in, her phone pressed to her chest. "Can you all keep it down in here! I'm on a call for work," she said in a hushed voice.

"Tori's cheating! She moved her ship!"

"Did not! And you are the one cheating! You told Quentin where you thought my ship was!"

"Kids!" my mom hissed at us. "This seems like something you can work out on your own, just be quiet!" She walked out of the room with a, "sorry," to whomever waited on the other side of the phone.

I looked at Quentin who sat there silently the whole time just watching the events play out. "I think we should just move on, because clearly Cole doesn't actually know where your ships are."

"No! She moved them!"

"I think that sounds like a good idea," I agreed. As the rain began to beat louder on the windows and I could hear as it rushed through the drainpipes outside, I had another idea. "Quentin! I have an idea. My mom is going to be on that call for a while."

I bounced out of my chair but remembered that he couldn't do the same. This didn't completely ruin my idea. I walked over to him, gently slipped my arms under his, then slowly and carefully lifted his body off the chair to make sure that he wouldn't pass out from standing. I supported his body with mine, and let him adjust himself for maximum support. "Where are we going?"

"Just you wait now, you need patience," I scolded.

I led him to the front door and opened it with my free hand. "We are going to get wet," he reminded me.

"That's the point!"

I took him outside and shut the door behind us. The rain pounded on the sidewalk and driveway in front of us. Each drop made a little splash and because there were so many drops so close together, it almost looked like the water hovered just the tiniest bit above the sidewalk.

I pointed to the water on the sidewalk. "Doesn't it look like it is floating?" I said to him.

"Yeah? Yeah, it does."

I walked him out from under the shelter of the roof, and the sheets of rain poured over us. Soon our clothes became stuck tightly to our bodies. I looked up at the sky and grinned. Letting go of my support under Quentin for a moment, I sang a song that ran through my head, but I couldn't remember the name of it. I could

feel the lightness in the singer's voice and I unconsciously swayed back and forth with his hands in mine.
I laughed at the dorky smile on his face and lifted up his
arm to do a little spin around underneath. He came
closer to me, supported himself with his arms around
my neck, and began to sway along to the song that I
sang and the beat that ran through our heads.

He lay his head on my shoulder. I wrapped my arms
around his thin body and held him. We stood there for
a while, me humming and swaying for the both of us,
and Quentin, even in his weak state, emanating enough
love, light, and happiness for the whole world like he
always did.

"I love the rain," he said, the warmth of his smile on
my shoulder.

"I know. Me too."

I took off my coat and wrapped it around Quentin. I
stuck my arm in the air and waved it in the wind like we
were the only audience at a silent concert. The cold
drops of rain stung my bare skin, but we were safe there
in the rain. The sound of the rain beating down on the
roof or the pavement had always made me feel at home.
The drops were familiar, they reminded me of the days
when Cole and I would run outside in our rainboots and
stomp in the puddles, squealing with laughter. Most of
all I enjoyed the rain because I always thought of the
days after the rain where all the dirt on the sidewalk
washed away, the soil smelled fresher, and all became
new and calm again.

QUENTIN'S HEALTH IMPROVED enough by the start of the
school year that he could attend the first day of our

fourth-grade year. We were not in the same class, which we both grumbled about in the days before school started because there were only two classes per grade. We lived in a really small town in Pennsylvania where everything felt small, and the people's minds felt small too. So, of course, we went to a small school, with small classes, and small amounts of them, too.

On the first day of fourth grade, I sat next to a boy, Spencer, who moved to our town from Colorado that summer. The teacher, a middle-aged guy who had a mean looking face, started us off with a worksheet to write about our summer.

Grinning, I got to work immediately, writing so hard that the tip of my pencil broke, and the lead smeared all over the paper. Later that week, I shoved the worksheet in the friendship box for us to find when we finally got to open it.

I spent the hole summer with my best friend Quentin. He is in Ms. Davis's class. We spent the first haf of the summer riding our bikes together in the forrest and eating sandwitches and watermellon every day. I wish my life could always be like that because school can be fun some times when we learn things that are usefull, but most of the time I would just rather spend time with Quentin or my little brother who I love alot when he is not being annoying. The second haf of the summer I spend watching TV and playing board games with Quentin, and sometimes talking to Quentin's mom. She says the people here aren't as colorfull as the people where she grew up. I gess I think she is more colorfull than the people here. I think Quentin is that's why I like him and his mom so much. I did not go anywhere with my family this summer. My mom says that is because daddy had to work alot but I just think she did not want to spend time with him. I do not reely care because I got to spend time with Quentin.

"Victoria?" The teacher saying my name interrupted my writing. "Will you share with the class what you wrote on your worksheet?"

"Uhm," I said, not wanting to share everything I had written. "This summer I went on a lot of bike rides with my best friend Quentin. And sometimes we watched TV." I looked up at the teacher to signify that I finished reading it.

"In this class we are going to practice reading our work aloud. Victoria, I would love it if you could read what you actually have written there." Hally, who sat diagonally in front of me raised her hand really high, her back straight, desperate to be called on. "Yes, Hally?" the teacher asked.

"Well, I heard that Quentin almost died this summer just like Victoria did last summer, except it happens to Quentin all the time and that's probably why she doesn't want to talk about it."

I slammed my hand down on the desk. "That's not true, Hally!"

"Maybe she wrote about it in her worksheet, let's see." She turned around and snatched it off my desk. I watched the expression on her face change as she read what I wrote. She slammed it back down on my desk, "You spelled half wrong; it's with an 'L'."

"Okay girls, can we move on now?"

Hally and I both nodded, finally agreeing on something. I saw Spencer's eyes on my worksheet, intently reading what I had written about Quentin. He looked up to see me watching him, "Can I meet him?" Spencer asked.

"Quentin?"

"Yes."

I smiled. Hally had made most of the kids in our school hate me and Quentin for some reason, maybe because of his disease, maybe for some other reason. I didn't really understand why she made fun of him for such a serious thing that he had no control over. I hated her intensely for it.

At lunch I took Spencer to meet Quentin. I ran up to Quentin who waited for me at our spot on the grass field. "Q! This is Spencer, he is from Colorado, and he said that the people here are much more boring than the people in the cities just like your mom. And he likes running and playing board games, and I think he should be our friend! What do you think?"

Quentin laughed, "Okay, sit with us Spencer."

Spencer sat with us at lunch that day and the next. I invited Spencer and Quentin to come over to my house after the second day of school so we could have a sea battle tournament, with the third person each round being the judge.

After Quentin and Spencer left that afternoon, my mom came into my room so we could have a talk. "Victoria," she said, "I'd really like it if you stopped making friends with all these boys. I don't think that they are a good influence on you. You are starting to become rebellious and entitled and you aren't doing things most girls your age are doing, and it is starting to worry me.”

“But I like Spencer and Quentin is my best friend!”

“Well, I’m not saying that you have to stop being friends with Quentin, it is already too late to go back on that one.”

I frowned, “Are you saying you did not want me to be friends with Quentin from the start?”

“I am saying that I wish you spent some time with girls, so you could be a little more normal.”

“But I wouldn’t be happy!”

“I’m saying I think you would be happier. Normal is normal for a reason, people act normal because it is what’s right and what makes them happy,” she said, trying to stay calm and not raise her voice at me.

“QUENTIN MAKES ME HAPPY!” I screamed.

“Honey, calm down,” she said and attempted to put her hand on mine, but I moved my hand before she could.

I looked at her with a fake smile, “I am calm,” I said and walked out of the room, and into my brother’s room down the hall.

He looked up from the Magic Tree House book in his hands, “Is Mommy mad at you?”

“Yes,” I said, sat down next to him and pulled him into me. “Cole?”

“Yes Tori?”

“You like Quentin right.”

“I love Quentin, it’s like I have a brother.”

“Oh, and I am not a good enough older sister?” I laughed.

“No! You are the best older sister.”

"Well, you only get one," I said and pulled him a little tighter to me.

WHEN THE LAST SNOW of the year fell, my family received some of the most devastating news I thought we could ever get. I remember the day so clearly, because when the snow fell on that day in late February, Quentin rode over to my house, bundled up in two coats and a hat, quiet because he knew it wouldn't snow again that year, but jumpy because he knew that it meant we were closer to the rain. We went on a bike ride. It was not one of our fast ones because the wind blew us back on the slippery roads and the cold pinched our skin, while the sun that emerged from behind the clouds burned it.

When we were out of breath from pedaling hard on our bikes the short distance against the wind, we sat down on a bench in the park. My throat ached from gasping in so much cold air as I panted, trying to catch my breath. Quentin bent down, scooped up a bunch of snow, and packed it together into a ball. "That better not be for me!" I told him, scooting away from him on the bench.

"Oh? Well, it's not. It is for me, to throw at you!" He laughed and threw the densely packed ball at my chest.

"Oh, you are going to pay for that one!" I put my gloved hands in the snow, lifted up as much as I could and threw it in his general direction. He shook his body so the snow fell to the ground. His freckled nose turned red with the cold of the snow. He reached down to pick up another ball of snow and packed it hard in between his hands.

I got up from my seat on the bench and started to run away from him, but the sharp cold of the snow hit the back of my neck as I attempted to make my escape. I tried to make another snowball to throw at him, but as I turned around to throw it, I got hit with a snowball right on the nose. A quick shock of a numb, metallic feeling went through my nose. I ran after him as he ran towards the play structure in the park. I caught up to him and pushed him into the pile of snow under a tree, but he grabbed my arm as I did and pulled me along with him.

We lay in the pile of snow, laughing and panting from our fight. As soon as he relaxed his body and settled in the snow, I reached my arm out into the snow next to me, grabbed a handful and brought it across my body and right onto his face. He wiped it off and laughed, "I deserved that," he said and gave me a little shove.

We let the wind carry us back to my house, laughing all the way up the steps and through the door, where our bright mood faded off our faces. My parents were sitting on the couch, my dad looking stunned and my mom with tears pouring down her cheeks.

"Victoria, can you sit down?" my mom said. I shrunk back away from her like a timid animal. The scene in front of me made my stomach turn in knots and my legs wouldn't let me sit down because they needed to run away.

"What happened?"

"Victoria, will you just sit down?"

"Will you just call me Tori?" I said pleadingly. The tears on my mom's face fell even faster and my dad stiffened up a little more, he hadn't even moved since I got home. The sight of my mom crying disturbed me. I never got any big emotions from my parents besides anger and disappointment. "What happened?"

"Victoria, your Aunt Jessica got in a really bad accident last night. A fire."

I knew what her next words were going to be, but I just stood there staring at her, dumbfounded. My Aunt Jessica had been the most alive person I knew. It couldn't be possible that she was dead. Maybe she just got injured, maybe the doctors were lying. She was a force of nature, as my dad liked to put it, she had to be alive. Aunt Jessica had her first kid, Charlotte, when she was twenty-five. Charlotte is 10 years older than me and had been my biggest role model in everything I did when I was little. She had two other kids, Alden and Owen. How could this happen? Where would my cousins go? Who would take care of them? My heart dropped into the pit of my stomach. I would never see her again or hear her tell stories about the places she had been. My aunt was an author, and she seemed to do whatever she wanted with her life, which I have always admired about her, even in her death. That is why it seemed so unreal to me that this could happen so suddenly. But it also made sense. My aunt had put so much out into the world and, knowing her, I don't even think she would be that upset about this. She had published three books, had three kids and was the only person that I knew who had been to all seven continents.

Remembering that Quentin still stood behind me, I grabbed his arm and brought him up the stairs and into my room. I laid on my floor with my feet up on my bed and stared at the ceiling like I always did. Quentin sat on my bed and folded his hands in his lap. He stared at the wall and waited for me to say something.

"She's dead, Quentin."

"When my grandpa died, my mom told me that people grieve in different ways, but there are stages, like denying it, and being angry and trying to trade or something. Then, being sad and accepting that they are dead. It's okay if it takes you a while, that's what she told me."

"I think I'm doing the last one you said. I don't think that she would have been sad that she died. I think it's okay."

Quentin placed his hand on my lower leg which rested on my bed, and we sat there in silence for the rest of the afternoon, not even flinching when we heard Cole crying in his room and my mom trying to comfort him.

I found myself wondering about what it had been like for her. My mom never told me if she died in the fire or afterwards, but my imagination filled with images of her caught in the flames yelling for help. My mind kept flashing back to a memory of her making us lunch and the tiny orange flames flickering under the skillet that held our grilled cheeses and back to her caught in the flames, coughing and screaming.

I must have fallen asleep like that, because I woke up around six laying on the ground with Quentin curled up in my bed. I got up and walked downstairs only to find out that my parents were nowhere to be found. I figured that my parents probably fell asleep, as well. Our grief caused the house to be eerily silent for the late afternoon and my ears rang with sleep. My stomach began to grumble so I went into the kitchen to make grilled cheese.

I pulled out a loaf of whole wheat bread, a block of orange cheddar cheese and the butter dish. I attempted to mimic the exact way that I had seen my aunt make grilled cheeses numerous times, but pretty much just succeeded in tearing up the bread with the cold butter.

"Hey," Quentin said sleepily as he walked into the room.

"Oh, you are awake," I said, angrily trying to spread the butter on the bread.

"What are you doing?"

"I'm trying to make grilled cheese, but I can't seem to spread this butter!"

"Here let me do it." He took the knife from my hand. "Go sit down."

"No, I can do it!" I said a little too loudly. I tried to spread the butter but made another large hole in the bread.

I felt his soothing touch on the back of my hand, "Let me do it."

I reluctantly walked over to one of the stools at the kitchen counter and pushed myself up onto it. Quentin somehow successfully made us grilled cheeses, and about five minutes later handed me one. "My mom would be mad," I said.

"Why?" he asked.

"Because she likes to tell me that I should stop being friends with so many boys so I will act more like a woman and do things like look pretty and cook."

He smiled at me, a bite of grilled cheese in his mouth, "I think you are pretty, and I'd much rather cook than eat whatever terrible thing you would make."

"Thanks, Q."

That night, as soon as Quentin left, I ran up to my room, threw myself on my pillow, and cried myself to sleep. I sobbed as I thought of everything that would change in the next few years. I mourned all the things I never got to do with Aunt Jessica. And I didn't realize it then, but the memories my parents told me we would keep close to our hearts and remember every day would start to fade. And later that year around Thanksgiving time, a time that we would normally go visit my aunt and my cousins, I realized that I hadn't thought about her in weeks, just like I hadn't constantly thought about her before she died.

Four

Spring came at full speed the year we were in fourth grade. After my birthday, March 2nd, the cold seemed to evaporate and the spring sun replaced it, baby birds chirped, and flowers began to bloom. Which for me also meant spring allergies. But, for everyone in our small town, it meant the spring carnival had come.

Everyone in our town seemed to look forward to the spring carnival year-round. Most of the moms in town, or all of the stay-at-home moms—Quentin's mom and my mom were the rare exceptions—would spend the whole year working on projects like painting, quilting, weaving, making jewelry, and so on, just to sell it all at a booth during spring carnival. The adults in town would walk around to all the booths for the whole day, while the kids ran around in the hay bale maze, ate cotton candy, hung out in the petting zoo, and went on rides.

My parents bought Cole and me tickets for the rides and told me I could go find my friends as long as I came back to the entrance by four. I ran off to go find Quentin, holding my string of tickets in one hand and the 10 dollars my dad slipped me before he walked off behind my mom and Cole in the other.

When I saw Quentin and Leah, I ran up behind them, "Quentin! What do you want to do first?"
He turned around and looked at me and looked back at his mom for permission to go with me, she nodded her head at us and as we ran away. "Be safe!" she yelled after us.

Quentin ran straight into the hay bale maze and I followed him, but stopped in my tracks as soon as I felt my nose fill with the itchy sensation of a sneeze, and my eyes water. Quentin turned the first corner in the maze, not realizing that I no longer trailed him. A couple of seconds later he walked back around the corner and cocked his head at me, "What are you doing?" I let out a huge sneeze and laughed. "C'mon," he said.

I ran after him again and another sneeze forced its way out. I heard him laugh from ahead of me. "Are you making fun of my allergies?"

"Let's play hide and seek!" he yelled back at me.

"Okay, you hide."

He started to run off but turned around, "Count to 30!"

"One, two, three..." I counted in my head. When he had gotten out of earshot I yelled, "30!" more like 20 seconds later.

I ran in the direction he had gone, and when I got to the first intersection I turned left. I remembered Quentin telling me that you should always go left in one of these mazes, but I had no idea why he thought that, and still don't. I turned left, then left again and a few more times, and found myself in the exact same spot as

I had been after the second left turn. So, I decided to turn right, and of course he stood there, pressed up against the wall, making a weird face at me.

"I saw you run by before!"

"You did?" I frowned.

"You just went left, didn't you?"

"Yes! But you basically told me to do that!"

"I know! So, I went the other way."

I shook my head at him, "I may have to use that one in the future."

"Okay your turn!"

I waited for him to close his eyes. I turned left, left again, and left again. I leaned against a wall panting, and tried not to let myself sneeze. My eyes started to water and I couldn't resist sneezing anymore. I let myself sneeze and, much to my chagrin, everyone in the maze could probably hear it. I braced myself waiting for Quentin to come running around the corner. I waited another moment and when he didn't come, I decided to walk down the maze. Suddenly I felt his hands on my shoulders with a loud, "Gotcha!"

"How did you find me?" I sighed.

"You sneezed!"

"Aw! C'mon," I whined, thinking I had gotten away with the sneeze. "Let's go get cotton candy," I said. "My dad gave me 10 dollars."

"Oh yes!" he said.

We attempted to make our way out of the maze, many times running into dead ends and having to turn around. After 10 or so minutes we retraced our steps and found our way out. I immediately ran to the cotton candy stand. I saw it on our way to the maze and made a mental note of exactly where it stood so we could go back.

"How many tickets did you get?" Quentin asked as we ran.

"20! What about you?"

"10," he said, sounding disappointed.

"Well, I guess we both have 15 now." I continued running towards the cotton candy booth.

We took our cotton candy and sat in the shade under the large cottonwood at the side of the fair. Quentin sat close to me so we could share the large cotton candy. We took turns ripping off pieces of the sweet fluff and shoving them into our mouths and licking our fingers one by one to make sure we consumed all the possible sugar we could.

"Let's play truth or dare!" Quentin said.

I looked at him skeptically, "What?"

"What? All the other kids play it!"

"That doesn't mean we have to," I said, taking a huge piece of cotton candy off of the stick and shoving it into my mouth.

"Come on!"

"Fine, just this once."

He gave me a big fake grin. "Truth or dare?"

"Hmm, truth," I said.

He thought for a second, "Who do you have a crush on?"

"Quentin!" I yelled, punching his arm a couple times.

"What? Why can't you just take this seriously?"

"I can!"

"Well then, answer!"

Trying to take him seriously, "Well, I guess I like Brayden," I said, thinking about how he always had kind words, didn't listen to Hally, and didn't smell gross like all the other boys. Despite being different from all the other boys, he found a way to fit in and I admired that about him. I noticed how they treated him differently, made little jokes and laughed at his dad. But they didn't look down on him like they did Oda's family for being Black or even Leah for being unmarried. After time passed, it seemed like everyone had forgotten Brayden's dad was Japanese.

"That's a good choice," Quentin said. Both of us nodded, not knowing what it actually meant to like someone.

"Truth or dare?" I asked.

He squinted his eyes at me and took a long time to respond. "Dare!" he finally exclaimed.

I thought for a second and remembered something Cole had done once, that my parents had scolded him for. "Scream penis!" I whispered to him, not wanting anyone else to hear, even though no one was within earshot.

He eyed me, "That's silly. Why would I do that?"

"Isn't that the whole point of the game," I said and punched him in the arm.

He took a deep breath in and with everything he had in him yelled, "PENIS!"

A mom holding the hand of her toddler turned around and gave us a death stare. A couple of teenagers with red eyes and tired looks on their faces who were sitting against a nearby tree fell into laughter and screamed back at us, "PENIS!"

Quentin looked at me, a smile creeping across his face, and burst out into huge fits of laughter. My body exploded with laughter too. I collapsed on top of Quentin, holding my stomach which ached with joy. He fell against me too, shaking with silent giggles.

"My... face... hurts..." Quentin said, trying to catch his breath.

I laid on the ground, my body tired from laughing, and tried to pull the smile off my face, but the corners of my mouth just wouldn't go down.

Quentin slowly picked himself up off the ground, "C'mon, Tori! We're wasting time! There's so much more to do!" And he was right; there was so much more we had to do.

FOR HIS 10TH BIRTHDAY, Quentin decided he wanted to go on a hike with his mom and me. Leah basically had to beg my mom to let me go; Quentin's birthday being on a Tuesday and all. None of it made my mom like Leah any more.

Quentin and I complained during the whole hike because Leah made us get up so early to leave. We had to drive over an hour to get there and apparently Quentin's birthday surprise would be waiting for us at the end. So, I got up before the sun rose with my dad who always woke up at five to prepare for work and drink his first cup of coffee. He made me breakfast as we waited for the Flasch's car to pull up in our driveway. When I heard the engine of their Subaru, I gave my dad a hug and quickly ran outside to meet them. I hopped in the backseat of the car, excitedly wished Quentin a happy birthday, and handed him the card I made the night before.

"Does your mom need to talk to me before we go?" Leah asked before pulling out of our driveway.

"Nope! She is still asleep."

"Okay, well you two are in for an adventure today! Buckle up and enjoy the ride!"

We drove out of the neighborhood and Leah pulled onto the only highway that ran past our town. In the beginning of the ride, we drove alone on the freeway and I got a clear view of the sun rising in the May sky as we listened to the only sound of the wind on the side of the car. I leaned my head against the cool window, and watched as the world passed by and faded into the distance. Quentin swayed along to the music playing on the radio in the seat next to me. "I can tell this is going to be a perfect day," he said.

A song came onto the radio. It started with the soft sound of a lone guitar, and a man's voice. More instruments came in to accompany him, and his voice sighed with disappointment in himself. He began to sing of all these places he had never been and the places that were familiar to him, how he would always be going back to where he started.

I looked over at Quentin, who leaned forward into the music, his eyes closed, breathing in every second and every word this man sang. I saw the way his heart felt the song. I watched him and smiled with the utmost joy to be witnessing this internally profound moment he was having. I understood later how he felt, like his soul was intertwined with something and it became difficult to tear it apart. Certain songs you can never unhear, movies you can never unsee, moments you can never unlive, people you can never unlove. They get stuck in your brain and can never come out.

"Hey Leah?" I asked quietly, trying not to interrupt Quentin's thoughts.

"What is it honey?"

"What is this song called?" I wanted to be able to find it for Quentin again.

She pointed to a little screen in the front of the car, that words were moving across. I leaned into the middle of the car so I could read it better, "Down in the Valley The Head and The Heart" the screen read, the same words circulating across the screen again and again.

I looked back over at Quentin, the moment had passed, he leaned on his hand, his elbow propped up in the place where the window went into the car door. We drove the rest of the way to the hike in silence, just listening to the radio and each other's breathing and watching the world pass by.

"Welcome to Riverview Park," Leah said as we pulled into our destination. The park had a big white house and a stone path with stairs. Another part had the trail that we were going to hike. "We are lucky, this place is usually packed on the weekends, but it looks like no one wanted to be here on Tuesday, May 26. Happy Birthday, Quentin."

Quentin hopped out of the car and went around to the back and tried to open it, but Leah ran around to him and quickly closed the trunk before we could see inside, which Leah had covered with a huge blanket. "No, no, no," she scolded, "Your surprise is in there."

Quentin narrowed his eyes at her, "I thought we were picking up my surprise in Pittsburgh this afternoon.

"We are, just," she shooed us away with her hand, "go over there; I will get the things for the hike."

We strolled mostly on paved paths, through emerald lawns in more of a developed park rather than the wilderness I expected. As we walked, Quentin and I talked about all the unimportant things in life and made jokes, trying to force the other one to laugh first. About halfway through the hike, when we were stopped at a bench eating lunch, completely out of the blue, Quentin asked, "Mom, do you think Dad is ever going to actually want to meet me again?"

The moment Leah heard this, it seemed I felt her heart drop in my body. She took a deep breath and with soft eyes said, "Quentin, honey, I am really not sure. You have to know that I believe your father is not a bad person. We just weren't ready for you to come along into our lives and he wanted to be successful before having kids and so he chose that."

"But isn't he successful now? And he has me now, isn't a father supposed to care and provide for their family like Mr. Bowen does?"

"Well, your father does provide for us, you know that's how we pay for all your medical bills when you're sick? And why you have a college fund. And, you know, that doesn't always have to be the way things are; I care and provide for you as well, and when Tori grows up and if she chooses to have kids, she can provide for them just as much as her husband would."

He shook his head, wanting more. "But isn't he supposed to love me?"

"I love you, Quentin. I love you! You are very lucky to have me, and to have him as well because without him we might not have our house or half the things we own." She suppressed anger in her clenched fists and her pursed lips, an anger at who, I didn't know.

Quentin looked up at her with wide eyes and a soft smile, he took her hand, "I love you too, Mom. I just don't understand why."

"Neither do I, sweetie."

We finished our hike in the early afternoon, me and Quentin complaining about how much our feet hurt and slinking our way back to the car, ready to fall asleep in the backseat. We both collapsed with our heads on the center seat and closed our eyes, exhausted. Leah energetically popped into the car with us, turned around to look at us and laughed out loud. "You two are going to have to get up, we still have to pick up the surprise!"

"Ugh," Quentin groaned, "do we really have to pick this thing up?"

She laughed again, "Trust me, you want this surprise."

This intrigued us and we spent the whole ride into the city discussing what the surprise could possibly be. Maybe she was taking us to the special ice cream place that we loved, but why would that require the secret supplies in the back of the car? Maybe we were going to have a picnic at the river, or maybe we were going to pick up a fancy birthday cake, or some elaborate gift that came in multiple parts.

As we got closer to our destination Leah reached into her bag and pulled out an eye mask for sleeping and handed it back to us. "Quentin put this on, no peeking, and Tori please don't ruin the surprise."

We pulled up to this huge modern-looking brick building that read "wellness clinic" on one of its sides and had huge glass windows and a turquoise overhang on the entrance.

"Wait here," Leah said and hopped out of the car. She walked swiftly into the building.

"Where are we?" Quentin asked.

I shook my head. "I have no idea."

About 10 minutes later I saw Leah come out with Quentin's present. A smile crept across my face, "Oh Q, you are going to be so excited."

She held the leash of a not yet full-grown boxer-greyhound mix with a smooth brindle coat and white markings on his face and chest. The dog bounced around Leah as they walked. Leah opened the car door on Quentin's side and put one finger on her lips to signal me to keep quiet. "What is going on?" Quentin asked, starting to get anxious.

Leah let the dog jump onto Quentin's lap, and, confused for a second, Quentin took off the blindfold. He looked at the dog, who had begun to aggressively lick his arm. He smiled a huge smile and wrapped his arms around the dog and pressed his face into its fur. "I love him, Mom!" he almost cried, his face still pressed into the dog's fur.

"Well, I'm glad," she said and grinned at him.

I reached over and pet the dog's boxy head. He turned his head away and began to lick Quentin's face. "Aw, Q, he already loves you!" I said.

"What's his name?"

"River," Leah replied. "But we can always change it if you don't like that, he is only five months old."

"I love it! Thank you! Thank you, Mom!"

Leah kissed him on the head, "Happy birthday, honey."

On the ride home Quentin spent the whole-time stroking River's head and pointing out all the little details of him at least twice each. After a very short discussion, we both came to the conclusion that River would be a much better pet and companion than my cat Pepper, who, in the seven years we had him, I only ever saw if he came in to eat or occasionally use his litter box. Some days he sat on our front porch in the sun, but didn't like it very much when I pet him.

When we got to Quentin's house, Leah made us her favorite chicken pot pie recipe while Quentin and I set up River's bed and things in Quentin's room. We spent the rest of the evening playing with playful, spirited River, eating chicken pot pie and vanilla cake that Leah had picked up from the store. She had attempted to write "Happy Birthday" on it with sprinkles, but it ended up looking more like "Hoppg 8inthdog." We spent the rest of the night serving ourselves seconds while laughing and cooing over everything River did.

Five

ONE DAY IN EARLY AUGUST, Quentin and I spent the morning biking, like almost every summer morning of our childhood. We spent that afternoon playing in the sprinklers in Oda's yard and eating popsicles. That evening, Quentin came with my family on a picnic at the park.

My mom packed all the necessities for a picnic: fruit and salad, bread and cheese, all sorts of sandwich meats, one of my dad's batches of cream cheese brownies, and a bottle of raspberry lemonade. She brought a blue and white gingham picnic blanket and packed all the food into two wicker picnic baskets. My mom laid out all the things just as she liked, while Quentin, Cole, and I ran off to play on the play structure in the park.

"Let's play lava monster!" Cole yelled. "Tori, you're it." He and Quentin ran away from me onto the play structure trying not to get caught.

I ran around in circles and my shoes began to fill with sand, trying to touch their feet from the ground, but my height didn't allow me to reach the high parts of the play structure where they had gone to get away from me. I reluctantly closed my eyes and got onto the play structure. I stuck out my arms and climbed up the stairs that led up to the tower I knew they were hiding in. I felt something brush past me. I reached out and grabbed my brother's arm. "Hah! Got you!" I laughed, opening my eyes.

"Aw come on!" Cole whined, and ran down the stairs and onto the red rubber underneath the play structure.

I turned and saw Quentin who still sat cross legged in the middle of the tower, shaking his head at me. "I have an idea," I said.

Cole made his way back onto the play structure, his eyes closed. "Your ideas are always really good or really terrible," Quentin said.

"This one may be both," I replied. "Follow me." I walked onto the rubber bridge that led to the other tower, and hoisted myself onto the railing, Quentin followed my lead. I walked across the railing until I got to the tower and attempted to lift my body on the top of the tower. When I finally got up onto the top of the tower, I pushed my body up and stood, my arms in the air.

Quentin looked up at me, "There is not nearly enough space for me up there." he said.

"That's okay!" I lifted my arms into the air again and let out a long "whoop!"

"I can hear you!" Cole yelled from the other side of the play structure.

"We're over here!" I yelled back. "Come get Quentin!"

Cole turned around and made his way over to my voice. Knowing I wouldn't get tagged, I looked at Quentin and cackled. Quentin made an annoyed face at me and shook his head. He carefully walked along the railing of the bridge and to the stairs. Once he got to the stairs, he jumped to the outside of the play structure and climbed down the stairs, using the railing like monkey bars.

Cole finally arrived at the tower only to figure out neither of us were there. He opened his eyes to look around, confused. "Cole!" I yelled from above him. "You are on the play structure! Lava monsters can't open their eyes on the land!"

"Hey! You can't be up there!"

"I'm still on the play structure," I taunted.

In the distance I heard my mom's call, "Victoria! Get down from there!"

"See!" Cole taunted back.

My mother's voice again, "All of you come get food now!"

We all jumped off the play structure and went running in the direction of the food, like wolves on the way to hunt their prey. We sat on the picnic blanket with my parents and quietly devoured our overflowing plates of food and sipped on our blue plastic cups of lemonade. My parents discussed work. They worked at the same law firm, my dad as a lawyer and my mom part-time as a paralegal. My dad talked about some of his recent cases and my mom just sat there and listened to him. These were the days when I realized why we were a family, and why my parents had gotten married in the first place; it was the look in my mom's eyes and

the way she leaned into him as he talked. I could finally
see they loved each other. I wondered if Quentin saw it
too, and if he envied me for having this. I remembered
Leah and the way my parents didn't ever seem to give a
damn about me, except in the moments where it really
mattered or didn't matter at all.

When I finished eating my food, I sighed and laid
down on my stomach, my head in my hands. "Daddy,
will you tell us the story about the bear?"

He looked at me and laughed his sweet laugh I
remembered from years earlier, a laugh that felt like a
long-lost memory, like déjà vu. "You have heard that
one so many times."

"But Quentin hasn't! Don't you want to hear the
story, Quentin?" I whined.

He settled into the same position as me and looked
up at my dad. "Yes."

"Well okay," my dad agreed. He cleared his throat
and put on his storytelling face. "When I was about
fifteen years old, my sister and I stayed at the lake house
in Michigan with my grandparents that they liked to
take us to every summer. The night that we saw the
bear, my sister Jessica begged my grandparents to let
us go on a drive in our neighbor's golf cart. They had a
boy who was sixteen, just like my sister, and a girl who
was two years younger than me.

"When we got to the neighbors' house, my sister
informed me we were going to go look for the bear that
liked to roam around the property, and also that I had
to drive. Once we started driving and looking for the
bear, the girl who was sitting in the passenger seat
started talking to me about the bear, and my sister sat

in the back with the boy, holding his hand and you know, being teenagers. I drove for about an hour in circles around the property, scared the whole time because I didn't have my driver's license yet." He picked up his finger and pointed it at us like he always did at this point in the story. "Don't you kids go driving without your driver's license!"

I looked at Quentin and furrowed my brow, "Don't you do it!"

Quentin put up his hands, "I promise!"

My dad continued, "Then, as we gave up, not being able to find the bear, I pulled into the driveway of the neighbor's house and guess what?"

"What?" Quentin asked.

Cole and I both laughed at Quentin and said together, "And there he was!"

My dad nodded, "And there he was! The big black bear, just sitting there in the neighbor's driveway, it was as if he had been waiting for us there the whole time!"

"Woah..." Quentin gawked, "That's so cool! He was just right there!"

"Yep," my dad chuckled.

"I have something for you kids," my mom said, pulling two Mason jars from the basket.

I took one of the Mason jars from my mom, knowing exactly what to do with it. "C'mon Q!" I said and ran into the field. It had begun to get dark, the sky turned to a sea of muted greys and blues and a few of the brightest stars lit up above us.

"What are we doing?" Quentin asked, running after me.

I stood in the middle of the field and did a little spin, "The lightning bugs are out! We are going to catch some!"

Quentin took the jar from my hand and examined the little holes that my mom had poked in the top of it. "Okay, but if you want to stay my friend you have to call them fireflies."

"Okay! Let's catch some fireflies!" I said, correcting the midwestern dialect I picked up from my parents.

I opened the jar, and carefully placed it in the grass with the lid next to it. Quentin and I ran around laughing for a while, crazily trying to scoop the little flashing creatures out of the air before they got dark and we couldn't find them anymore. When one that we were chasing stopped flashing its little light, we would move on to the next, desperately following it until it got too high in the air for us to reach.

Within about twenty minutes of our chase, we had successfully captured about 10 fireflies in our jar. We sat on the dewy grass, our legs crossed and the jar set in-between us. Quentin leaned forward, and pressed the top of his head against the top of mine. We sat there for a minute just looking at the little bugs bumping around in the jar and trying to escape. A few of the fireflies settled at the bottom, giving up.

"Do you think they have enough air?" Quentin asked.

"Yeah, there are holes in the top."

"But look at that one." He pointed at a firefly that had settled at the bottom of the jar and hadn't flashed in a little while, "he looks dead."

I flicked the bottom of the jar and the firefly crawled away from the place I flicked. "I think he is just tired."

"Don't you think we should let them go?" Quentin pleaded.

"Why? They are just little bugs."

"I mean look at them," he said, the top of our heads still pressed together as we stared at them. "They look so much prettier when they are free. Did you know that they use their flashing lights to tell each other that they like each other? They are barely flashing anymore. I don't know, if I were them, I would want to be let free."

I surprised myself by not laughing at his odd sentiment. I listened, "You aren't a firefly, though."

He shrugged, "But maybe we aren't too different from them. I mean think about it."

I did think about it, and I have come back to thinking about it so many times over the years. I know Quentin did, too, because after those words left his mouth the silence between us spoke volumes. I understood what he was telling me. In the years after I might forget it for a while, but those words always come back to me. "Okay," I said, "let's let them go."

We moved so we lay on our stomachs in the freshly-cut grass with our faces in front of the jar. Quentin placed his hand on the top of the jar, "Ready?"

"Ready."

He slowly unscrewed the top of the jar and placed it in the grass. The fireflies began to flash again. Each one floated from the jar, a little ball of light taking off into the beyond. We watched them intently, until the last one opened its wings and flew, following all the other fireflies into the night. "Goodbye, friends," Quentin said softly to the air above us.

Six

"DINNER, KIDS!" my mom yelled at us from the bottom of the stairs. Cole, who sat on the landing, playing with plastic dinosaurs, jumped up, scattering his dinosaurs and ran down the stairs. My mom stopped him with her hand, put her hands on his shoulders and turned him around. "Go pick up your toys. And don't run, please."

Cole hung his head and started back up the stairs. When he passed me, he looked up into my eyes. "I'm really hungry, though."

I hopped down a couple of the stairs and used the railing to push myself up in the air and swing down a couple more steps. I looked back up at Quentin with a grin, but he just walked down the stairs normally. I sighed and pushed past my mother who gave me a stern look but didn't say anything. The air smelled wonderful, like warm bread and all sorts of herbs. I took in a huge breath of the smell wafting from the kitchen and let my socked feet slide along the hard-wood floor. "Oh, did Dad make dinner?" I asked my mom.

She nodded her head and I grinned, but quickly turned it into a frown. My mom took great offense when

I insulted her cooking, but her food just didn't make me want to eat it ever. We always had the same sorts of things for every meal. A vegetable, a meat and maybe a starch if my mom felt generous. It all tasted the same to me at that point because it seemed the only flavors my mom knew existed were salt and pepper. My dad's cooking, however, always put everyone in a good mood. Just smelling it made my stomach grumble.

I leaned up against the counter and gazed up at my dad. "Oh, what is it? It smells so good."

"Quiche and garlic bread."

"Oh, my mom has made quiche before," Quentin came up behind me. "But, yours smells a lot better than hers, Mr. Bowen."

"Thank you, Quentin. That is very kind," my dad nodded his head in Quentin's direction. "I just had some extra time today and I thought I would try out a new recipe for you all."

"Thanks, Dad. I'm excited."

"Well, let's get it served up!"

My dad sliced the quiche and placed a piece on each of our plates along with a chunk of garlic bread that he pulled out of the oven wrapped in tin foil. We sat down at the table and my mom asked us about what we were doing in school.

"Well Quentin and me are—"

"Quentin and I are," my mom corrected.

"We are starting a project about American history. Quentin and I are doing ours together. We have to pick a subject about the founding of the thirteen colonies and research it."

My dad tore a piece of his bread off and began to chew it. "I think it is a good skill for you to learn that at your age. If you can use the internet to research history, you can also use it to get ahead in other parts of your studies. Imagine how much more they can know now than we did when we were their age. Isn't that great, Amy?"

"No." My mom clenched her fist around her fork. "If they can get information about history, then they can get information about anything. When we were kids, there were boundaries, certain things that were controlled. And now these children are able to go rogue and we might never know. I think it is just horrible."

"They can actually limit what someone can search for, so I don't think that should be so much of a problem."

"We're not using the internet," Quentin butted in. I had stayed silent because I knew my mom would have just told me that it didn't detract from the point she wanted to make. Most of the time, I would rather have my parents go on arguing about something pointless than have them be mad at me.

My mom clenched her fork even tighter, "So, what is your topic going to be?"

"I don't know, we were thinking maybe smallpox. You know it killed a lot of the people that lived here before us? And that it wasn't just smallpox that killed the Native Americans, but that the British people did it on purpose? That's horrible I think."

"Yeah. The story they tell us about the first Thanksgiving isn't even true. The Pilgrims hated the Indians," Quentin added.

"And who taught you that?" my mom asked.

"A book," I frowned at her.

"The Pilgrims came here to escape religious persecution and you should be grateful, because without them you wouldn't be here."

I tilted my head at her, "But they murdered people who didn't do anything wrong. And children. The Native Americans were doing perfectly fine without them, you know. They were living just fine."

My mom took a bite of her quiche and chewed. She took an insanely long time to chew one bite of food. "The Pilgrims are the reason that you get to live in a democracy, where you can have luxuries like this food and this house. The Indians were not better off without us, they couldn't even build themselves good shelter and now our government gives them land to live on."

I shrugged, "I guess I'll do the research for my topic."

"I think you should do a different topic. Did you know that Thomas Jefferson wrote the Declaration of Independence right here in Pennsylvania?"

"Yes. We did Pennsylvania history last year, and anyway that's not until later. It is still the beginning of the school year."

My dad coughed, "So Cole, what are you doing in school?"

"Well, in geography we are learning about all the different types of landforms. Have you ever seen a butte?" Cole asked.

"I have in fact seen a butte," my dad raised one eyebrow at him.

"Really? Where?"

"In Utah, while I was in college." He took a sip of water. "It was really nice, maybe we should go there sometime."

"Maybe Tori will go to college there!"

My dad turned to me, "Are you interested in law school Victoria?"

"No." Both my parents remained silent. Next to me Quentin bit his lip to keep himself from smiling. I kicked his foot under the table and he looked up at me. He raised one eyebrow and turned down the corners of his mouth. I knew exactly what his intentions were, but I wouldn't let him get to me. If he started this battle, I guess I couldn't back out now.

I shoved a piece of quiche in my mouth and chewed it up. I opened my lips at Quentin so he could see the excess egg bits around my teeth. "Victoria!" My mom scolded me.

I closed my mouth and burst out into laughter.

"Victoria that is not appropriate for the dinner table."

Quentin burst out into laughter too.

QUENTIN JERKED HIS HAND around above the papers that he had laid out around the floor of his bedroom. "Okay so it starts here," he pointed to the farthest panel of his comic, "and then you read that way." He motioned to the right, down, and to the left.

"That doesn't make any sense, you should read top left to right, then bottom left to right."

"Whatever! I like it better this way you don't have to look around so much."

"What is it about?"

"It's about a knight who went to training school, but all the other knights were stronger than him. When they all went on a journey to slay a dragon that burned down a nearby village," he raised his hand up and slammed it down on the paper, "BOOM! The dragon stole the strongest knight of all!"

"Then what happened?" I urged.

"Well, I can't tell you that would be a spoiler."

"I want to know!"

"You have to read it!"

I started reading where he told me to start and immediately recognized the main character. All the knights were standing in a line, strong and put together, but second from the end of the line was a smaller knight, who stood tilted just slightly to one side. I witnessed him fail at many of the training exercises, but do enough just to scrape by. He became the laughing stock of the whole training academy. When they went to save the village from the dragon, the most horrible of all the knights who made fun of him got snatched up by the dragon and taken away. All the knights went on a perilous journey to find him and when they did, they found him barely alive. They managed to get him and escape from the dragon's lair, but their best knight was dying. The small knight came forward and placed his hands on the shoulders of the dying knight, and before everyone's eyes, the dying knight woke up and miraculously, he healed! The small knight became the hero and it turned out being a knight might not have been his purpose after all.

"Wow! It was good. I just wish instead of healing the mean knight he would have stolen all his strength and then he could be the greatest knight of all!"

"Tori! That's not the point!" Quentin sighed. "He is the hero, just not how they thought he had to be!"

"But what happened to the dragon? Did he keep burning the village down?"

"No, the great knight went back to his lair and slayed him!"

"What happened to the small knight?"

"He went back to the village and became a healer, but once the glory wore off everyone made fun of him again because all the other healers were girls."

"Are you going to draw that comic too?"

"Yes, it's going to be the sequel. In the end, he is going to save the king of the whole land because none of the other healers were able to do it!" he exclaimed. "It teaches the rest of the people that made fun of him that they're not so great after all!"

"Children," Leah poked her head into Quentin's room. "I called you for dinner 10 minutes ago, it will be cold if you don't come soon."

"But Mom, we were talking about my comic!"

"And it will still be there when dinner is over."

"Fine," Quentin groaned, "but don't let it get out of order."

I jumped up from the floor and ran into the kitchen. "Ooo, spaghetti! I love spaghetti," I smiled when I saw the pot of noodles covered in red sauce.

"Ugh, Mom, spaghetti again?" Quentin groaned.

"I'm sorry, hon, it has been a long day at work. Tori is excited!"

"Yeah! We never have spaghetti!"

I scooped up a large serving of noodles and brought my plate to the table. I breathed in the scent of the tangy sauce that felt so simple yet for some reason so special to me. "Leah, can you pass the cheese?" She handed a tiny bowl of parmesan cheese to me and I sprinkled it over my pasta.

Quentin slid his plate onto the placemat next to me. He slammed his elbow down as he sat, shaking the table. I leaned my stomach into the edge of the round table to eat, careful not to let my sleeves catch on the places where it had splintered. When Quentin leaned on his side of the table, it bent just a little from the fold in the middle, making the side of my plate hover above the other side of the table. "Hey, put the table down," I whined at him.

"I'm not picking it up. I would have to be a goliath for that."

"Oh, I definitely think you could pick up this table in a couple years," Leah said. "I can pick up this table."

"Just take your elbows off, it makes this side higher than the other one."

Quentin slurped up a piece of spaghetti. "Just move your plate to one side."

Leah sighed, "Quentin, will you please take your elbows off the table?"

"Fine," he groaned and slurped another few pieces of spaghetti.

I twisted a bunch of noodles around my fork and shoved them all in my mouth. "Leah, what's communists?"

Leah had just put a big bite of pasta in her mouth and had to cover it with her hand. She chewed for a second. "Who told you about communists?"

"No one. That is why I asked you, obviously."

Leah laughed again, "Who did you hear talking about communists?"

"My dad. He thinks they are the worst thing ever."

"Did he say that?"

"Kind of?"

"Is that a question?"

"No. What is communists?"

"Well," she sighed, "there are different ways of organizing your economy and political system. One very controversial way is called communism. Basically, communism means that everyone works in society together and gets exactly the same amount of resources. At least that's how I understand it. You would probably do better asking someone like your teacher."

"Do any places have communism?"

"Not really," she told me. "There are some places that believe in it, but don't really have it."

"Why does my dad hate it so much?"

She sighed, "Well, all systems like that have a lot of problems because there are so many people that are controlled and so much corruption and inequality."

"But if everyone got all the same resources doesn't that mean they are all equal?"

"In a way, but imagine it like this: Quentin needs his medication to be healthy, but if you both got his medication it would be a waste of resources and if neither of you did then Quentin wouldn't be healthy."

"Hmm, what does our country have?"

"Our country has capitalism. That is another reason why your father probably hates communism so much, because capitalism greatly benefits him."

"Capitalism means that everyone's work has value and they get paid based on the value of their work," Quentin chimed in. "You told me that before."

"Yes, and they get to choose what work they want to do. Most people in America value that as well, free will."

"I don't understand, they both sound good." My mind felt twisted over upon itself. Shouldn't everyone have equal resources, but also be paid for the work they do?

"Finish your food," Leah commanded.

"What?" Quentin and I asked.

"Finish your food and then clear the table," she said.

"Why?" Quentin asked.

"Just do it; I'm going to show you something."

We shoveled the rest of our pasta in our faces and while still chewing cleared all the dishes off the table. Leah stacked the placemats and moved them to the kitchen counter. She went over to the cabinet and pulled out a tub of letter alphabet cookies. She slammed it down on the table and sat down in the chair across from me. She peeled the lid off the top of the tub and placed it down next to her.

"So, imagine I am a dictator. Do you know what that means?" I shook my head no. "A dictator is a person who has complete control over a country, kind of like a king or a queen. So, I am a dictator who thinks my country should be a communist country. On paper, that means that we each get one third of the cookies, right?"

"Right," Quentin agreed.

"So, imagine Quentin is a farmer and he grew all the ingredients that Tori used to bake into the cookies, then the cookies were given to the government to redistribute to the people. That means that as the dictator I now have possession of all the resources. Both of you did your part so you should be given your equal share of the resources, but I could just do this." She pulled the tub of cookies over to herself and took out a few and dropped them in front of Quentin, then the same amount and dropped them in front of me. "Now the idea behind communism is that any kind of government would fade out and that it would be done in a democratic way, but it never seems to happen that way. See, both of you are equal right? You have the same amount of resources, but are you being paid justly for the work you did?

"Now, Quentin might not want to be a farmer, but he knows he will still get his food, so he just doesn't make as much food anymore. And then eventually there won't be enough food to feed everyone."

"That's all the cookies we get?" Quentin whined, holding up a G.

"Okay, so you don't like that?"

"No!" I said.

"Well maybe let's try capitalism." She took a big handful of cookies and placed them in front of me. "Okay, your cookies are money. In order to get more, you have to do certain tasks. You don't have to do them, but if you do you can get money."

"Okay what do we have to do?"

"Hmm," she thought for a second, "I'll pay you to do a push-up."

"Okay!" I said. I hopped out of my chair and did a push-up. Quentin did the same.

"Good job," Leah said. She placed three cookies in front of me and only two in front of Quentin. "Now, in order to do tasks that get you more money, you have to go to school and learn how to do the tasks. In order to go to school, you have to pay me seven cookies, but remember if you want to pay for meals and housing you have to keep some cookies."

"I only have six cookies!" Quentin whined, "That's not fair."

"Well, you can continue to do tasks that earn you less cookies or you could get a loan of four cookies from me."

"Okay I'll have a loan."

"Remember when you pay back your loan you have to give me five cookies instead of four."

He furrowed his brow, "But Tori started with more cookies than me."

Leah shrugged, "Do you want to go to school or not?"

"No," Quentin crossed his arms.

"I want to go to school!" I handed Leah seven of my 15 cookies.

"Good," Leah said. "Go get me a glass of water."

I walked over to the kitchen and filled a glass with water. I placed it in front of Leah. She put five cookies in front of me. "Quentin, I'll pay you a cookie for every push-up you do."

He got down on the ground to do push-ups, but already started to struggle by the sixth one. Leah gave him six cookies. "Tori, will you call River for me?" I called him and she gave me six cookies.

"I could have called River," Quentin groaned.

Leah shook her head, "No, you couldn't, Tori learned that in school." He frowned. "Oh! I forgot, it's time to pay taxes. Quentin, you owe me four cookies and Tori, you owe me five."

"This is so stupid!" Quentin slammed his fist down on the table.

I popped a cookie into my mouth, "I like it!"

"Tori, you aren't supposed to eat the money," Leah scolded with a smile.

"Can we stop now?" Quentin moaned.

"Do you get it?"

"Yeah! I get it. They're both stupid."

Leah and I both laughed at him. "Tori, do you understand what I meant now?"

I nodded, "I think so."

"Okay great. Now give Quentin some of your cookies," she chuckled.

I pushed a few of my cookies over to Quentin, and he happily popped one in his mouth. "I like it better when I just get to eat the cookies."

A smile ran across my face, "I don't know, my brain hurts, in a good way."

"That's a nice feeling," Leah agreed. "I wish school would do that for you guys more often."

"School is stupid," Quentin said with his mouth full of cookies.

"I agree," I nodded my head up and down.

"Well, I wish there was something I could do about that," Leah frowned.

"You should be our teacher!" I suggested. "School would be a lot better if our teachers did lessons like that."

"Well, I regret to inform you that I don't have a college degree, so it would be impossible for me to be hired."

"*That's* stupid, you're so much smarter than all the adults I know."

"Thanks, Tori," she laughed.

Seven

The day he showed up must have been Saturday or maybe Sunday. The wind outside howled as we approached our 10th winter. Quentin and I had been watching TV and playing with River all day, cozied up in his house. River grew a lot since we had picked him on Quentin's birthday and the amount of energy he had also only increased.

Quentin and I snuggled up under a blanket with a space heater in front of us to make up for his house's lack of good insulation. River, who sat in between us, also watched the TV. The doorbell rang just as an ad break went on. Leah had gone out to get groceries, so Quentin looked at me and said, "If you get it, I will give you a lollipop from my Halloween candy."

I didn't want to get up from my spot on the couch either. "Okay, but it better be cherry flavored," I said, knowing how much he treasured anything cherry.

The doorbell rang again and River jumped up from the couch, barking at the door. "Okay, fine," Quentin agreed.

I walked over to the door and pulled it open, leaving the screen door closed, a thin barrier between me and whoever stood on the other side. The person I saw wore a brown coat, a blue button up shirt, and khaki pants. He stood at about five foot 11 and when I looked up at his face, something churned in my stomach. He had dirty blonde hair, green eyes and an expensive watch that caught my eye when the sun peeked through a cloud and its light glinted off the minute hand. He must have been about thirty and clearly not from anywhere around here. I could sense the tension he held in the way he stiffened his back. On the path up to the house stood a young woman who must have been his wife, also nicely dressed in a blouse and knee length skirt with a long black coat bundled around her, holding a baby tightly in her arms.

I looked up at the man. "What can I help you with sir?" I asked. "If you are trying to sell something, unfortunately I will not be able to buy anything from you today," I enunciated.

"How old are you?" he leaned forward and back on his heels. He kept turning his head around and around like someone might jump out at him and attack him.

"I don't think I should tell you that, sir. But, if you must know, I am 27 at heart."

He left out a sharp breath through his nose. "Is Leah Flasch your mother?"

I shook my head, and he turned to go, "She's not here right now, she went to the grocery store."

He turned back around; I couldn't read the look on his face. His eyebrows were curved down and his eyes questioning, one corner of his mouth turned into a smile but he kept unconsciously digging his teeth into his lips. "So, she is your mother? Is your brother here?"

"No, no, and yes," I replied.

He took a breath in through gritted teeth, "What?"

I decided to stop messing with him, "Leah is not my mother and my brother is not here, but if I *was* her daughter, then yes, Quentin is here."

He took a deep breath and repeated his name, "Quentin."

I turned around and looked at Quentin, who seemed to not be hearing any of the conversation. "Yes? What do you want with Quentin?" I said this not understanding, but now that I look back on it, I laugh at my stupidity. Quentin never really looked much like Leah. Except for the way he held himself and walked, they barely resembled each other at all. But there I stood, staring at a grown-up version of Quentin, not understanding at all. They had the same wavy dirty blonde hair and electrically green eyes. They were built exactly the same way, lean with legs that were unnaturally long compared to the rest of their body. Except this man felt different, not at all like my best friend. He did not feel like a cool summer's breeze the way Quentin did or have the same sunny smile like Quentin. He felt like a rock that had only partially been worn smooth by the ocean. And he had a close-cut beard that made his features look sharper and more masculine, unlike Quentin's boyish softness.

Before he had a chance to respond to me, which took him a while, Quentin came up behind me, "What's taking so long?" he complained.

The man's eyes widened as he took in everything, they flickered across Quentin's face. I looked between them a couple of times and the realization started to swell inside me.

Before I could say anything, I heard a car door slam and Leah's voice, "Saul?"

He turned around, "Leah?"

Leah looked horrified, "What are you doing here? Why didn't you call? Didn't you think to call?"

He walked over to her and tried to put his hand on her arm, a comforting gesture, but she swatted his hand away from her. "Leah, come on," he pleaded.

She turned away from him and to his wife. "Hi, you must be the wife I have heard nothing about," Leah said and stuck out her hand to Saul's wife.

"Hi, I'm Riya," she said and shook Leah's hand.

"Very nice to meet you Riya, I'm sorry it is under these extremely uncomfortable circumstances." She turned towards us, "Kids, can you take the groceries into the house?"

Quentin and I walked to the car and as I loaded my arms with groceries, I looked over to Quentin. He looked as if he had just been hit by a bus. "Are you okay?" I asked.

He shrugged, "That's my father."

"I know," I replied. I wished I knew what to do, that maybe he would show me an inkling of what was going on in his head, but he kept his arms straight at his sides and his mouth pursed in a line.

We carried all the groceries inside and Leah told us to show Riya around the house while she talked to Saul. We took Riya inside and stood unmoving in the living room for a couple seconds. Quentin motioned around the room, "This is the living room." He pointed to his room, "That's my bedroom, and across the hall is my mom's room and the bathroom, through that hall is the kitchen, and that's it."

"It's lovely," she smiled.

"Can I meet the baby?" Quentin asked.

"Yeah of course," Riya said, "go sit down and I'll let you hold him."

Quentin quickly walked over to the couch and sat down. Riya followed him and placed the baby in Quentin's arms. "What's his name?" he asked.

"Peter," Riya said.

"Hi Peter, I'm your brother Quentin," he cooed softly at the baby. "Tori, come meet my brother."

I walked around to the couch from the place in the corner I had been standing. I sat down next to Quentin. "Why hello, Peter," I whispered. I turned to Riya, "How old is he?"

She smiled, "Five months and a half, his birthday is May 29th."

"Aww, Peter," I said. "Your birthday is only three days after your brother's!"

"Oh really, I didn't know that!" Riya chimed in, her voice a little too loud and chipper.

The room fell cold with the unintended harshness of these words, a father that didn't celebrate his son's birthday. Until Peter grasped Quentin's finger with his baby hand. "Look at his little finger nails, Tori." Peter widened his little brown eyes and made a small burbling noise that sounded halfway between a laugh and a cough.

"I think he likes you, Quentin," Riya said. She tried so hard for the sake of all of us to be nice, but the suddenness of their appearance made everything all too uncomfortable. Quentin ignored her and continued to make faces at Peter.

We sat there in silence for a while until we heard Leah yell from outside, "So you thought you could just walk into our lives, just show up out of the blue, and we would be fine with it?!" I could hear Saul respond, but I couldn't hear what he said. We heard Leah again, "We were doing fine without you Saul!" Again, I couldn't hear his response. "Of course, we appreciate you helping pay for Quentin's treatment, Saul. But that is just what a father is supposed to do, Saul." The way she said his name made it sound like poison on her lips.

They lowered their voices again. A couple minutes later the door knob turned and they walked in, Leah with red eyes and a fake smile on her face and Saul with a real seeming smile on his. "Okay, Quentin, your dad is going to spend an hour with us, and that's it, after today maybe we can have a phone call to figure out when else you can see him. Tori, would it be okay if you went home now?"

"Yeah," I said and started to leave.

Quentin gripped my wrist and held onto it, "No, I want her to stay."

"Quentin—"

"Hey, it's okay if you want her here," Saul interjected.

Leah gave him a death stare, but Quentin smiled at his dad and I sat back down on the couch next to Quentin. Riya lifted Peter from Quentin's lap and pulled up a chair. Saul did the same and Leah sat down on the other side of Quentin. Quentin's fingernails dug deep into my arms, almost enough to draw blood but I didn't move.

"So, Saul, can I call you Saul? My mom says I should never call an adult by their first name, but Leah said I could call her Leah."

Saul chuckled awkwardly. "It's all good. Where I live in California, everyone goes by their first name unless we are being really formal."

"Where do you live?" I asked.

"San Jose. Have you heard of that? It is in the San Francisco Bay Area."

I nodded, "Leah is from San Francisco."

We spent the majority of the hour just sitting there and making uncomfortable conversation. Saul and I did the majority of the talking. Quentin didn't loosen his grip on my wrist for the first half an hour and when Saul asked him about school he just shrugged, not making eye contact. I learned all about Saul though; he worked for a technology company and he had been living in San Jose for five years. He and Riya had been married for two years. He loved to go into San Francisco and watch their baseball team. He told Quentin that he would definitely take him and Peter to go see a game sometime. Quentin's hand clenched my arm a little tighter when he said that. I told Saul about how we liked to go on bike rides and all about our *friendship* after he had jokingly asked Quentin if we were dating. Of course, Quentin just stared at him in response.

Finally, after an excruciating hour, Leah said, "I think it's time for you to go now, Saul."

They gave their goodbyes and Saul gave Quentin a stiff hug. Saul shook my hand and told me he was glad to have met me, and Riya shook Leah's hand and thanked her for everything. Saul patted Quentin on the shoulder and said, "I really hope I can see you again soon, son." A long pause followed his words.

And then they were gone. Leah looked angry, Quentin looked horrified and I didn't know what to do with myself, so when Quentin told me I could leave and ran off to his room, I listened to him and walked home in the cold.

A FEW MONTHS AFTER Saul's unexpected arrival, Quentin and Leah's normal had been completely turned on its head. "He keeps flying out here unannounced and apparently, he wants to move to the city to be closer to me. My mom is really mad at him because he refuses to make a plan or anything, but says he wants to be in my life." Quentin sighed and spun around in the chair at my desk. "Also, he is just so weird, like he keeps trying to make these jokes and I have to pretend to laugh even though they aren't funny, but it makes me like him more and want to hate him more. I mean he says he wants to get to know me, but it's been four months since I met him and I still feel like I know nothing about him besides what he told you on the first day."

I laid on the ground and just listened to Quentin rant. Of course, I had no advice to give him because I had only met Saul once, and I had never experienced having my father leave me and come back into my life randomly. "Oh, I have something to show you," I said. I got up off my floor and went over to my bookshelf, where I pulled out the latest addition to my CD collection. I clicked open the brittle plastic of the CD case and pushed out the CD. *In Between Dreams* by Jack Johnson. "It's not The Head and the Heart," I said, knowing that his favorite band had been The Head and the Heart ever since his birthday when we heard "Down in the Valley" on our way to the walk at Riverview Park.

I opened the top of the clock next to my bed that had a CD player in it, popped the yellow disk in and hit play. The slow yet joyful music filled the room and I stood back from the CD player and moved my hips, swaying to the music. I grabbed Quentin's hand to dance with him, pulling him into me and pushing him away to the beat of the song. We moved our arms in the air and danced circles around each other laughing. Quentin took my hand and spun me in circles around him. The album's tempo wouldn't make most people want to dance, but it made my fingers dance on the empty CD case and it made us want to feel the happiness in its words.

I sang along to the third song on the album, my hands on Quentin's shoulders, smiling into his laughing face. "'Wake up slow, wake up slow,'" I sang. He swayed his body along with the words and I motioned for him to sing along with me, he shook his head and put his hands on my waist. He danced me in circles around the room.

We collapsed on my floor laughing by the fourth song, amused by our little private performance. He turned towards me and laid on his side, he looked at me with his electric green eyes, closer to me than he ever had been. I began to notice the tiny yellow flecks mixed in with the green of his eyes that I never saw before. I squinted my eyes at him and pinched my face into a smile. He quietly let out a laugh and smiled back at me, "Thanks, Tori."

EVERY DAY FEELS SIGNIFICANT until you forget it a week later. Every day was the same in our little town, every night was the same, every class, every meal, every lunch. Nothing really stands out in my mind about lunch. I mean every American child basically has the same experience in the cafeteria. They sit, maybe with their friends, maybe not, the food sucks but they pick at it anyway and the cafeteria smells like sticky children and something else that you can never quite place.

I usually sat with Oda, Spencer, Quentin, and a few other people that rotated groups. I noticed that Hally's group of friends slowly dissipated over time that year. She had so much power in my eyes, an endless pick of friends, or maybe they were just people she could control.

"Hah, Queen Bee is all alone today," I said to Oda.

That day, Hally sat alone with her face close to her tray of food; she occasionally took a small bite of food. Her long blonde hair fell down in sheets around her face, "Look at her, finally getting a taste of her own medicine. Pathetic," I laughed.

"I heard her parents are getting divorced," Oda said.

"So?" I scoffed.

Oda shrugged, "My mom says divorce can be really hard on a kid, and her parents' one is really bad."

"Do you even remember what she did to us?"

"It really wasn't that bad," Quentin said softly.

"What are you talking about? She was the worst to us. She is the worst. People get divorced all the time. Why do you all care so much?"

"What if your parents got divorced?"

"It wouldn't be that bad. I would get to have two rooms and two sets of clothes and two houses. Anyways, my parents already don't love each other the way Oda's do," I said remembering the way Oda's parents embraced and looked into each other's eyes all the time. You knew that was real love, not the passive aggressiveness and constant need for approval, not forcing your kids to be people they weren't and constantly checking each other on everything the other one does. No, love is selfless. The only thing my parents care for is themselves.

"Was it bad when your parents got divorced?" Oda asked.

Quentin shrugged, "I don't know, I was a baby and they were never married anyway."

"My parents wanted to make it seem like we would all still be friends," Spencer chimed in, "but my mom decided to move us all the way here, which didn't make my dad very happy."

"Your parents are divorced?" I asked.

He nodded, "A year before we moved here."

"I'm sorry, Spencer," I said sympathetically. "But Hally is still awful," I glared at her as I said it.

At that moment Hally got up, walked by and slid her half-empty tray towards us with one harsh movement, "Look its sick boy and his caretaker. You think you can take care of my tray too?" The tray hit Quentin hard in the chest and spilled spaghetti all over his front, staining his new white graphic t-shirt with tomato sauce. "Oops," Hally smiled, "I wouldn't want to hurt him. You better clean that up." She walked away with her head up. Right before she got to the door she slumped back down

"I don't know how you can be nice to such a bad person. I doubt she is even human."

JUNE 10TH WAS a date I definitely would not remember for the rest of my life – in fact, I just had to look that up right now – but I guess the day seemed very important to us at the time. Fifth grade promotion felt like the end of an era.

Even if I didn't remember the date, I do remember the day very clearly because of how excited we were to be growing up and getting out of elementary school. Looking back on that day, my heart still sinks when I remember how quick we were to get out of there. Even now, years later, I still miss every second of elementary school. Quentin and I may have been through more than your average fifth grader in our town, especially Quentin, but we still carried an air of unconditional happiness; just being with each other and listening to Jack Johnson or dancing in the rain or hugging his crazy dog would make all our problems go away. I miss the constant bike rides and our conversations about the world that we knew nothing about. Of course, I took all this for granted at the time.

I got dressed up in a floral dress and flats for once. I allowed my mom to braid the top half of my hair and excitedly I met Quentin in the front of school. He wore a purple button-down shirt and black dress pants. We went to our fifth-grade classroom to sign our yearbooks that were filled with pictures from our whole elementary school experience and to give our teacher flowers and gifts that our moms shoved in our arms before we walked into school that morning. The ceremony started at eleven, so we spent the morning playing games with our classmates and trying not to mess up our clothes.

At ten-thirty, we brought our chairs onto the field and sat in alphabetical order by last name. I turned around in my chair to see Quentin who sat two rows behind me with a last name that started with F, and mine starting with B. The parents and siblings started arriving to watch us graduate. My dad waved at me, holding the hand of Cole, whom they pulled out of his third-grade class.

We sat through the ceremony, all getting burnt in the early summer sun and sweating in our dress clothes as we waited for our turn to get promoted. When they said my name, I hopped up from my chair and walked across the makeshift stage that they set up that morning. I took the elementary certificate from my principal and walked down the other side of the stage. When Quentin's name got called, I stood up, clapped, and cheered for him as loud as I could, Leah doing the same from the middle of the audience.

After everyone got their certificate and the families finished cheering, the time came for the student speeches which Quentin and I had volunteered to do together. We spent the past month working on the speech we were supposed to give that day. I wrote most of it because I had a way with words and I made sure

Quentin knew it. In our dynamic duo, Quentin took more control over the artistic and creative side of things.

We both walked up the stage and stood stiffly in front of the microphone. I cleared my throat for dramatic effect. "Hi, I'm Victoria Bowen," I said.

"And I'm Quentin Flasch," Quentin said nervously.

"We have both been going to this school since kindergarten!"

"And we are here to tell you all about why it was so great!"

We went on about how we had met at school and how we were best friends, how the school had helped us learn, and grow and how amazing our teachers were. I do not remember the speech word for word or have a copy of it anywhere, but I remember the writing of that speech. About half of the sentences ended with an exclamation mark and the whole thing sounded overly enthusiastic and fake. The parents ate it up though. I hated that they probably all thought we were so cute; I wanted them to listen to my words. At the end of the speech, we held hands and bowed, a finishing touch that my mom made sure we did after we practiced our speech in front of my family.

After the ceremony, everyone went around and hugged their kids, giving them flowers and calling their grandparents. A whirlwind of flowers and hugs blew my way as well. "Good job, sweetie!" my mom kissed me on the top of the head and shoved a bouquet of summery looking daisies into my hands.

"We are so proud of you Victoria Lucas Bowen," my dad said in a fake serious voice.

Cole stuck out his hand to me and smiled with his lips turned down but his teeth showing, I hit his hand out of the way, "Oh shut up," I joked. He ran into me and wrapped his arms around my waist. I laughed and rubbed my knuckles into the top of his head.

Quentin and Leah walked over to us and Leah handed me a card with my name written on the pastel blue envelope, similar to one Quentin held in his hand. "Okay, you two get together for a picture!" my mom exclaimed and pushed me to the side so I stood next to Quentin.

Completely ignoring my mom trying to take a picture, my dad said, "So Quentin, how does it feel to be a middle school man?"

Through his smiling teeth, "We aren't in middle school yet, Mr. Bowen."

Also ignoring Quentin's response, "bet it feels good. Wow they grow up so fast," he said to Leah. She nodded. "I hope they will start to learn how to become productive members of society in middle school."

"Now one with Cole!" my mom yelled happily.

Cole stepped between us and smiled, showing all of his crooked teeth.

MIDDLE SCHOOL

"What we have once enjoyed deeply we can never lose. All that we love deeply becomes a part of us."

Helen Keller

Eight

"TORI, CAN YOU PUT your arm around your brother, please?"

We stood on our front porch as my mom took our annual first day of school pictures. I touched the tips of my long brown hair that stretched all the way to the middle of my new sweater. My mom had told me that morning, "Victoria, you have to start to grow up and care about the way you look, like a real woman." Of course, I just mocked her and asked why I didn't just cut off all my hair. But she walked away and left me with a brush and a tangled head of hair.

I put my arm around Cole, "Happy first day of fourth grade little brother!" I said. "Can I go now, Mom? I told Quentin I would meet him at his house."

"Okay, fine. Have a nice day."

I slung my nearly empty backpack over my shoulder and jumped on my bike. I rode as fast as I could to Quentin's house, my hair already messed up from the helmet and wind as I biked. I knocked on the door and River barked for a while before Quentin opened the door, backpack slung over one shoulder and helmet in hand. "Tori is here, Mom!" Quentin yelled back into the house.

I moved my shoulders back and forth, antsy, excited for the first day of middle school and what it might entail for us. Leah came up behind Quentin, kissed him on the top of the head. "Have fun," she said. "Be safe."

Quentin stepped out of his house and closed the door behind him. I gave him a quick hug, pulled away, and bounced up and down in front of him. We hadn't seen each other for a month because my parents had decided it would do Cole and me some good to spend time with my grandparents at their lake house learning how to be proper kids because, apparently, we lived in an environment that allowed us to go wild, an environment that our parents created. I think they realized it but didn't want to say it aloud.

Quentin looked me up and down. "You aren't a proper young lady now, are you?" he asked skeptically.

"No! I'm just as wild as ever! I'm just a good actor. I convinced my parents that I am civilized." I reached into my pocket and pulled out my dad's old smartphone. "Look what they let me have!"

Quentin turned his backpack around and pulled out a shiny new grey flip phone. "Hey! We can text now if I can figure out how to make words on this thing." He flipped it open and pointed to the numbers on the keypad. "Maybe we can just make a code with the numbers or something."

"Let's go! Let's go!" I said excitedly, wanting to make it to school early.

We jumped on our bikes and raced all the way to school. When we got there, we locked our bikes in the giant bike racks in front of the school, trying to catch our breath. I took off my helmet and attached it to the outside of my backpack and followed Quentin to the school. We sat down on a bench in front of the building and pulled out our schedules. Already knowing that we only had history together, I looked over Quentin's schedule, just to make sure.

The first bell rang and we got up and walked into the building. Immediately, I felt my hands start to sweat as the noise of the crowded hallways filled my ears and I looked up at the eighth graders who must have been giants. Quentin had to go to the second floor for his first class, so I told him good luck and waited until he disappeared up the stairs. I remember walking into my first class and seeing that all the desks were set up in pairs facing towards the front of the room. I missed the table groupings I had most of elementary school.

I sat next to a girl from the other elementary school in the district. She played on my soccer team the season before we went to middle school. I tried to make conversation with her by saying, "Hey, Harper!" when I sat down, but she completely ignored me to talk to her friend sitting behind us.

I don't remember much of the rest of the day except running up to Quentin in the hallway during the passing period before history. "Quentin! This is so weird and awkward and awful!" I almost yelled, so relieved to see him.

"I don't know, it's kind of cool. I have talked to a few new people in my classes and they were nice, even Hally is being nice to me!"

At lunch, as we sat with Oda and a few other people from elementary school, Quentin informed me that he might be joining the track team with Spencer since he had gone to practice over the summer when I was at my grandparents' house.

After school we rode home to Quentin's house. Leah had left us a note telling Quentin she was proud of him along with a huge bowl of cheese puffs. We sunk into his couch and watched our TV show while eating the cheese puffs.

"Hey, Quentin?" I asked during an ad break.

"Yeah?"

"My teacher kept talking about how we were all going to become different because everyone changes during middle school."

He nodded his head, "Mhmm."

"Do you think we are going to change?"

"Well, I think it would be a little weird if we didn't, because if we were exactly like this as adults that would be kind of creepy."

"But would that change us?"

He tilted his chin in the air, "Well, I think that might be about the silliest thing you have ever said."

I stared down at my hands. "I know," I said, "it is pretty silly."

The show went back on and I put my head on his shoulder. "Can we put a cheese puff in our box?"

He laughed, "What?"

"Well, I just couldn't think of anything else to put in the box to mark the first day of sixth grade."

"I think it would probably rot."

"It would most definitely rot," I agreed and looked up at him. One of the corners of his mouth tilted up a little and his eyes smiled as he tried not to laugh at me. "Hey shut up!" I said and pushed him a little.

He lifted his arms in the air, "I didn't say anything!"

"But I could tell you wanted to laugh at me!" I threw a cheese puff at his head.

He picked it up off his lap and put it in his mouth. "Hey, don't waste this perfectly good cheese puff!"

"Oh! I'm just trying to be a good friend here, that cheese puff could have most certainly gone in our box, but now it is inside you!"

"It's not my fault you threw it at me!"

"It's not my fault either!"

He furrowed his brow and made a concerned face at me. "You make no sense."

"That's the point!" I yelled and reached out to tickle him.

"What?" he yelled back.

"Exactly!" I laughed and stopped tickling him.

He pounced back at me, and knocked the bowl of cheese puffs that were on my lap onto the ground. He tried to tickle me under my armpits. I squealed with laughter and pushed him away from me.

We heard Leah's key in the door and both looked at it surprised; Leah normally didn't get off work for another hour. She opened the door, a white box in one hand and her bag in the other. She dropped her keys on the shelf next to the door, looked up at us and laughed out loud, "I see neither of you have grown up one bit!"

Quentin stuck his chin in the air again and crossed his arms with a smug look on his face, "I have no idea what you are talking about. We are officially middle schoolers now, that means we are officially grown up."

Leah laughed again, "Oh, does it?"

"Well, of course it does," I said, taking Quentin's side.

"Tori, I think your mom might want you to be on your way home soon."

"Yeah," I frowned.

"But not before you both have huge slices of this pie I brought you!" she exclaimed.

"Pie?" Quentin asked intrigued.

Leah walked into the kitchen. "Yes! C'mon."

We followed her into the kitchen and sat down at the table. She placed huge slices of lemon meringue pie on little plates in front of us. "Don't tell your mom, Tori!" she said. I licked my lips as I sunk my fork into the two inches of meringue that jiggled above the tart lemon custard which made my lips pinch when it touched my tongue. As we sat around their table, I tried to take as long as I could to eat the pie and Quentin rambled on about the first day of school.

I rode my bike home, the sun still hovering above the horizon. I knew the summer still lingered when I could see the sun this late. It must have been at least seven. The sun's fading rays shone in my eyes and I had to squint as I rode towards my house. I felt different, things were going to change.

I CLAPPED MY HAND over my mouth and ran out of the bathroom. Quentin would be over any minute and I really did not want this to happen right now. I could have thought, "at least I wasn't at school or about to go swimming," but no, I couldn't help myself. This didn't really have to be happening now, when a *boy* was supposed to be here. Anger already simmered in my stomach at my mom for making me wash my bed sheets the day before. I would probably have to wash every day for the next week now.

"MOM!" I screamed down the stairs.

"What do you need?" I heard her respond.

"Get up here right now!"

I heard her sigh loudly, "Honey, what is it that you need?"

"I need you to get up here right now!"

She stomped her feet to the top of the stairs and put her hands on her hips, "What do you need?"

I leaned my head into her and whispered, "I got my period." She smiled and a wave of excitement went through her body. "What? Have you been waiting for me to just start bleeding out of my vagina since the moment you found out you were having a daughter?" my anger simmered.

"Yes, that's exactly what I have been doing," she responded, matching my tone.

"Well, let's just get on with this. Quentin is going to be here soon."

She brought me into the bathroom, and went over the basics with me for about the one hundredth time. As she demonstrated how to use a tampon, I heard the doorbell ring, my dad open it, and him tell Quentin to just go to my room.

"Quick get out!" I told my mom and pushed her out of the bathroom. I slammed the bathroom door as I saw Quentin at the top of the stairs and my mom ushering him into my room. I put on a pad as fast as I could and walked nonchalantly into my bedroom, squeezing my legs together as tightly as possible. I sat down stiffly on my chair and crossed my legs.

"Hi," Quentin said and looked at me skeptically.

"What?" I said angrily.

"You are acting weird," he stated.

"How?" I asked and crossed my arms.

"Well, number one, you hid in the bathroom for like 10 minutes without saying hi to me. I saw you slam the door when I came upstairs. And normally you would lay on the ground, I don't know why you do that, but you always lay on the ground. And you didn't tell me to shut up, and you are twisted up," he said mimicking the way I had my arms and legs crossed.

"I am acting perfectly normal!" I said while crossing my arms around me even tighter.

"Well, if that's true, let's just have a normal conversation."

"Okay!"

"Hally asked me to go to Dimond Cafe with her."

"Why would you go to the Dimond Cafe with Hally?"

"Because she is nice to me!" he shrugged. "And because they have better pastries than Abigail's."

"But do you not remember the way she treated you in elementary school?"

"She's changed! People change!"

"But it's Hally."

"Why are you acting so weird?"

I huffed, "Am I not allowed to be mad that you have befriended your elementary school bully?"

"No! You are just acting so weird," he groaned.

"Leave!" I pointed at the door.

"What?" he asked.

"Get out of my room!" I yelled.

He put his hands up and walked out of the room. I slammed the door behind him and ran to my bed. I shoved my face into my pillow and screamed. Why did things have to be like this? He made me so mad! A couple minutes later my door opened and I yelled, "Go away, Mom!" into my pillow.

"It's not your mom," I heard Quentin's voice say.

I scoffed, "I told you to go away too!"

"Well, whaddya know, I didn't!" Quentin said, and I felt him sit down at the end of my bed. "I brought you some things."

I didn't respond. He pulled my phone out of my back pocket, and "Down in the Valley" started playing. I finally took my face out of the pillow and looked at him. He gave me a big smile. I flipped my head back onto the pillow and sighed. He sang shakily to the music, his voice cracking like a teenage boy, but this time because he just had a terrible singing voice.

"Just because you sing your favorite song really badly isn't going to make me not mad!" I said, stubbornly trying to maintain my anger at him, even though my head already felt less heavy.

"I seem to remember it being *our* favorite song, not just mine," he corrected.

I flipped over onto my back and squinted skeptically at him again. He began singing the "oh, oh, oh, oh," part at the top of his lungs.

"Shut up!" I interrupted his awful voice and threw a pillow at his face. "I can't listen to another second of that!"

"There she is!" he laughed and scrunched his nose at me.

I sat up and held my knees to my chest with my arms, let myself fall against him, and placed my head on his shoulder. We sat there for a few moments and the song started over again. "So, what else did you bring me besides your awful voice?"

He reached into his pocket and pulled out a chocolate bar. "Your mom said that you might enjoy this."

"She told you, didn't she?" I pinched my lips into a fake frown.

"Told me what? All she told me was to come back up here and bring you this!" he said sarcastically.

"Wow, she's really reinforcing those stereotypes," I laughed.

He shrugged, "I have absolutely no idea what you are talking about."

I looked at him with a fake serious expression on my face, "Why haven't you heard? I am a woman now!"

He cocked his head at me. "And you weren't before?"

"Oh no. Of course not. I was just a humble young boy!"

"I see, I see," he laughed, trying to match my fake sophisticated voice.

I spread my arms in the air, "And now I have transformed into this creature called a woman! And my only fuel is chocolate, now you must feed me!" I smiled at him and opened my mouth like a baby bird.

He peeled open the chocolate bar, broke off a piece, and dropped it into my mouth. I chewed for a second, it felt good and smooth in my mouth and for a second felt like it might ease the cramps in my stomach, but it probably just distracted me. I scrunched my face at Quentin, "This seems like it is of the dark variety."

Quentin nodded, "Yes, yes. I hear that is the best variety for fueling these creatures called women."

"I see," I said and flopped backwards into his lap. "Now all I need is a creature called a man."

Quentin looked around, "I'm not sure I see any of those around here." We both laughed.

Nine

In March, everyone seemed to be going crazy about one thing or another. Leah kept apologizing that the world had to be this way when our minds were developing and looking like she might cry when she talked about how the state of the world might affect us in the long run. She would mutter under her breath that she didn't know how it wouldn't, and apologize again for something she didn't even bring upon us. My parents didn't seem to give a damn about the country and whenever I brought it up, my mom would shush me and tell me that we don't discuss politics at the dinner table, but I never got any other chances to bring it up because I really only ever talked to my parents at dinner. My dad began a big case, so he rarely even got home in time for dinner, forcing me to suffer through my mom's bland meals. When he finally got the chance to come home, the air in the house became too tight to breathe. We all felt it, even the cat.

On Saturday I went to one of Quentin's first track meets with Leah and apparently Saul, too. I got to the meet and I sat on the bleachers next to Leah. We watched as our team warmed up on the opposite side of the field in their bright red track jerseys. A bunch of other teams ran and did warm ups, but I kept my eyes intensely focused on our team, trying to find Quentin. They were too far away and blurry, so I gave up.

Leah laughed. I looked at her, "What?"

"Quentin just started dancing, looks like he's showing off for that girl."

"What?" I exclaimed. "What girl? And how can you see him? They all look the same from this far away!"

"No, they don't. You can totally see him, long legs, skinny boy butt, short blonde hair. That's my son." She pointed in the direction of the team. "See, right there."

"I do not see!" I said and crossed my arms.

Leah gave me a concerned look, "Well, I hate to say it, Tori, but I think that you might need glasses."

"What!" I responded. A few seconds later, "Well, that might explain not being able to see the board in class very well." Leah chuckled a little. "Which girl!?" I asked.

"You know the one that you went to elementary school with? I remember you didn't like her very much. The tall one with the wavy light brown hair, maybe blonde." She moved her hand back and forth next to her head to show wavy hair.

"HALLY!" I exclaimed in disgust.

"Ah, yes, Hally, that's her name."

"Hello everyone!" Saul said as he sauntered towards us on the bleachers.

"Hi Saul!" I said and made room for him on the bench next to me.

To everyone's surprise, Saul's first visit wasn't his last. He had actually followed through. That autumn, he and Riya moved to Pittsburgh, the city closest to our town with Peter. And with their move, Quentin had gotten to spend much more time with Saul. They saw each other every other weekend. Sometimes they would just spend the day together, but sometimes Quentin even stayed for the whole weekend at Saul's house. It took a lot out of my time with Quentin, but I decided to be alright with it one day when Quentin told me about going to a baseball game with Saul. Saul had taken him to a Giants vs. Pirates game and cheered every time the Giants got on base, causing many dirty looks from a stadium crowded with Pirates fans.

Quentin still called Saul by his first name and referred to Riya as "Saul's wife," or just Riya, never his step-mom, but he couldn't hide his excitement about his little brother. I hadn't met Peter very many times, but I think Quentin had always wished for a little brother. Cole had only weakly attempted to fill that void for him.

"Have you ever been to one of these things before, Tori?" Saul asked me.

"Nope," I replied.

"Well, so basically what we do is we sit here looking like we are paying attention, but we aren't, then when it is time for Quentin's events, we actually pay attention. When he wins, we stand up and scream until our asses fall off. Does that sound good?"

I nodded my head, "Whatever you say."

"What about you Leah? You in?" Saul asked.

She sighed, "Well, everything but your use of profanity in front of a twelve-year old whose parents entrusted me with her safety and wellbeing."

I snorted.

"What is it, Tori?" Saul asked.

"Well, it's just that Leah is the only adult that swears in front of me on a regular basis, except if we're including my parents fighting."

Saul looked across me at Leah, "did you hear that, Leah?"

"Yeah, yeah, I hear you."

We sat there awkwardly for a while. Leah handed me a granola bar from her bag and I chewed it slowly. "So, Quentin is a pretty quiet kid, but all he ever talks about is you," Saul said, trying to make conversation.

I smiled, "Yes?"

He rubbed his hands together and stared at them for a second. "Well, I hate to do this, but there are so many things that you get to know about a kid watching them grow up and getting to know them that way. And because I wasn't with Quentin, I haven't gotten the chance to really be a friend to him. I just wanted you to help me know what he was like. And maybe help me out with some activity ideas for the two of us."

I had an urge to tell him he should feel terrible for asking me this and that he should have been there, but I turned and saw that Leah's face didn't seem angry like it should. "Well, he wasn't very much different. He has always been a likable guy, not that people in elementary school ever noticed!" I said and turned to Leah. "People like Hally."

She raised one eyebrow at me, "Hally?"

"The girl that you said he was showing off to earlier!"

"Quentin has a girl?" Saul interjected.

I ignored him, "Leah, don't let him hang out with her."

"And why shouldn't I let that happen?" she laughed.

"She's evil!"

Leah let out another laugh, "I doubt it!"

I put my hand on Leah's leg and looked at her seriously, "She spent all of elementary school teasing Q for his Thalassemia and trying to turn everyone against us."

"Sorry to interrupt, but Quentin is lining up for his first race." Saul pointed to the sixth-grade boys lined up for the 200-meter dash. They were finally on our side of the field and I could identify Quentin stretching and pulling his arms across his body and into the air. The boys lined up, we heard a whistle blow and they were off.

I kept my eyes focused on Quentin as his legs took the longest strides I had ever seen someone take who wasn't on TV. He ran with his back straight and his head tilted back just the tiniest bit. Each breath he took seemed to carry him a few more gliding steps forward. He started off in one of the outside lanes, behind most of the other runners, but he soon progressed ahead of them and crossed the finish line with full force, thrusting himself forward at the end for the big finish.

All three of us stood up immediately and cheered. We were screaming his name and whooping as loud as we could. Leah screamed at the top of her lungs, "That's my son!" And I screamed, "That's my best friend!" A few people turned around and gave us annoyed looks. Quentin turned and waved very aggressively back at us.

"Go Flasch!" Saul yelled.

We finally sat back down, enormous smiles taking over our faces. "Wow! He's good," Leah said, "I did not know he could do that."

Saul nodded, "I did, I ran exactly like that when I was in middle and high school."

Quentin ran up to us after the meet ended covered in sweat and breathing hard because he had just run in another event. I gave him a fist bump and told him he did really well.

"Thanks! Did you see that Spencer won the 800?"

"Yeah, but just barely."

"You did great, hun," Leah congratulated him.

"Yeah, really good," Saul added.

Quentin looked pale, he closed his eyes and took a deep breath. "Are you okay Quentin?" Leah asked.

He nodded, "I think I'm just hot."

"Why don't you sit down for a second?" Leah and I both knew that this could be a very bad sign, he looked faint and dizzy. We both worried whether or not it could be because his anemia could be getting worse again and we hoped the heat was just getting to him, but we both assumed the former.

"I'm fine, Mom!" he said, "I'm just hot and I haven't drunk enough."

"We can never be too careful. You will tell me if anything is wrong tomorrow? Okay honey?" she reached out to touch his face, and he swatted her hand away.

"Mom! I really am just hot."

"Well, I know how to fix that problem," Saul interjected.

"How?" Quentin asked.

Saul raised one eyebrow, "I think I'm going to have to buy you ice cream!"

"That sounds like the best fix to my problem." Quentin nodded, very happy about Saul's idea.

"Waddya say, Tori you in?" Saul asked me chipperly.

"Well, I'm always up for ice cream!" I exclaimed.

"Leah?"

She sighed, "I think I'm gonna leave this one to you, Saul. I've got some work to do."

"Let's go!" Quentin grinned.

I DROPPED MY BIKE and smiled back at Quentin. It had been a while since we had the chance to ride to the clearing. The sun shone in the sky, not a single cloud around it, but its light still felt cool on my skin. As we were biking to the clearing, the soil and soggy sticks squished under our tires, spraying bits of rainwater up at our ankles. I threw my backpack on the ground and stared up at the sky; the color reminded me of the blue jay I had heard crowing on a branch above me a few minutes earlier.

We could feel the summer approaching because the mornings were warm enough for us to walk to school in our shorts. My allergies were dying down and we would come home from school covered in sweat from the heat and a little bit more sun baked.

"Look there's the moon." I pointed at the dim outline of the moon in the early afternoon sky.

Quentin craned his neck at the sky as he stood over me, "I don't see it."

"Well, that's because you aren't even looking at it." I reached up and grabbed the bottom hem of his shirt,

"Get down here stupid." I said and pulled him down beside me.

He traced his eyes along my arm and to the sky. "Oh, I see it now. It's not very impressive."

"Shut up!" I said and pushed him away from me.

"Hey! I'm just saying." He got up and brushed dirt off himself. He walked around for a couple seconds and bent down to pick something up off the ground. He turned to me and held it up, a spoon. "How strange," he remarked.

I sat up, "Yeah it's kind of weird to think that other people have been coming to our spot."

"And leaving their *spoons*!" He shook his head and laughed at his joke.

"I don't know but it feels so much like this is our spot, we have spent what feels like forever here and never seen another soul, but there are people coming here and leaving their spoons."

"I wish we could spend forever here, Tori." "Yeah, that would be nice," I chortled. "No school, no parents, just us."

He circled around me once and sat down next to me, "Tori, do me a favor and when I die, take me on a bike ride here and spread my ashes. I think this is the only place I can be truly free. Please don't let them bury me."

"Okay," I promised, "but they are going to have to do that for the both of us. We are going to die at the same time, remember?"

He moved closer to me and rested his head on the backpack next to mine, "Of course, we will have to tell our parents."

"It would be so nice, us here together forever."

He nuzzled his head into mine, "Yeah."

"I don't think I believe in heaven anymore Q," I blurted. "It's just I've been thinking about it a lot and I just don't think so anymore."

"Yeah?" he asked.

"Well, here's the thing," I took a deep breath preparing myself to explain. "Heaven means that there is a God and I don't think that I can believe in God. There are so many things wrong with the world, as your mom loves to point out, and if God did exist, why would he allow things to be the way they are? Why would he even allow your dad to leave you or for you to have thalassemia, or my aunt to die, or my parents to hate each other and not care enough about their kids?"

"Well, maybe God makes mistakes. And he tries to fix them, like my dad came back, and my disease hardly even affects me anymore, and you said your aunt was happy when she died. Or maybe God doesn't have control of what happens in the world at all."

I countered this, "maybe everything in our lives has turned out okay so far, but there are people whose lives are terrible and don't deserve any of it. I feel the world would at least be a little better if there was some being that controlled everything."

"Maybe if we changed some of the things that were happening, they would affect other things and make them worse and there really is no possible perfect world. I mean, the way I see a perfect world is different from the way you see it. Maybe there is someone in the world that sees it as perfect now."

"That person would really have to not give a damn about other people. And isn't there just some level of basic morals that all good people have. And if God has the power to fix his mistakes, then shouldn't he have the ability to go back and make them never happen?"

He scooted away from me and looked into my eyes, "Take my dad leaving, for example. If he hadn't left us, then Peter most definitely wouldn't be born, and he probably wouldn't have gotten the opportunity to be successful and maybe we would have had to move by now into a cheaper neighborhood and we might not be friends anymore."

"You don't believe that good things like that would stay the same. That our friendship is meant to be?"

"Well, isn't everything based on chance?"

"Not if God existed, that would mean that everything is purposeful, that things are meant to be. Think about it, if there was some being controlling everything, don't you think it knows what it's doing? It makes decisions like you and me. Don't you want to believe that our friendship is meant to be or on purpose for some reason?"

He looked back and forth between my eyes, "You realize you are disproving your own point?"

I scrunched up my face, "Because I want to believe what I'm saying, but I don't."

"I don't completely believe everything I am saying. I believe that we have souls, that there is more to us than a breathing mass of flesh, and that human connection is more than just nature. That when I look into your eyes and feel things for you it's more than just a need for survival or companionship or whatever. I feel like we must be connected in some way so that we can have a relationship like this and it could last this long. Maybe that's God. Maybe God isn't the all-powerful being we are all told he is."

I could feel it too, what he was saying. The way his green eyes felt like more than just eyes, the way his words meant more to me than anyone else's, and how I knew we would never lose what we had. He had a small sideways smile on his lips and wouldn't stop holding eye contact with me. I noticed his face had moved close enough that I could see every freckle, some of them were lighter than others, but overall, there were just way too many of them to count. I looked at his nose and traced it over with my eyes and down to the subtle dip in the top of his thin lips.

I felt each of his warm breaths on my forehead, and let my eyes settle back into his gaze. "Thank you for being such a good friend Q," I smiled.

He flickered his gaze around my face, "Like I just said, it's not all about us!"

I hit his shoulder and pushed him away from me, "Shut up, Quentin!"

"I was just contributing to the conversation!" he said and rolled back into the exact same position from before, face right in front of mine.

"Yes, and contributing to the downfall of the moment!"

"Well, that's what I'm here for isn't it?!"

"To do what? Be your irritating self?"

He bopped me on the forehead with the spoon, which I had completely forgotten about.

I bopped him on the head with my hand. "Hey, no weapons!"

"Your hand is just as much a weapon as this spoon is."

"Well I am not made of metal."

He looked at me, jokingly confused, "Really?"

"What?" I laughed.

"I could have sworn that head of yours was made out of metal." He grabbed my new glasses off my face and placed them on the tip of his nose. "Oh! I see her now! If it isn't Victoria Bowen! I thought I was looking at the tin man from the Wizard of Oz, entirely made of metal. But alas it is just Tori."

I grabbed my glasses back from him. "Can you ever find the chance to just shut up?!" I laughed and pushed him away from me again.

As I pushed him, he grabbed onto my arm and pulled me on top of him. He quickly rolled us over and put his hands on my upper arms so I couldn't get out of his hold. He laughed as I tried to get out of his grip, he just shook his head and waited for me to stop struggling.

"Wow, you have gotten a lot bigger," I said. "You used to be so small I had to protect you!" I pushed up with all my weight and countered him. We fell back onto the ground. I lay on his chest laughing at my success.

He struggled a little and groaned, "You're crushing me!"

"I'll get off if you halt your attack."

Between strained breaths he yelled, "Okay! Okay!"

I rolled over and lay next to him. We lay in peace for a second, lost in thoughts about life and spirituality and our friendship. I held my breath, listening to the sound of Quentin's and the wind blowing through the trees around us. I let my breath go and matched it to the sound of Quentin's. I stared at the sky again and my eyes landed on the thin outline of the moon, "So you are really telling me that you don't appreciate the moon?"

"Oh my god! Can't you just shut up for a second?"

"I did! I shut up for way more than one second."

He didn't respond and I didn't care. I could feel him living next to me and hear him taking in each breath as I took in my own.

Ten

MY MOM AND a few of Cole's friends' moms were having a fundraising event for all the fifth-graders and their parents, so my mom left my dad, Quentin, and me in the house for the night, telling us not to destroy anything. We decided against doing anything too crazy and as soon as my mom and Cole left to set up for the event, my dad pulled out the cook books.

My dad, having been great at cooking before, used to make many of our meals on the weekdays and cook with Cole and me every weekend when we were little. As we got older, he got stuck at work more and my mom began to make our meals, which all tasted the same to me. So that night, Quentin and I begged my dad to help us cook a big fancy meal. My dad decided to teach us how to make pasta.

I used the pasta roller to flatten out the dough into sheets. I placed the cheese mixture that my dad made in blobs about an inch away from each other. My dad helped me place the other piece of dough on top of my cheese blobs. Quentin struggled while trying to make tomato sauce.

"Mr. Bowen? When do I put the garlic in?" he asked as he cooked the tomatoes.

My dad stood beside him and watched as Quentin clumsily mashed the garlic into his tomato mixture. "You are doing perfectly fine." He took a deep breath in and rubbed his hand on his chest.

"Are you okay Dad?" I asked.

"Yeah, it's just indigestion, I'm going to go take an antacid." Before he left the room, he turned around and said, "No funny business while I'm gone."

"Dad!" I yelled after him, my cheeks turning red.

I turned back, laughing, and cut out the ravioli with a pasta roller that makes little curvy edges. Quentin walked up behind me, "What is defined as funny business?"

"I don't know!" I chortled, "Maybe this," I grabbed a handful of flour off the counter and hit him in the cheek with it.

"Very funny," he said. He began to lean into me, flickering his eyes across my face, he put his hand on the counter right next to my waist. It almost felt like... but no. Except that he got closer to me and I could feel his hot breath on my face, and I didn't have to keep myself from laughing at the flour smeared across his face because everything felt so wrong.

"Hey, my dad said no funny business!" I joked, trying to deter the moment, but he didn't flinch or move one bit.

"It's just that you have something on your face."

Forgetting all about what I had just done to him, I put my clean hand up to my face and wiped at my cheek, "Where?" I asked.

"Everywhere," he said calmly. He brought his hand that had been resting on the counter up to my face, coating it all over with flour.

"Hey!" I said and pushed him away from me with my floured hand, leaving a clear handprint on his chest. I walked over to the pot full of Quentin's sauce concoction, "So is the tomato sauce going to kill me?"

"I hope not," I heard my dad's voice say from the doorway, "then I would have to kill Quentin, and I like him a little too much to do that."

Quentin and I both turned around and looked at him, wondering how long he had been leaning in the doorway like that, watching us. I rubbed my hand against my jeans over and over again thinking about if my dad saw what I just felt. "How long have you been there?" I asked my dad, biting my lip.

"Well, it only takes me a couple seconds to walk into the bathroom and open the medicine cabinet, but why would you ask that? Were you two doing something suspicious to the food?" he joked.

I struggled to come up with how to answer but Quentin saved me. "It's just that it's a little creepy to have someone be watching you and you don't know. You know, like a stalker."

He laughed, "So you are calling me a stalker?"

"Not exactly," defended Quentin.

My dad and I both laughed at him. We laughed all the way through the rest of the cooking process and to dinner. We set up the table and sat down, just the three of us at my family's ten-person dining room table.

After we had our initial bites of food and words of praise, Quentin attempted to bring conversation to the dinner table, "So, Mr. Bowen. Tori and I have been having this ongoing discussion since fourth grade about heaven and God. I know your family is Christian, but I just wanted to know what you personally thought about all that?"

He chuckled, "It's funny that you think we're Christian."

"Well, that's what Mrs. Bowen said."

He laughed louder this time, "We are what some people would call C and E Christians."

"What?" Quentin asked.

"Christmas and Easter Christians. We only go to church on Christmas and Easter. And that's not the type of thing I think about very much."

"Do you think there is an all-controlling eternal being or an afterlife?"

"Well, in my life, I have never experienced anything that has led me to believe any of that isn't real. I think that we should all believe in something, it gives a man morals. In my job, there is a right and a wrong and it isn't always easy to find what that is, but it is there. I personally don't feel such a religious or spiritual connection to it all. But Amy sure does have a lot of spirituality. She believes that praying actually helps the person you are praying for, and I think it helps the people who are praying believe, so I guess it can be good." He sighed and pulled at the collar of his shirt, sweat gathered on his forehead and I looked down curiously at my coat. "But why are we talking about this serious stuff? I thought we were going to have fun tonight!"

"Yeah, Quentin!" I agreed.

"So how is that girlfriend of yours, Quentin?"

He froze in the middle of chewing, "What?"

"You know the one you were dating over the summer, and Tori spent so much time with Oda because you were off with that other girl."

"Hally?"

My father pointed his finger at Quentin, "Yes, that's the one! You made Tori very jealous with that one!"

I blushed, "Dad! That's so not true!"

"If you say so, but I thought you seemed pretty mad about it!"

"That's only because I don't like Hally!" I argued.

Quentin shook his head, "Tori doesn't think people can change."

"Quentin! I said stop with the seriousness!" My dad interjected. "Now put your dishes in the sink, it's time to watch one of the greatest movies ever made."

We rinsed our dishes as my dad poured a bag of popcorn into a big plastic bowl and pulled out a bag of Oreos. He kept massaging his shoulder, "Tori, I think I'm gonna go sit down... I'm having a little trouble breathing. Nothing too bad." He walked off into the living room with the bowl of popcorn.

"You know I do think people can change! I just don't trust Hally, she went from bullying you to having a crush on you and wanting to date you in like two seconds," I said to Quentin.

"You know she wasn't acting like that because she wanted to make fun of my disease? She told me when we were dating that it was because her parents were going through a divorce and she felt lonely and envied our friendship. Well, she didn't say those exact words, because she is Hally, but I broke up with her anyway, so why do you care so much?" Quentin seemed to plead with me. "You don't understand."

I opened my mouth to respond, but my dad's voice interrupted me, "Victoria, get in here!" His voice was weak yet urgent sounding.

Quentin and I both immediately rushed into the living room, my dad slouched over on the couch with his hand on his shoulder. His face dripped with sweat and he seemed to struggle to get air with every breath he took. He looked at us and said very calmly, "Call an ambulance, tell them you think I am having a heart attack, and remember I am a forty-six-year-old man whose family has a history of heart disease."

I looked back and forth between him and the phone, "Dad? What's going on?"

"I should have realized it sooner. I am having a heart attack and I need you to help me, okay?" he said, still remaining extremely calm but his voice straining with every word.

I reached into my pocket to pull out my cell phone, only to see that Quentin had already dialed 911 and had his phone up to his ear. I watched Quentin and tried to match my dad's calm mood. "What else can I do Dad?"

"Go get me aspirin from the medicine cabinet, and bring it to me, I don't need water."

I tried to walk away calmly, but my hands were sweating and my head felt full and muddled making it hard for me to think. My heart felt like a hand reached inside my chest to squeeze it and with every beat it had to work faster to keep going. I tried as hard as I could to keep my breaths steady and prevent my hands from shaking. I shook the aspirin container into my hand, and a few of them fell on the bathroom floor, clicking and rolling into the corners. I didn't bother to pick them up.

I dropped the pill bottle on the side of the sink and ran back into the living room, holding the pills tightly in my hand.

I sat down on the couch next to him and handed him the aspirin.

"I'm twelve, we're both twelve," Quentin said to the phone. His pointer finger tapped absent-mindedly on the back of his cell phone. Up and down, up and down, faster and faster, like your heartbeat when you know something bad is going to happen. He listened for a second and walked quickly to the front door and let it swing wide open. "They're on their way, Tori, it's gonna be okay," he said to me. *Tlat, tat, tat, tat*, his finger kept tapping on the back of his phone.

My dad's breaths became shallower and his face contorted with the difficulty of each one. I felt like I couldn't breathe either, but I tried as hard as I could to stay calm until the ambulance got there. "Stay awake Dad, stay awake," I breathed, "stay awake." I could hear Quentin's finger still tapping the back of his phone.

I wrapped my arms around his shoulders and pressed my face into his neck. I waited for each of his breaths, each one reminding me I still had my dad. The world seemed to be ringing and turning, I could hear the sound of my heart beating in the back of my head, and Quentin saying into the phone, "He is still awake, he is barely awake. How long? It's getting really bad."

I felt his body collapse in my arms just as I heard the sound of the sirens in front of the house. I touched his sweaty hot face and watched his unmoving chest. I desperately shook his shoulder and cried. I couldn't breathe anymore. My brain filled with the sound of my heart beat and my own voice screaming for him to wake up. I kept shaking his shoulders, but he didn't respond, he didn't move, he didn't wake up.

I remember the paramedic pulling me away from him, and watching as they lifted him into the ambulance. I remember sitting on a bench in the ambulance as they tried to save his life. We got to the emergency room about 10 minutes after we had left my house. The paramedic immediately jumped out of the ambulance and took my dad with him. A doctor from the emergency room came and got Quentin and me. She escorted us to go sit in the waiting room with a social worker in the ER waiting area. My memories go completely fuzzy after that.

I must have somehow fallen asleep with all the stress of it. I woke up with my head on Quentin's shoulder and my legs tucked up next to me on the chair, to the shrill sound of my mom worrying. "Tori! You're awake, finally!"

"What happened?"

"Your father is in surgery, we have to move up to another floor to wait, let's go."

"Is he going to be okay?" I asked.

She sighed, "We can't be sure, we can only hope," my mom said, trying to remain calm.

"We can only hope? That's so stupid," I yelled. "Hope isn't going to do anything for Dad! Hope can't save him!" I wanted to throw something at her.

"Let's just go up to the other waiting room and we can pray." I could see the exhaustion in her face and her begging me to just listen to her for once.

"Okay Mom," I sighed.

We walked up to the other waiting room and Leah came to pick up Quentin. He told me he would be back and that he would bring me all the things we could possibly need. I curled my legs up on a chair in the waiting room and I let Cole lean up against me. Cole still wore his suit and tie from the event, but the tie hung loosely around his neck. My mom crossed her legs and pulled her dress tightly over her knees. She rested her head in her hand and didn't move. We all didn't move. My mom and I stared at the walls and Cole slept on my shoulder. They came out to update us on his surgery a few times without telling us much at all.

Quentin and Leah came back about two hours later with clothes for my mom and Cole. Quentin sat next to me. He handed me a water bottle, reached up and swiped softly at my cheek. "You still had flour there," he frowned. "Hardly feels like the same day, does it?" I looked down at his shirt, which he had changed, no more hand print. He widened his eyes at me and swiped at my cheek again, this time letting his hand linger on my face for a moment. "I made you something a while ago and I was waiting to give it to you until you really needed it. I decided it's probably the right time." He pulled a thick sheet of paper from the bag in his arms. When I looked at it, I saw four panels of Quentin's drawings.

The first panel showed us on the hill at dusk riding our bikes. I rode ahead of Quentin, leaned over my handle bars while Quentin stood on his pedals as he tried to catch up to me. He remembered the evening of the accident as clearly as I did; I saw the colors of the sky and the warmth of the air. In the second panel we lay in the clearing, Quentin stared up at the sky, and I had my eyes closed with my head resting on his chest. The light hit us just so it made us look like we were glowing.

My favorite one of all showed us lying on our stomachs in the grass in the dark, with the firefly jar in front of us. We had just opened the jar and the fireflies were floating up in front of us. As the fireflies flew into the sky, they were the only light on a pitch-black background.

The last image showed the two of us, but not of a memory we had. It showed the future. We were standing next to each other, posing for a picture, huge smiles across our faces. We were wearing the cap and gown of the high school we were supposed to go to, our arms wrapped around each other tightly.

"Aw, Quentin, this is amazing!" I said and snuggled my head into the crook of his neck. I pressed the piece of paper to my chest and crossed my arms over it, "I'm gonna frame it. And when you become a famous comic book artist and runner, I will have an original Quentin Flasch."

"Family of Cory Bowen," I heard a doctor say.

My mom rushed over to him, while I grabbed Cole's hand and walked over to the doctor. I looked back and realized that Leah had been sitting with my mom, comforting her. Maybe my mom didn't hate Leah that much after all. I turned my attention back to the doctor.

My mom wrapped her arm around my shoulder and pulled me into her.

The doctor started, "So there was a complication in his surgery." Immediately my thoughts went to the worst. A complication could mean so many things, like that his heart stopped again, that he lost a lot of blood, that the surgery didn't work, or that they weren't able to revive him. That I might never see him again, my last memory of him would be his body collapsed in my arms. I wouldn't ever hear the bear story again or taste his barbecue, or learn recipes from him, or watch *The Breakfast Club* like he had wanted so badly to do that night, or was it the night before? It must have been way past midnight. And it seemed, worst of all, I would never hear my parents fight again, or hear him come home from work at ten o'clock at night, or contradict my mom's decisions for me again. My life would never be the same. I wouldn't have a father anymore, only a mother who would wallow in her own sorrow and care even less about her kids than she had before. And I had let this happen, I saw his condition get worse but didn't do anything.

My mom hugged me tightly and said, "Oh thank the lord!" I looked up. I didn't hear what the doctor said.

"What?" I asked, my heart pounding in my chest.

"Your father made it out of surgery, now we just have to wait for him to wake up."

A huge rush of air filled my lungs and I burst into tears. I clung onto my mom's arm and pulled Cole into me tightly. For once in my lifetime, the spirituality that my mother always claimed would help us through

everything made sense. I loved her and I loved Cole and
I loved my dad; everything would be alright.

Eleven

IT'S HARD TO BE someone you know you aren't supposed to be. It's easier to hide that you are the person you aren't supposed to be. And it's easier to become someone you don't want to be. It's easy to become disconnected from reality and trapped in your own dark mind. It is easy to make your parents hate you, but the memories of your dad not breathing still plague your mind. It's easy to think that no one can understand, that no one can help you. It's easy to be alone even if you don't want to be. It's easy to tell yourself you aren't allowed to feel the way you do. It's easy to forget who you really are, to get lost in who you want to be and who you think you have to be. It's easy to lie to yourself and even easier to lie to everyone else.

But it's so much harder to lie to Quentin.

One of the things that certainly is easy is lying in bed. So that's what I did. I laid on my bed, curled up in a ball. I had no energy left in me to even answer my phone which kept incessantly buzzing in my pocket. Quentin probably wanted to come over because his dad had canceled their plans. The messages sat there for a moment as I contemplated my options. I could let him sleep over and lie to him some more. I could tell him that I had a lot of homework, a stupid lie that he would see right through, or I could let him come over and just be honest. I tried to curl my body even tighter into a ball, intense pressure on my chest forced me to shut my eyes. I couldn't do this anymore. I jumped up from my position and sat upright on the bed, like I had just woken up from a nightmare. And I knew I had to tell him.

I picked up the phone and told him to come over as soon as he wanted.

I yelled as loud as I could, "MOM! Quentin is going to stay over tonight!"

"WHAT?" I heard her yell back from the bottom of the stairs.

"QUENTIN IS GOING TO STAY OVER!" I screamed.

I heard her footsteps coming up the stairs and towards my room. When she burst through my bedroom door, I gave my perfect *annoyed teenager* face just to make sure she would be extra insufferable. "Honey, we need to talk about this."

"About my best friend sleeping over like he has done since third grade." She sat down on the bed next to me. "You don't have to sit down, I already told him that he could come over," I berated.

She folded her hands in her lap. "Your father and I have been having some concerns about you and Quentin spending the night together."

"Why? Do you think I'm going to end up pregnant or something?"

"It's just that when you have a boyfriend in the future, we want to make sure that we are not allowing you to be alone in that way with him."

"Well, what if I don't have a boyfriend ever?"

She gave me her *please shut up and listen to me* smile, "It's just that, honey, we know that it will happen eventually, and when it does, we want to be cautious."

"What if I didn't have a boyfriend? Leah says I could have a girlfriend if I wanted to," I said, testing to see what she would do. "You could never know if I was letting a girl sleepover."

She scoffed, "Leah shouldn't be telling you things like that."

"Why?"

"It's just some people think it is normal to be like that."

"To be like what? In a relationship with someone you love?" I raised my voice.

"I think that they can do it as long as they are not disturbing people like us. They can go off and be their *colorful* selves as long as they don't try to bother God-fearing people like us," she attempted to defend herself.

"We're not even Christians, Mom!"

"Tori," she tried to calm me down with a soothing tone.

"Mom, what do you want from me anyways?"

She took a deep breath, "I am just saying, if you were having these feelings for Quentin or if he were to have them for you, I would want you to tell me so we could deal with it properly."

The doorbell rang, and Cole opened it and chattered to Quentin. "Quentin is here," I said.

"Will you at least acknowledge what I said, Victoria?"

"Yep, but that's never going to happen, so can you go now?"

"I just don't think you are really hearing what I am telling you."

Quentin appeared in the doorway of my room. "We are going. C'mon Quentin." I grabbed his arm and dragged him out of the house behind me.

"What's going on?"

I walked over to my bike. "My mom. Come on, we can go back when she has come to her senses. Which might be never," I mumbled and jumped onto my bike, pedaling once before remembering that my tire had been popped on a nail in the garage. "Let's go, we're walking."

"Go where?" Quentin ran after me.

"Does it matter?" I kept going up the street, my head pounding and my heart racing. I walked as fast as I could, and Quentin struggled to catch up with me.

"Tori? Tori! C'mon! What's happening?"

I stopped and looked him, "Quentin, I told you, it's my mom just being stupid as always, I'm not gonna repeat *exactly* what she said." I slowed down, giving Quentin a chance to catch up.

He tilted his head at me, trying to catch my eye contact. When I kept my eyes glued to my feet, he let up and matched his steps with mine. "Riya convinced Saul to go with them on Peter's preschool camping trip."

I used all my energy to flip my mind onto him. "Oh Q, I'm sure he wants to be there with you, he just doesn't want to miss out on all that kind of stuff with Peter."

"Yeah, but you would think that he would want to make up for all that stuff he missed with me. Peter is always his priority, even though Peter probably won't even remember if he went on that camping trip or not."

"Do you remember every trip you went on that Saul didn't?"

"That's so different, he was never there with me, he lives with Peter." He furrowed his brow and stared down at his feet. It felt wrong for me to tell him that I knew what he was going through because I had both my parents my whole life, but I did know what it felt like not to feel loved by someone who should. I remember every moment that I saw Leah fussing over Quentin and praising him as much as I remember every moment that I felt my mom's discontentment in everything I had done. I remembered every Halloween and Valentine's Day that I spent time with Cole and not my parents. Every Halloween costume that my mom bought on October 30th, every Valentine's card I made for my parents and didn't get one back, until I only made them for Cole, and every store-bought birthday card with a shorter note on it than the ones from my aunt. I didn't remember all the field trips my mom went on or PTA meetings she spoke at without even asking how I felt about what happened at my school.

"I know Q, I know it sucks a lot."

"Yeah, it sure does. It sucks."

I laughed, "Well why don't we talk about something else then?"

"I think Lara likes me," he said with a smile.

"Really?" I laughed, "Lara."

"Yeah, she asked me for my phone number and she tried to make it seem like she needed help with homework, but I could tell it's because she likes me, she acts super weird around me now."

I laughed, "Well, Lara's... *sweet.*"

He furrowed his brow. "I can't tell if you are joking or not."

I pushed him, "I was trying to be nice!"

"Hey! I'm just making sure!" He put his hands in the air.

"You know, like, I like, like love being on like phone calls like the entire day because like I'm so popular and my daddy is like so rich," I flipped my hair behind my shoulder, mimicking the way Lara always talked.

"So, you were being sarcastic!"

"Hey I'm not a nice person. I admit it!"

"And 'I'm also selfish and stubborn and arrogant,'" he cajoled. "'Oh, and Quentin is better than me!'"

I snorted, "Well, I wouldn't admit all those things."

"C'mon, you know it's true! But I still love you for it."

"For it or despite it?"

He shrugged, "Maybe both."

"Do you have any money?" I asked.

"I don't think so. I left my stuff in your room. Nice segue by the way; selfish and arrogant people definitely don't want other people's money."

"It's okay, I have 10 dollars in my phone case."

He shook his head, "Way to make up for it."

We drifted to the grocery store and the conversation made me forget whatever kept making me clench my jaw so tightly. I immediately went over to the aisle that had fresh bread behind a plastic door. I unlatched the door and grabbed a bag from the top of the shelf. I took a circle of French bread and placed it in the bag.

"Do you want cheese?" I asked Quentin.

He shook his head no. I placed the loaf of bread on the conveyor belt. No one stood in line in front of us, a strange occurrence for a Saturday afternoon. It left my mind boggled at how lovely the air smelled. The sun glared in the sliding glass doors and the grass had just begun to peep up after the snow melted. If I hadn't been inside, I swear I would have heard birds chirping.

A girl I recognized from the high school stood behind the checkout counter. "Marissa", her name tag read. She typed something into the computer that hung next to her. I paid with the emergency money I kept in my phone case and we walked out of the store.

Quentin and I found a bench at the park and sat down to eat our loaf of bread. I grinned as I tore through the crust with my teeth and felt the cool inside of the loaf on my tongue. I absolutely loved bread, especially ones that came in perfect loaves like this one. If I were to pick any food to eat forever it would have to be bread, or maybe my dad's homemade mac and cheese. He hadn't been making it a lot since he got home from the hospital—too much cholesterol. It had gooey sauce that stretched a little when you ate it, with an endless variety of cheeses inside. And the best layer of cheese and bread crumbs on the top that I always pulled off and set to the side of my plate to save for the end of the meal.

"Quentin," I said.

"Yeah?" He said with his mouth full of bread. I clenched my hands into fists to try to prevent them from shaking, but my wrists were weak and my head bobbled loosely on my neck, feeling like it could roll off at any second. I looked down at my sweaty palms and put them together, deep breath in, "This bread is really good." I breathed out. I didn't have to tell him, or at least not right then. I would tell him later that night. He was going to be okay with it. I had to at least tell myself that.

We walked back to my house in silence, the entire time with my mind screaming, *I like girls! I like girls! I'm not straight! I like girls!* As if screaming it repeatedly in my head enough times would cause Quentin to finally hear me and he would know. If I didn't have to say the words maybe it wouldn't be true. Everything would be alright with Quentin and me, I already knew that. We were us. Tori and Quentin. The dynamic duo. Inseparable. One piece of information couldn't change that. It couldn't possibly change.

We ate dinner with my family, in complete silence. My mom had either forgotten our conversation from before I left, submitted to failure, or somehow decided that I got her message. She made us chili, but messed it up so badly its spices burned my tongue as soon as the spoon left my mouth. Cole kept picking up his spoon, touching it to his lips and placing it back down in the chili without eating anything. I just glared at my mom. She tilted her head at me and smiled, occasionally taking a spoonful of chili and trying not to wince.

I caught Quentin's eye contact and inhaled with all the force I could muster, bared my teeth at him and exhaled over my food. I looked down at my bowl and back up at him, my eyes wide. He bit his lip, holding back a smile. It was a game we often played during meals with my family; I made myself look like an idiot trying to make him laugh, while my parents ignored the entire exchange. I turned my head to Cole and forced both my eyes to look down at my nose. Cole giggled as he took a sip of his water and let the water dribble back into the cup.

My mom jerked another spoonful of chili to her mouth, the spoon rattling against her teeth before she pulled it out of her mouth. Her fingers gripped tightly to the table cloth as she swallowed her food.

My dad hadn't taken a bite of the food since he had desperately washed his mouth out with beer after his first bite. He looked up at me, "Tori, remember this for when you have your own husband and kids to cook for, add spices slowly."

I nodded, "Okay Dad."

"Maybe when Tori has her own husband and kids, she won't make them sit through an entire inedible meal." My dad chuckled and eyed my mom, who grimaced into her bowl.

No one else laughed. "I think when I have a wife and kids, I will cook for them, like Dad used to cook for us!" Cole said.

After an eternity, Quentin and I escaped to my room to watch a movie on the laptop that Cole and I shared. We squished together on my bed and placed the laptop on one leg each.

About halfway through the movie, my mom walked up stairs and opened my bedroom door, leaving it open and walking away without saying anything. "What was that?" Quentin asked.

"Don't mind her," I scoffed. I didn't see a point in telling Quentin why she did that.

"Should I close it?"

I sighed, "No, if you do, she will probably just come open it again."

After we finished the movie and my parents had gone to sleep, I closed my bedroom door and sat Quentin down on my bed in front of me. Immediately my hands began to sweat and shake. I chastised myself for being a coward but I just couldn't stop thinking about how one thing would lead to another and soon there would be no turning back, and *wasn't it better to just keep it a secret?*

I spent the previous months researching my feelings because I didn't know what else to do. I found other people on the internet saying that they felt the same way I did. I found a community of people that shared the quality that my mom let me know she found so distasteful just hours before. My brain replayed the moment Leah had urged me not to tell my mom, the first time I found out people like me existed. My mind was like a scratched record. The same thoughts and memories playing over and over again. The silence in the room when the topic was inconveniently brought up. I could feel the hostility in my mom clearing her throat and staring at the ground when Oda corrected her once after she assumed Oda's female cousin was marrying a man, my mother's sharp eyes, the tension in the silence, secretive, unwanted, wrong. I just didn't understand the pride of other people who were like me. Why couldn't it just not matter at all? I wanted to live my life without thinking about it, but I couldn't. I wanted this to just be my secret, I wanted it to just disappear and maybe I wanted to disappear along with it.

"Quentin?" I sighed and looked into his big green eyes. Telling him this would break his heart. "I need to tell you something."

He nodded, and the kindness that he held in his face made my heart swirl. Each breath that I took fluttered with my shaking hand on Quentin's knee. I tried to pull my hand away before he noticed but I waited too long. He grabbed my hand and sandwiched it between his. "It's okay, you can tell me."

"I like girls!" I blurted. My hand clapped over my mouth. Some part of me still thought I wouldn't do it. A huge knot formed in my throat and I held my breath with everything I had in me, waiting for Quentin's response.

He pulled me into a tight hug. "I love you," he said into my shoulder, and squeezed me a little tighter. A smile warmed my face, but my stomach dropped. I felt unsettled and another feeling I didn't expect.

Dread.

"Thank you, Quentin." I choked on my words.

He pulled away from me, "Can I ask you something?"

"Yeah, anything."

"Do you still like boys?"

I smiled at him, "Yeah, I think I am bisexual. You know, I look at girls and I am like holy shit, then I look at guys and feel the same way."

"Good," he said.

"What?"

Without warning he leaned into me and placed his lips on mine. It surprised me how soft they were. The mint toothpaste that lingered on his inner lip swirled from his mouth to mine and for some odd reason my body urged me to kiss him back. I pressed my lips harder onto his and felt him breathe me in. His lips were colder than I expected, much different from the warmth of his cheek that pressed up against mine. I knew how much he wanted it to happen and understood how much I didn't. Not because he was a boy, or because he was him. Those were the very reasons I had let myself kiss him back in the first place. I knew I didn't want this because we were never supposed to be anything other than friends. I let him kiss me one last time and detached my lips from his.

I placed my hand on his chest. "Quentin. What are you doing."

He looked up at me with his bright green eyes and his huge smile. "That didn't sound like a question," he said and leaned closer into me.

I straightened my elbow and kept my hand pressed firmly against his chest. I laughed. I laughed with my whole body, the fear that had paralyzed me just moments earlier now dissipated from my chest. I loved him, but I sure as hell didn't like him like that, not that I hadn't spent many hours of my life thinking about it. We were never meant to fall in love and live happily ever after, we weren't even supposed to experiment with each other. It would ruin what we had. I was too stubborn. I hold grudges. As soon as he wasn't just the Quentin, I knew it would be too hard to get back what we had right then.

Quentin frowned. "Well, I'm sorry you think this is funny, but you kissed me back, so I don't know what you are laughing at," he whined like I took away his favorite toy.

"Why don't you just go lay on your bed," I said and pointed to the blow-up mattress on my floor.

"So, you don't—"

"No."

"I just..." his voice trailed off, and he slid off of my bed and onto the blow-up mattress.

"I know." I pulled my blanket over me.

"Tori?" Quentin said, softly.

"Yep?"

"Things aren't going to be weird?"

"Not unless you make them weird." I turned off the light next to my bed and rolled over.

I could tell Quentin I was bi, but how would Oda and Spencer react? What would happen when I wanted to be with a girl? Or my parents eventually found out? Would I have to tell every new person I met? Would I ever tell anyone else? What if people figured it out on their own? Could I keep this a secret forever?

It took me hours to fall asleep, the dread in the pit of my stomach again consuming my thoughts.

Twelve

The skirt of my dress wouldn't stay flat. I kept jerking it forward to straighten it, but it just wanted to be wrinkled. Spencer snorted when he saw me pulling on it for the hundredth time. We sat in the second row, behind Saul and Leah's families. People on the ceremony stage rushed around, trying to get everything set up in time.

"Can I sit with you all?" I looked up to see Oda standing over us.

"Sure," I said, scooting closer to Spencer.

"Is your family here?" Spencer asked me.

"Yes, why?"

"Your mom doesn't like me very much."

I chuckled. Quentin walked out onto the podium. I flailed my arms at him and gave him a huge smile. Quentin made eye contact with me, smiled a little and gave me a timid thumbs up.

"Don't mind my mom, her opinions are very questionable though," I said to Spencer.

Spencer and Oda laughed. "That's kind of true," Oda said. "I've known Mrs. Bowen for a really long time now, and I never agree with her on anything and neither do my parents."

"To be fair, your parents and Leah are the most liberal in the entire town," I replied.

"Maybe that's why your mom hates your taste in friends so much."

I laughed, "She just wants me to make friends with at least one white girl with conservative parents."

"I fit all but one of those requirements," Spencer said.

"I fit one of those requirements," Oda said.

"I fit all of those requirements," I laughed. "I should probably add Christian to that list too."

"Yeah, Quentin only fits one of your mom's requirements, too," added Oda.

Quentin and the Rabbi both started singing in Hebrew. Everyone in the room besides the three of us and my family joined in and sang along with them. The song drew a harmony of voices from around me, its simple melody sounding complicated when such a variety of voices came together to sing it.

They stopped singing and the Rabbi said, "Shabbat shalom."

I didn't understand most of the ceremony, but a few times I hummed along with the tunes of the songs or read along in the prayer books because the songs were too beautiful not to join in. I loved this community so much, not just because of the people like those at the Chanukah party, but how warm and welcoming it felt to be here and how supportive they were of Quentin.

Quentin gave a speech about the part of the Torah they were reading that week. I am still not entirely sure what he wanted us to learn from his speech. He told me that it is better to have your Bar Mitzvah from October to January because that is when they read the most famous Bible stories that a lot of people know, and after that it is mostly just rules and retellings of the stories.

After a while we got bored and read the English in the book we found in the chair in front of Oda. We found many questionable things, like a father having sex with his dead son's wife and a whole bunch of rules that made absolutely no sense.

The three-hour ceremony finally came to an end and we went to have lunch in the social hall. Before we were able to eat, we had to bless the wine and bread. They had identical platters of wine and grape juice, and somehow Oda, Spencer and I all grabbed cups of wine and not grape juice. We drank it after the blessing and all three of us spit it back into our cups.

"That is *not* grape juice," Oda laughed.

The initial shock wore off and I decided to drink mine again. "It's not that bad."

Spencer followed my lead and downed his glass, "Yeah, it's not that bad."

Oda laughed at us and swallowed a few sips of her wine with a pinched face. "Maybe we should get more."

We blessed the bread, then sat at the table sipping our cups of wine, looking like we enjoyed our grape juice a little too much. We ate bagels with cream cheese, served with all kinds of sliced vegetables and salmon. I don't know what kind of person would want raw onions on their bagels.

I got up from my seat to go get us a few more glasses of wine, when the woman from the Chanukah party came up to me. "Well, well, well," she said, squeezing my shoulders, "if it isn't young Victoria. You were a lot younger the last time I saw you."

I nodded and smiled at her, hoping she wouldn't notice the three plastic cups of wine in my hands. "About four and a half years younger," I said awkwardly.

"Well, I would recognize Quentin's best friend anywhere. Even with those big glasses and blue dye in your hair!" I adjusted my glasses and pushed my long hair onto my back. She laughed this big laugh and placed her hand on my shoulder.

She was about to tell me something very important when Quentin walked up behind us. "Ms. Meyer! It's so nice to see you here!"

She gave Quentin a huge smile. "Mazel Tov!" she exclaimed and pulled him into a hug. "I'm so proud of you."

"Thanks so much," Quentin said for the millionth time that day.

"Will you tell your mom that I think she has done the most terrific job raising you?" Ms. Meyer bubbled while staring intently at Quentin.

"You should go tell her yourself! I'm afraid I'm going to have to take Tori away now," Quentin directed.

"Tori, now that's much less fitting than Vic. Have you always gone by Tori?" she asked, concerned. I nodded, "But I go by Victoria at school and with most adults."

"I think I'm still going to call you Vic, it suits you better," she pondered.

I nodded even though I completely disagreed and didn't know anyone who would agree. "Ms. Meyer, we really gotta get going, it was so nice to see you."

Quentin put his hand on my back and led me away from Ms. Meyer. "I should change my name to Vic officially."

"You should definitely do that."

As we walked to the table my legs started to feel a bit wobbly and my eyelids began to feel heavier. I giggled, "She's actually really interesting."

"You looked like you needed rescuing," Quentin chuckled.

"Why? I like her!"

"Because that isn't grape juice in your hands and I don't know how much you all have already had to drink." I laughed, "Want some? No one has noticed."

"I have to host this goddamn party," he sighed.

"All the more reason to have some," I pushed one of the cups into his hand.

"Okay, I guess I'm not chanting any more Torah." He took one of the cups from me and gulped down about half of it. "But you probably shouldn't drink more Tori, your parents are here, remember?"

"You really think my parents would notice if I got drunk?"

"Fine, my mom is here. And I don't need you to embarrass me, we are only thirteen, you probably would get drunk really fast."

I nodded, "My mom can drink three or four glasses of wine without even acting tipsy and I only drank two cups and I feel pretty weird."

"Just don't talk to too many adults, okay?" He downed the rest of the cup.

I slowly smiled at him, "Sounds like a plan." We walked over to the table with Oda and Spencer, "What took you so long?" Spencer asked and grabbed one of the remaining cups from my hand.

"I had to get saved by Quentin," I said and plopped down into the chair next to Spencer. I took a huge bite of my bagel and slouched down lower in my chair. "Sit down and eat with us for a while, Quentin."

"I've got to walk around and say hi to people again."

"Fuck those people who want you to say 'hi' to them twice." I wrapped my arm around his neck, "You've gotta hang out with your best friend on your birthday! You turned 13 today and all anyone cares about is this ceremony!"

"This ceremony is about me turning 13 and becoming a Jewish adult."

"Well, you are supposed to spend your birthday with me like always. Sit down," I commanded.

He sat down on the half of my chair I left open for him. "Give me a bagel, I'm starving." I grabbed a bagel from the middle of the table and slapped it into Quentin's hand. He spread cream cheese on it. "I almost forgot today is also my birthday. I had to wake up at six to get ready and set up here."

"Well, we are going to have a really good party tonight." I leaned into Quentin. Everything around me felt slow and a blur. The rest of the world seemed further away than normal, except Quentin, sitting there next to me. He felt warm and present. I took a breath of his happiness and the pride emanating off his body. "I'm proud of you Q," I told him, realizing that I had never told him that before.

The party started around seven, but I arrived at six-thirty despite what Quentin had told me about being a proper Jew. I walked into the hall which had dim lighting and saw Leah running around desperately making the final adjustments. The decorations had Leah written all over them, complete with blue lights strung across the walls and blue helium balloons in the corners. Each of the tables, which were gathered on one side of the room, had a glass jar filled with candy in the center.

I danced over to Leah in my flowy dress that I loved so much. It had long sleeves that flared out at the wrists and two layers, the bottom one tighter and dark purple with spaghetti straps, the one over mesh, the same deep tone of purple with little, embroidered flowers scattered all over. The outer layer went down to my mid thighs, only an inch below where the sleeves ended, and when I spun in circles the skirt blew out around me.

Leah looked me up and down. "I love the dress." She pointed to a flower on my arm, "these flowers look beautiful with your hair."

"Maybe you should've had a daughter. I'm sure dress shopping is much more fun than trying to find a suit."

"Well, maybe I should force Quentin to come dress shopping with me."

I laughed, "I'm sure he would enjoy that very much. Can I come?"

"Quentin!" Leah yelled across the room to him, "Tori and I are taking you dress shopping!"

We both burst out into laughter at the look on his face. "So, what can I do to help?" I asked Leah.

"Just go keep my son occupied," she chuckled and continued to straighten the decorations on the table.

I ran over to Quentin and slipped my arm around his, linking us together by our elbows. "We're matching," I said pointing to his dark purple bow tie.

"It's like you are my date to a fancy ball." He tapped my arm and grinned at me.

I pulled my arm away from his and straightened a piece of candy in a jar on the table next to us. Occasionally things like this would happen and I would have to be reminded of the way he had kissed me and looked at me as if I possessed the key to happiness. "Your mom wants everything to be perfect," I said and straightened another piece of candy.

"Yes, I know, she's driving me insane." I squinted at him in the dim light. He had the I'm-ready-to-mess-with-Tori face on, but the look faded and soon he raised one eyebrow at me and smiled. "Stop fixing things. Come with me."

He led me out of the room and back to the entrance of the building, then back up the big stairs that creaked under our feet as we tip-toed. "We aren't allowed to go up here Q."

"And when today have you followed the rules?"

I hit his shoulder. "Shut up!"

"You always tell me to shut up, but look at me, I'm still talking. I have overcome the adversity of your verbal suppression."

"Wow, look at the new man, using his big boy words!" I teased him.

"Shut up!" he scrunched his face at me.

I waved my arms in the air, "Oh how the tables have turned!"

The stairs ended at an attic full of dust, old furniture, and boxes. "Look," Quentin said with a wave of his arm.

"What? There is nothing here."

"Nothing but peace and quiet!"

I chuckled, "You might have to attend your own party."

He walked over to the chair and dusted it off with one hand. As he threw himself into it, the base made a loud creak. A concerned smile appeared on his face and he burst out laughing. I ran over to him and threw myself across his lap. The chair made a huge creaking noise and a couple of small popping noises before settling closer to the ground than before. I tilted my head back and wiggled my legs around off the edge of the chair, I allowed my hair to touch the dusty floor.

"I'm sorry," Quentin said solemnly.

"For what?"

"For earlier, for making things weird between us." He struggled for the right words. "It's just that before, before I... you know. It's just that things were normal and now it feels like they can't be. I just want things to be normal again. I promise I don't feel that way anymore."

I pulled myself up and looked at him, "It's okay if you do, just know that it can never happen."

"I don't though," he avoided making eye contact with me, "and I do know! I just want things to be normal again," he pleaded.

"Yes!" I said and wrapped my arms around his neck.

"Quentin! Tori!" We heard Leah yelling from another part of the building.

I let go of Quentin. "We better go down before people start arriving and wondering where the new Jewish man is."

We hurried down the stairs and into the party room. Leah turned around with a concerned look on her face, "Where have you two been?"

"Just around," Quentin said.

Leah's mom came through the front door and rushed our way like a whirlwind. She placed her hands on Quentin's cheeks. "My darling grandson has grown up to be so handsome," she cooed.

She encompassed him in a big hug full of sequined blue sleeves and pride. When she pulled away, she reached to straighten a pin in her wispy silver hair that probably took hours to do every day. She always smelled of sharp sweetness, like cinnamon candy and limeade.

"It's nice to see you," I said and gave Mrs. Flasch a hug.

"Oh, how wonderful it is to see you, Victoria!" She smothered me in her tight hug.

More people arrived, some of Quentin's close family, but mostly our friends from school. We ate a whole assortment of wonderful things for dinner, like tiny pizzas and little dishes of mac and cheese. Quentin told me that Saul's parents had paid for it all, despite much protesting from Leah. We sat around the tables and laughed about Quentin while periodically shoving candy into our mouths, pockets, bags, and any other place we could store it for later.

Once we were done eating, someone turned on this song, which consisted mostly of these joyful sounding horns, but for some reason all of Quentin's family knew this meant that they must jump up from their seats and make a circle on the dance floor. Leah waved for me to come join them. A few more of our friends joined me. One of Quentin's cousins grabbed my hand and we were off.

Everyone began to dance, one foot forward, then back, holding hands, round and around in a circle. My dress moved around me as I copied everyone else's movements. Side to side, forward-back, round and around in circles we went. The circle became more and more full, until we were barely even dancing anymore and rather shuffling our feet around in circles with the utmost joy. The room filled with laughing and cheering and even singing words I didn't understand. Everyone stopped moving and clapped their hands along to the quick beat of the song.

I saw Saul break off from the circle along with Leah's brother and a few of Quentin's older cousins. They returned pridefully, Saul with a chair raised above a huge smile on his face. Saul set the chair down in the middle of the circle of people and Quentin threw himself on top of it, ready for a moment he had been waiting for his whole childhood.

Leah grabbed my arm and led me to the chair. "It's supposed to be the men who do this, but I think it should be the people who raised him and made him," she said, and placed my hands on one of the chair legs.

Saul, Leah, and Leah's brother held onto the other legs of the chair. They started lifting it into the air.

Startled, I attempted to raise it along with them, but we were all very different heights, Saul standing at a towering six foot two, me at my almost full grown five foot five, Leah's brother no more than two inches taller and Leah at her meek five foot one, it didn't bode well for Quentin's safety.

We lifted him, once, twice, again, and again, while everyone else laughed and cheered and clapped around us. Joy and pride echoed throughout the room and allowed me to hear nothing else but happiness. My face felt warm and a smile, not letting up, reached from one side to the other.

Quentin let out a loud whoop and let go of the arms of the chair he had been gripping onto so tightly. He raised his arms in the air and allowed his body to rise up from the chair as we lifted it. His body lingered as we brought the chair back down, stuck flying for just a split second. When he fell, we lifted him again and he flew.

Our arms got tired of lifting eventually and we set the chair back onto the ground. Quentin jumped off of it and grabbed my hands with his. Everyone else around us rejoined hands and began to dance again. Quentin pulled me around in circles with only him, leaning back so we kept each other from falling. People continued to dance and dance in circles around us, alive with the excitement and exhilaration of it all. Quentin tilted his head back to look up at the ceiling, then stopped moving in circles with me, sending me tumbling backwards, almost to the ground but he grabbed onto my hand and spun me around him again, pulling me back and forth with his arm, skipping around and holding onto me tightly. Our bodies were ablaze with movement, our heads filled with our laughter. When the song finally came to an end, we collapsed into each other, shaking with giggles.

Then we danced until we couldn't anymore, and laughed until our chests and cheeks ached with joy. We cheered and sang at the top of our lungs until our voices broke. We spun and played for as long as we could still stand and we fell into folding chairs on the edge of the room. After all our friends left, my mom stood in the doorway waiting for me to come with her.

"Bye Quentin! Bye Leah! I can't wait to go dress shopping!" I yelled as I followed my mom out to our car.

Thirteen

"I CAN'T BELIEVE you are actually making me do this!" Quentin complained as we pulled into the parking lot of the department store.

"Don't worry we aren't going to buy anything! Just make you try it on!" I grinned at him.

He crossed his arms. "This is pure torture."

"Oh, come on! Tori and I will try on boy's clothes for you!" Leah countered.

"That's different, girls wear boys' clothes all the time!" Quentin whined.

"But why does it have to be different?" Leah laughed.

Quentin scrunched his face angrily, "You're such a hippie! Why do you act like you are from California all the time! No one here likes it."

Leah laughed, "I'll take that as a compliment, I don't agree with the views of most of the people in this town."

"People are going to think I'm gay!"

My chest twinged. "So let them!" Leah said, looking back at me. "There is no one here that we know. We are fifty miles away from anyone that could possibly say something to you about it."

"We will try on the most ugly dresses!" I added.

We hopped out of the car and walked into the department store. Leah led us up to the floor with women's clothing and immediately we were met by the sight of a million sequins. I walked over to the closest dress and wrapped it around my body, it hung down to my toes and it had a modest structure, but it looked like an easter egg painted by a child.

Quentin laughed, "What is that thing?"

"A beautiful ball gown, fit for a queen!" I said sarcastically.

"A foofy pastel queen."

I jumped to the next dress and held it up. Its navy, tulle skirt only reached my upper thighs and giant yellow flowers protruded from the fabric of the bodice. "This one makes me look like a five-year-old whose parents want her to be the girlish girl ever."

"I'm sure your parents wish you would wear that!" Quentin chuckled.

"Quentin!" Leah scolded.

I nodded, "That is the truth. Now grab as many ugly dresses as possible and meet me in the dressing room!"

I laid dress after ugly dress over my arm and when I felt like I had scoured a good portion of the dress selection I walked to the dressing room. Quentin already sat outside on one of the huge cushioned chairs, with one dress in his hands. "I'm very disappointed in you Quentin, I told you to get as many ugly dresses as possible." I shook my head at him.

He shrugged, "I didn't feel like being stared at."

"How many times do we have to tell you, no one cares!"

Leah appeared next to me, her arms and hands laden with too many dresses to count, some in multiple sizes. "I thought I would get multiple of some so you two could be matching."

"Mom! How many times do I have to tell you that I don't want to do this! You and Tori can have all the fun you want but I will not try on all those dresses."

"Take a step outside of your masculinity for a second hon, and just have fun with us!" Leah laughed.

He furrowed his brow, "It's not my masculinity, it's my dignity. I don't want to feel like an idiot."

I held a bright yellow jumpsuit up from Leah's pile and placed the hanger over my head, "Look, I feel like an idiot too."

"I really don't want to do this, Tori. Don't you get it?"

"I get it hon," Leah said. She picked up a matching jumpsuit to the one I had hanging on my arm and hung it over his head. "It's hard being a teenager. Everything is a competition and a test to be normal. Trust me sweetie, normal isn't so admired in the real world. It's okay to let go and have a little fun."

"YOLO!" I added.

He looked up at us angrily. "I will try on this dress, and this dress only," he grumbled, while holding up the dress in his hands. I have to admit, Quentin had pretty great taste in ugly dresses, this one had a tight black and yellow striped bodice with a mock turtleneck and short sleeves. The sleeves had red lace around the armband for an extra finishing touch. The waistline had alternating red, yellow and white rhinestones around it, which turned into a mid-calf, red and yellow mesh skirt. This kind of dress made me question what kind of people were coming to these stores and how they could possibly be making money.

"I have to admit that dress is the most terrible dress I have ever seen."

"Well let's see it on you then!" Leah grinned.

A few minutes later Quentin emerged from the dressing room, the look on his face half way between a grimace and a smile. I immediately pulled out my phone and took a picture of him in order to make sure I captured his initial reaction to how that horrific thing looked on him. "Do you think anyone would actually wear this?" he frowned down at himself.

"Only someone who wanted to get bullied or beat up."

We continued to try on dresses and other items of clothing that proved to be just as horrific. My favorite out of everything was the bright yellow jumpsuit made out of jersey that clung to my thighs like I had just jumped in a pool wearing it. We finally convinced Quentin to try one on with me and we looked like we were wearing bananas with a scooped neckline.

"This looks terrible!" Quentin laughed at us in the mirror. The yellow fabric hung about half a foot below where it should on him, every fold wrinkled and loose.

I smiled, "You look gorgeous!"

"YOU LOOK FINE!" Oda said and straightened out my hair for me.

I swatted her hand away from my head, "Do you have a sweater or something? All mine are too small."

"No, and you look fine!"

"You can see my scar though." I touched my shoulder uncomfortably, feeling the long, thick line of raised skin.

"So?" Oda argued.

I turned to her and pressed the tips of my fingers to her shoulder. "You look beautiful." She wore a red dress that accentuated her curves perfectly. She had her curls pulled back into a little puff on the top of her head, and the ends of a thick black ribbon that she used as a headband hung down the open back of the dress. Her mom had done her makeup with just the subtlest amount of eyeshadow and highlight that made her skin shimmer.

She touched my shoulder, "You look beautiful too, Tori."

I frowned and felt a harsh twinge in my chest, "Everyone is going to see it." I grabbed her hand and removed it from my scar. I looked over to Quentin, who sat quietly on my bed. "Quentin?"

He shrugged and looked down at his hands, "I don't have a sweater."

I took a deep breath and smiled, the tension in my chest lifted a little. "Very helpful," I said and threw myself on the bed, across his lap. My eyes met his and he gave me a huge goofy smile, we both laughed and he squeezed my chin between his fingers. I sighed, "Let's go!"

"Finally!"

"Dad! Can you drive us to school now?" I yelled, then ran down the stairs and slipped on my shoes.

"Wow my beautiful grown-up little girl," my dad said, emerging from the kitchen.

"Dad..." I said, my cheeks hot, holding back an embarrassed smile. "Let's go! Quentin, Oda, you ready?"

"Yes, and we have been for hours," Oda complained.

"I'm sorry!"

That year, only the seventh and eighth-graders could attend the winter formal because of an incident with the sixth graders a few years before. I hadn't gone when we were in seventh grade because my dad had just gotten out of the hospital, but Oda informed me that she had no fun and that the eighth graders had forced them off the dance floor.

We arrived at the dance bundled up in all our winter clothing, but immediately had to take off our coats because of the body heat of eighty sweaty teens. As we walked in and I saw how many people there were, I immediately put my hand up to my shoulder in an attempt to cover up my scar. Oda ran off to go say hello to someone across the room, I looked around, trying to find a group of people I could fit in with.

Quentin came up next to me, looked me up and down, then took my hand from my shoulder and held onto it tightly, "I think your scar makes you look cool, it shows that you have been through something."

"And I think it looks gross and that no one actually cares what I've been through," I attempted to pull my hand away from him, but he tightened his grip on my hand.

"You look good! And it is dark in here anyways. C'mon Tori!"

I squeezed his hand back and felt a wave of warmth travel through my body. I shivered and smiled at Quentin, then pulled him into the middle of the gym. "People are watching us," I whispered loudly at him.

"Perfect! Let them stare!" He pulled my hand into him and spun me in circles around him.

I laughed, "Sometimes I don't understand you."

"What?" he yelled back.

"Sometimes I don't understand you!" I yelled, matching his pitch.

"You understand me perfectly!"

"Better than you understand me."

"What?" he teased me.

I dropped his hand and crossed my arms around my body, "This is so stupid. I can't dance."

He jumped in circles around me laughing. He threw his hands up in the air and allowed the music to overtake his body. He grabbed one of my arms and tried desperately to make me jump up and down with him, but I wouldn't move. I pulled my arm away from him and back across my body. "Quentin! Stop," I pleaded, my face red with embarrassment.

"All you gotta do is jump up and down and put your arms in the air." He demonstrated for me, fists in the air, going higher and higher with each jump. A huge grin spread across his face as he jumped up and down and attracted many gazes from around the room.

"You are enjoying all the attention, aren't you?" I teased.

"Quentin!" A boy's voice yelled from behind us. Quentin looked over to the voice that yelled his name. I felt someone's hand on my elbow and I turned to see

Harper, a girl from my soccer team, leading me away from Quentin, who spun around the room for whoever called his name.

"Where are you taking me?" I asked Harper.

She smiled a wry smile at me and moved her hand down to mine. A shiver ran through my body and up to my face, making the corners of my mouth rise and my cheeks turn red hot. I saw her blue eyes flicker in the dim light. I pressed myself closer into her and allowed her to pull me along through all the people. She pulled me out of the gym and into the bathroom, where the air felt cooler and easier to breathe, except that I couldn't breathe. My chest moved up and down quickly, heart beating faster than a racehorse. I clenched my hands, hiding my palms which were filled with sweat.

Harper shakily put her hand on the wall next to my head and I looked up and down her perfect face. I guess I now have to admit that I had liked Harper for quite some time. I remember watching her at soccer practice and being completely entranced by the way she moved so perfectly with the ball, and her long strawberry-blonde hair swung behind her as she played, so concentrated on making every step right. And then her face hovered close to mine and a huge smile spread across her lips and her eyes flickered between mine. Her lips were on mine. And it all felt right and so wrong at the same time.

I don't quite remember what happened with Harper after that, except that my arms shook with excitement and I wanted to go dance with Quentin. I walked out of the bathroom and ran into the gym, desperately searching for him. I felt his hand on my shoulder and turned around, so excited to see him.

"Where were you?" A huge smile crept across my face and I squeezed my arms to my chest. "What?" Quentin laughed at me.

I leaned into him and whispered loudly, "Harper kissed me!"

He laughed again, "Yeah right!"

"She did!" I nodded vigorously.

"Wait, for real?" He looked so surprised.

"Yes! Let's go dance!" I yelled and dragged him with me back to the center of the gym. I threw my arms up in the air and embraced the fluttery warmth that filled my body.

Quentin mimicked my hands in the air and began to jump up and down around me. A few more of our friends followed our lead and gathered around us in the center of the room, barely dancing but jumping and laughing our hearts out. For once I could be me and no one noticed.

Fourteen

Every day I was finding it harder to breathe. Even the good days felt clouded over by a sheen of my wavering perception of myself. There would be days I couldn't move and days where I would go about everything as I normally would, but feeling lightheaded. My ears felt clogged and my head spun even when I laid down. I couldn't control it and I couldn't make sense of it and I couldn't bring myself to talk about it. I wasn't me anymore. I couldn't find an escape from my own head and self-loathing.

One day the thoughts were particularly dark, screaming at me that I didn't deserve to be here anymore. My chest ached like every day before and each breath took so much effort. I lay flat on my back in my bed when a sudden urge told me to get up. Before the brief thought could go away, I rolled out of my bed and onto the ground. I sighed with my nose pressed into the hardwood floor and reached up to grab my phone off of the bedside table.

I pushed myself up from the ground and did the only thing that I could think of left to do. I walked out of my house and down the street to Quentin's, trudging my way along and shivering from the cool evening air. I only wore a thin long sleeve shirt and pajama bottoms and the wind bit at my skin. I knocked on his door so lazily for a moment I didn't know if they would even hear it, but then River started barking and a moment later Quentin stood in the doorway with a surprised look on his face. A smile turned into a concerned frown.

"What are you doing here, Tori?"

I stood there on the doorstep staring at him and quivering. Quentin looked me up and down, then took my hand and led me inside. He sat me down on the couch, then walked back to the doorway to kick off his shoes. I noticed his clothes, he looked nicer than usual in an untucked button-down shirt. He had even combed his hair into place.

Someone rang the doorbell a few minutes later. Quentin raced to answer it and when he opened it I heard a voice say, "You look nice." I didn't bother to try to figure out who spoke on the other side of the door because then I would have felt bad for taking over his night. He slipped through the crack in the door and shut it behind him. I heard whispered voices on the porch and then eventually Quentin came back in, shutting the door quietly behind him.

"Are you alright?" Quentin whispered from behind me.

I forced my lips to smile, "Yes. Yes. I am fine. TV?"

Quentin flopped down on the couch beside me, threw his legs up on the coffee table and clicked the TV on. "I assume I know what we are watching," he said while finding our show on the TV. I curled my legs up close to my aching chest and leaned into the corner, taking up as little space as I could.

Even our show couldn't make me laugh that night. My body throbbed with my pain. I couldn't even reach the temporary happiness that I usually found with Quentin. Sometime into watching the show I moved over to put my head on his shoulder, I wanted to feel his warmth, his breath, his life. Quentin put his arm around me and sighed.

I must have fallen asleep around that time because I woke up to the sound of Leah walking in the door. At some point I had taken over the couch and I noticed a pillow under my head.

"Hi sweetie!" I heard Leah say loudly when she saw Quentin. She switched on the lights in the living room, "What are you doing sitting here in the dark?"

Quentin rushed over to her and turned off the lights, "Shhh," he whispered.

I felt Leah's footsteps come near me and a quiet, "Oh." She walked over to the chair and sat down, "Didn't you have that—"

"Yes," Quentin interrupted, "but she just showed up here and didn't say anything. I don't know what's wrong, but she's been like this for a while."

"Like what?" Leah whispered.

"Just down all the time, she isn't the same."

"Yeah," Leah agreed. "You're doing the right thing sweetie. I'm proud of you."

"Why?"

I couldn't see her, but I knew Leah smiled, "You're a great friend."

"Thanks, Mom."

I heard Leah's footsteps go into the other room and then come back. She laid another blanket on me, then kneeled down next to the couch, "I know it's hard, you'll get through it. You are strong and you are smart and you are beautiful." She pushed herself off the ground and said to Quentin, "Get some sleep."

So many days I felt like I did that day, but I didn't have the strength to find Quentin to keep me safe from myself. I felt wrong. Everything about me felt wrong. I looked in the mirror. I wore only my bra and my soccer shorts which fit the curve of my hips too tight and were uncomfortably short. I pulled my shorts down a bit so they fit looser on my thighs, only until I realized that this revealed my belly button. I turned to the side to look at the small bulge of my lower belly. I felt bloated even though I had only lost weight since I stopped growing. I turned back to the mirror and looked into my eyes. They were the most boring brown you will ever see. I pulled down my lower lids and looked up, seeing bloodshot veins when I did. My hair lay stick straight on my shoulders looking unnatural and stiff. I pulled it back into a tight ponytail so no one had to see.

I touched my shoulder, my biggest of all imperfections, my scar. I touched the bumpy skin with my fingertips and ran my pointer finger down the curve of my shoulder where the scar sank into my skin. I couldn't remember how I felt when it happened, only that day and the days that followed with Quentin. It didn't used to agonize me like that; I used to show it off like I'd received a trophy. But now I only saw my imperfections. I pulled my jersey over my head to cover my shoulder. I tried to pull down my shirt sleeve over the area that the scar peaked out, but I knew it would just slide back into place.

It seemed my faults were the only things I could find. I should have better grades. I should try harder. I should spend less time with my friends. I should be kinder to my friends. I shouldn't like girls. I shouldn't be with Harper. I shouldn't be me. I should just suck it up and become who my mom told me I should be. I might be happier? At least I wouldn't be me.

"Victoria!" my dad yelled from the bottom of the stairs, snapping my brain out of its cloud. I quickly slapped my shin guards on my legs and pulled my socks on as I hopped down the stairs on one foot then the other.

My dad stood at the bottom of the stairs in a t-shirt and shorts while my mom rummaged around in her purse. Her clothes were way too nice to be going to my soccer game. She glanced up from her purse and made a tutting noise with her tongue, then pulled down on my shirt, "Have you been doing those exercises I sent you?"

I shooed her hand away, "Yeah Mom, the shirt just shrunk in the wash or something."

"It's just they can help with this," she waved her hand in a circle around my midsection.

The muscles in my forearms tensed, "I said I tried them, Mom."

"It's for your own good."

"Are you not coming to my game?"

"No, sorry sweetie." My face hardened when she called me sweetie. "I have an event that I remembered at the last moment. Lisa just called me. I have to help set it up. I hope you don't mind."

Of course I minded. I had only asked them to come to one game. It should have been easy for them, it was simple, just one game. "No, it's fine," I gave her a stiff smile.

"We're gonna be late if you don't hurry up," said my dad.

I looked at the clock in the entryway, two minutes until my game. I shoved my foot into one of my cleats without tying and grabbed the other one in my hand, "Coming, coming," I said in an annoyed tone.

My mom gave me a look, "Victoria, your father—"

"Yeah mom!" I cut her off and ran out the door behind my dad, not wanting to hear her lecture me for about the twentieth time that week.

I hopped out of the car after the three-minute drive to the field to see my team already done with warmups and standing in a huddle on the sidelines, listening to my coach. I ran up to them apologizing for my lateness.

"Victoria, thank the lord you're here! Go run around the track then do your stretches, we only have 11 today, so you are going to have to be on the field!"

I took off on the track that went around the field, like he had instructed and noticed as I passed the families sitting on the other side of the field, Quentin, sitting next to a blonde woman who looked very familiar but I couldn't place. It seemed off that he was sitting with the families from the away team and that he hadn't told me that he would be there at all. Maybe he had a family friend that lived in a different town or something, but I didn't see Leah anywhere.

When I finished my lap around the track I ran to my position, center back. I got to control the field. As the last person before the goalie, it was my job to stop people before they could shoot. I would run at the people with all I had, not afraid to use all my weight against them so I could turn the ball around and my team could score.

I looked down the field at the other team, they were wearing dark purple shirts with gold shorts that made us look stupid in our bright red shorts and yellow shirts. I finally realized why Quentin was here and also why he hadn't told me. We were playing Hally's team. I remembered now that her mom drove her an hour away so she could be on this team with their family friend. Heat rose in my chest as I stared at Hally, one of the strikers for their team. I readied myself to destroy her, she wouldn't get any goals on my watch. I turned my head and saw Harper, standing alert and ready to start.

My eyes stayed glued on her. Even when the whistle blew and Hally kicked the ball to her teammate, I kept my eyes on Harper, who sprinted after the ball. She took long strides and I noticed how her shorts weren't too tight on her like mine or too loose, they hugged the slight curve of her hips in just the right way, then fell loosely to her mid-thigh. Her hair swished around behind her in a long ponytail.

Without warning, the other team stole the ball and ran down the field towards me. I forced myself to snap out of it and watch the ball instead of Harper. I shuffled my feet over so I had a clearer view of the game, then I saw that Hally had the ball and she had begun to run down the field with a clear path that my idiotic team-mates had left open.

"Get to her!" I screamed at my team before running at her, but it was too late and she had already shot the ball, which had landed smoothly in the corner of the goal. The goalie lay on the ground in her feeble attempt to dive for the ball that my entire team had somehow missed. "C'mon you guys!" I yelled, knowing that all eyes went to me when we missed a shot.

I looked at my dad on one side of the field and my heart clenched, he had to see me at my worst. I looked to the other side of the field at Quentin whose expression was unreadable, until Hally waved at him, jumped up and down with glee at her goal and Quentin's face turned into a bright smile. The woman next to him clapped lightly and gave Hally a nod of approval, she looked awkward next to him and he looked out of place.

I looked angrily back at the field, where Harper and a girl named Robin were kicking off. Our team barely ever had enough players. More than half the girls in my grade and the grades above and below me had played on my soccer team at some time or another because our town always had a lack of players.

I couldn't blame my team. My slip had caused the goal. I had to concentrate on the game, not on Quentin whose presence only further agitated the heat in my chest, or my dad who filled my head with the pressure to be the daughter he wanted, or Harper who had her eyes on me in fleeting moments. I knew those moments were valuable.

Again, the game moved without my head being in the right place. Hally came running down the field, except this time she tried to pass the ball to her teammate. Before the girl could receive the ball, a girl on my team, Jules, intercepted it and passed it to Harper who began dribbling up the field. She was perfect. She moved flawlessly with the ball, dodging between the opposing players with ease and then a smooth shot with her left foot. The goalie dived and caught it just before it went in.

Harper was beautiful. Her beautiful face with its sharp edges, short frame and sky-blue eyes. Her beautiful body with its slight curves and the spattering of freckles all over that gave her clear skin perfect depth. Her agility in soccer, her strides that seemed ever so easy and effortless and her shots on goal that nearly always went to the corner and slid down the net with a satisfying swish. The way she could convince me that she cared only the right amount, how I couldn't hold her anger in my hands, and how she could get me to do anything for her because I had become so blind to her imperfections. Yet, she saw all of mine.

My brain snapped out of its haze when Jules yelled my name. This time instead of Hally I saw the team's other striker. She dribbled with the ball close to her feet and was approaching the goal fast. I ran at her with everything I could muster and got to her right as she took the shot that sent the ball flying the few feet to my nose at full speed.

My nose felt numb for a second until the burning pain arrived. I shook my head but knew I couldn't stop. I would not screw up this time. I kicked the ball from in front of the girl's feet, who stood there stunned, and dribbled past her. I got a couple yards when I saw that I had an open shot across the field to Jules. I sent the ball skipping right in front of her feet. She caught it and with one swift motion she sprinted down the field, then took a soaring shot at the goal. The ball hit the tips of the goalie's fingers and went flying over the crossbar.

"Tori! Come off!" My coach yelled.

I wiped my nose to find a streak of blood on the back of my hand. "I'm fine!" I yelled back at him, sniffing the blood back in as hard as I could.

The rest of the half went smoothly, no one scored and I didn't make any drastic mistakes. My obnoxiously yellow shirt had become speckled with drops of blood. When the referee blew the whistle, I ran as fast as I could to Quentin before Hally could get to him.

"Tori..." Quentin said.

I threw my arms up in the air, "What are you doing here?"

"I think you know..."

"Of course I know, but," I grabbed him by the arm and dragged him away from Hally's mom. "Why?"

"Hally asked me to come."

"But Hally—"

Quentin cut me off, "Tori I really don't need this right now." He lowered his voice, "Her mom is right there."

"Fine, then we can talk about it later."

"No! We always talk about it! And we never end up understanding each other. You are the one that doesn't understand, why don't you just give her a chance?"

"Why *do you* give her a chance?"

He started to say something, then shut his mouth and stormed away to Hally and her mom. "Good job, Halls," I heard him say.

I grimaced and jogged over to my team.

"That wasn't too bad..." my coach said. As my coach discussed what we could do better, my brain wandered back to raging at Hally until he dismissed us. "Okay, go get water."

I walked over to my dad to grab my water bottle from him. He reached up and knocked on my head with his fist, "You need to get your head in the game! You could have saved that first goal."

I took a long drink of water. "Maybe if my team knew where to be," I said indignantly.

"You have to take responsibility for your own actions, not blame them on other people. That mentality will make you lazy and you will never get anywhere if you always place the blame somewhere else. Learn from your mistakes. You can't lean on people."

I frowned and took another drawn out sip of my water. "I have to get back to the field," I said and dropped the water bottle at his feet.

"Hey Tori," Harper's soft voice said from behind me. She had come up next to me close enough that I could feel the hairs on the back of her hand touching mine. I moved away, knowing that my dad could probably still see me. "You seemed a bit distracted out there." She moved closer to me.

I moved away again, "My dad is right there Harper."

"And? It's not like he's ever gonna suspect anything," she laughed. "The old people here are too homophobic to even think that's possible."

"But other people might," I stepped away again.

"It's fine," she reassured, her voice's soothing tone unsettling my stomach, but I let her press her arm against mine.

"Girls, get on the field!" Coach yelled.

The second half of the game moved quickly. The ball stayed in the middle of the field at the start. Each team kept missing their passes, then Harper saw an opening and made a run. Our other striker, Lily, saw the opening too. Pass, pass, then Harper shot and it landed beautifully in the corner of the goal, just past the tip of the goalie's fingers.

Harper and Lily jogged back to the center with an extra pep in their step. As Harper passed Hally, I swear I saw Hally turn her foot out sending Harper stumbling forward. Harper turned around to glare at Hally but she kept going to our side. Hally's team had the kick-off, they were concentrated and determined, ready for anything. We were scattered, our minds not connected to our feet and our thoughts focused on winning, not on playing right.

My uncoordinated team couldn't seem to manage the other striker on Hally's team and she scored before we even knew what was happening. At our kick-off, the other team stole the ball immediately, only for one of their midfielders to shoot and miss. This shot just jangled my team's nerves even more. The next time she had an opportunity, the same midfielder scored. The sweat that poured off my skin brought sunscreen with it and the back of my neck started to burn. I yelled at my team more than my brain was yelling at me, which relieved the noise in my head a little.

Harper almost had another shot until the defender stole the ball and passed it to one of the midfielders, who dribbled with it for a bit. She passed it to Hally who had a clear break away.

I took off towards Hally, my head dizzy with competition. I sprinted as fast as I could, but my momentum didn't allow me to stop. I ran full force into her just after she passed the ball to her teammate and took us both down. I tried to catch myself with one hand but my face still hit the ground on impact and my nose began to bleed again. My head throbbed and I couldn't bring myself to move off her. I heard cheering from the other side of the field.

"Get off me," Hally growled and pushed me off her onto my back.

The other team had scored and my wrist, my head and my nose were all throbbing from the fall. I pushed myself up with my other hand, making myself light headed with the sudden movement and stumbled off to the nearest side of the field, where I lay down on my back, clutching my wrist in my hand.

"Tori!" I opened my eyes and saw Quentin's face looking down over me. "Pick your head up so the blood doesn't go down your throat."

A second later Harper's face appeared next to his, "Is she okay?"

"I don't know." Quentin lifted me up from under my armpits, "I'm just going to lean you up against the bleachers," he told me. Harper tried to grab my other arm, but he shooed her hand away. He sat down next to me and used his shirt to stop my nosebleed. "How are you feeling?"

I laughed, "Hally is going to be upset that you are helping me, not her."

"That's okay."

Fifteen

"DON'T TALK TO STRANGERS!" Leah yelled at us from the car.

"Mom, we are 13, not three. Actually, Tori is 14!" Quentin whined.

"And I have a weapon!" I held up my casted wrist.

Leah sighed loudly, "Yes, but still don't do it, and get to your father's before the sun sets. Do you have your meds?"

He reached into his backpack and pulled out the orange bottle, "I'm not stupid, Mom."

"Okay, okay. And call me if you need anything. And you can call Saul, too. He said Riya could pick you two up if you needed."

"Bye, Mom! Don't you have a meeting to get to?"

She looked at her watch frantically then blew a kiss in our direction, "I love you! Be safe!" she said and drove off, leaving us on some random street in the closest city to our town, which was still over an hour away. The buildings above us stretched much farther into the sky than any building in our tiny town.

I breathed in a gust of wind that blew our way. "Where to first?" I asked Quentin.

"Let's just wander."

For a while we did just that. We meandered our way around the streets of downtown in the way that we would have done in the woods outside of our town, except here people buzzed around us and pushed past each other to get to their destination.

I pointed to a middle-aged woman with curly black hair and a nervous look on her face, "What do you think her story is?"

"What do you mean?"

"Don't you ever just see people and think up their whole life's story because you have nothing better to do?"

"No," he frowned at me.

"C'mon, it's fun. Like that man," I motioned to an older white man who sat on a bench holding a briefcase in his lap. "Obviously I know nothing about him, but I can imagine. He got married when he was in his twenties after he got home from fighting in Vietnam. He was never in direct combat, but he still takes pride in being a veteran. His wife was a teacher and he worked at some unimportant desk job. When they were younger, before they moved here, they went to California, lived near Yosemite and did drugs all the time and went on hikes and jumped off cliffs into lakes. They had their daughter and she now has a boyfriend and a daughter herself, but she hasn't called him very much since her mother died a few years ago. Now he is waiting to meet her for brunch, but he is very nervous."

Quentin grinned, "But you know nothing about him."

"That's why it is fun and completely harmless."

He nodded in the direction of a young woman with a tiny baby strapped onto her chest, holding the hand of a toddler. "She doesn't have a job, but she has always wished to be an author ever since she was a little kid. She met the father of her kids when she was in high school and they got married, planning to get her career in motion before they had any kids. He was in law school, so they didn't really have very much money to support her becoming an author, but as soon as he graduated, she became pregnant with the first baby and it kinda ruined her plans. Now she has two kids whom she loves, but she resents them for being born, and her husband for making them, and herself for ruining her chances."

"Woah, that took a turn for the worse."

"That's exactly how she feels, I mean you saw how stressed she looked."

We continued this for a while. Making up stories of lives that mostly seemed worthy of the movies or people whose stories desperately needed to be told. The majority of the people we knew had the same life painted a different shade of beige. On the outside everyone in our town had done everything right. They achieved the classic American dream: gone to college, gotten married, worked some boring job, and had kids. A cookie cutter house with a cookie cutter family, a cookie cutter life. They all had enough that they could put up a facade, they could pretend that the cookie wasn't crumbling in their fingertips. Sure, some of them thought they were happy but they lived their lives the same every day. I doubt most of them were ever completely satisfied with not doing the things they wanted to do and settling for the things they were supposed to. None of it was real. All we knew were these kinds of people, with the exception of Leah. Every person that we created in our stories we found to be different. Every person in our stories had hopes, dreams, pain, and an interesting life that didn't come out of a mold made by generations of societal pressure. We both wished to be anything other than those kinds of people, the exact kind of people my parents were and wished for me to be.

"I want to move to Montana," I said.

"What? Why?"

"Or maybe Idaho. I want to live in the middle of nowhere."

Quentin tilted his head at me. "I'm not sure if you remember this, but we already kind of live in the middle of nowhere."

"But not in the kind of place with middle-of-nowhere people. I want to live with people who are so different from any other person you have ever met and ever thought you would meet. The kind of people who you can only find wandering in the wilderness or living in some middle-of-nowhere town in Montana and spending their days in the forest reading under the oldest trees and growing all their meals from a garden in their backyard."

"I would really love to have a burrito tree." Quentin chuckled at himself.

I ignored him, "I want to be a middle-of-nowhere person."

Giving up on his joke, "I'll come to visit you, but I am going to be a city boy and live in a tiny apartment with three roommates and spend all my time going out and experiencing everything that I can. I don't think I'll ever settle. I think I will become a famous comic book artist, then spend my whole life traveling the world and doing interviews, then visiting you in your middle-of-nowhere town in Montana."

"Do you want ice cream?" I said as we walked by this small shop with big glass windows and a big purple circle with the white outline of an ice cream cone advertising their homemade ice cream.

"Sure," said Quentin.

I pushed open the door, the little shop bell jingling jovially above me. The worker was in the backroom. While we waited for her, I took in the sweet smell of freshly baked waffle cones that drifted through the air. Eventually she came out and took my order, then I went to sit on the stools that were lined up on a counter on the side of the shop. Quentin came and sat down next to me a few minutes later. "What did you get?"

"Cookie dough. What about you?" I asked. "Wait no, let me guess," I cut him off before he got the chance to respond.

"Okay," he said and covered the top of his ice cream cup so I couldn't see it.

"Hmm, salted caramel?" I guessed.

He laughed sarcastically, "Wow, how did you know? It's not like I get the same thing every time."

"Salted caramel in a cup, of course!"

"It's as if we have been friends for seven years."

I nodded, playing along with the joke. "As if. I just met you when your mom dropped me off in this city and I saw a boy and had to spend the whole day with him."

"And I was like who is this strange creature that is following me around? And who has been following me around for seven years." He laughed.

I smiled at him and then sighed. I didn't know why he hadn't brought up what happened with Harper yet. I didn't want to think about it though.

He never told me, but I always knew that after Harper and I broke up he had begged his mom to allow us to have that day in the city, away from everyone in town.

"Really? I felt the same way the whole time. There was always this weird boy around me and I didn't know what to do with him, because I didn't want to hurt his feelings and his mom was so nice to me. You might know him. His name is Quentin Flasch, I think. Everyone at school calls him Flasch because he is a good runner or something, I don't really know."

"Oh! I think I do know him; he seems kind of weird, mostly because he is always hanging out with this really lame girl named Victoria."

"Oh yeah, she does seem very lame."

He laughed and gave me a half smile that really seemed like more of a frown. "This is a very creative way to make fun of yourself," he said.

I shrugged, "I bet I could do better, except there is not too much to make fun of! But you, however, oh I could do that forever!"

"Shush," he said with his mouth full of ice cream.

I gave him an endearing smile, "You just do so many questionable things."

"Is it possible for you to be nice to me!?"

"Of course not, it is my instinct to be mean to your face. But what you don't know is that to all my other friends I talk about you as if you are a superhero."

"And what do you say to these so-called other friends?"

"Oh, just that you are the greatest person ever."

"Well, I'm nice to you to your face sometimes."

"That's because you are a better person than me."

He tilted his head to the side, "Do you actually think that?"

"That you are a better person than me? Yes, definitely. You are so much nicer and more caring than me."

"No, that some people are actually better than others?"

"Well, yeah, don't you think you are a better person than a murderer or a rapist? I think that's just logic."

"I think we can't control our circumstances."

"You are saying that if you were in the position of a murderer then you would still murder someone?"

"I'm saying I can't know because I am not that person."

"Hmm," I mulled it over.

"I mean we both have been through different things that the other one doesn't understand and that makes us different people. Just because someone has made some bad choices doesn't mean that they are a bad person. Tori, you aren't a bad person," Quentin reassured me.

"Hmm," I said again, then shoved a big spoonful of ice cream in my mouth.

He put his hand on the counter closer to me, in a motion to defuse whatever harm he'd done, "Tori."

"I'm done, do you want to go?"

"Okay," he said and hopped off the stool, still holding his ice cream in his hands.

I jumped off my stool and walked swiftly out the door, the bell hanging from the doorway pinging again as I walked out. I yanked down on the strings of the drawstring bag on my back and crossed my arms over my chest, shivering from the wind. I walked quickly away from the ice cream place. Quentin struggled to keep up with me while still eating his ice cream.

"Tori! Slow down," yelled Quentin. I didn't slow down or respond; I wanted to lift my face to the sky and scream, at Harper, at myself for letting any of it happen, and at the world, at everything that ever went wrong. Maybe it was because I knew how stuck I was in my own head all the time and because every day of that year had just been a struggle to get up in the morning. Maybe I noticed the way Quentin tried to help me and I couldn't let him because I couldn't hurt him. I had already caused myself enough pain.

"Tori!" He caught up to me and stopped me with a hand on my shoulder. "Can you just slow down?"

I stopped walking and looked at him angrily, slowing down physically, but still not giving him what he wanted from me. He let it go, and the air relaxed. "I don't want to talk about it."

"Okay," he agreed. We walked in silence for a few moments, "What about her?" He pointed at a woman standing across the street from us, waiting for the traffic to slow down enough for her to run across the street. She had her long black hair in a braid down her back and a wild look in her eyes.

"Hmm," I took a deep breath, allowing my body to relax a little more. "She is from a Southern European country, I can't tell which one, but she moved to New York City a few years ago to experience the world and be a photographer. She enjoyed the city, but only in small doses, so she started to explore the mountains and she found that she enjoyed nature photography much more. Last year she moved to Yellowstone for the summer and she did a lot of photography and nature writing. She ran out of money and had to move back to the country that she came from, but her older brother got a job in the city and now she lives with him and his girlfriend. She is going to get a job and make enough money to go traveling again," I smiled and looked up at Quentin, very satisfied with my story.

We walked to a small park sandwiched between urban areas and sat down on a bench next to a tree hoping to shelter ourselves a bit from the wind that had picked up significantly and blew my hair all over my face and into my mouth. In a meager attempt to get my hair out of my face I pulled it into a knotted cross between a bun and a ponytail.

We sat in the park for a while. Quentin didn't bring up what had happened before or Harper in any way, but I could sense with everything he said to me his need for me to open up to him. We talked about nothing. The simplicity of small talk was all I needed from him.

It reminded me of a day after the accident. I think it must have been the first time Quentin showed me his comics. I sat in my hospital bed and weakly doodled on his cast. We didn't talk about anything personal when we were at that age, probably because we had nothing personal to discuss, and I had tried to keep it that way, although not very successfully, as we got older. I assume he must have been telling me about his day camp or something. He had laughed at the drawing I did on his cast, then pulled out a piece of paper he saved for me.

It was a comic strip of us playing with Legos. It showed our strategy of attack against the evil Lego village which we had also built from our imagination, and didn't really look much like a village at all.

Now, Quentin chattered about something that had happened in his English class and laughed about how he hated the novel they had to read.

"You really don't have any appreciation for literature, do you?" I scolded him.

"What?"

"You know, you draw everything and you only read comic books. Don't you have any appreciation for real books?"

"You don't even like reading," he laughed at me.

"But I appreciate literature, it's so amazing to analyze a good book and pick up on all the clues an author is giving. You spend the whole time trying to figure out what every word means. Then, when you finish it, everything comes together and it just leaves you feeling right. I just love stories. I love hearing them.

I love making them up. And I love to find them everywhere. Maybe I will even become an author."

He looked puzzled, "Do you even write?"

I shrug, "Sometimes. I'll show you if you want. But, it's like I'm constantly writing in my head."

"What do you mean?"

"It's like every moment, I am narrating in my head as if I am writing my own autobiography and someone is going to read it, so every line must be perfect. Do you not do that? I thought it was just how people thought." I grinned, "Sometimes I write things down for the box."

"No? Explain."

"Did you have to do the pacer test in P.E. yet?"

He sighed, "We only have to do that in seventh and fifth-grade, don't we?"

"What? Really!"

He dipped his head and furrowed his brow, "Yeah, those are the years we have to do all that testing."

I huffed, "Mr. Hyde! I hate him. I swear he only has that job because he hates teenagers and likes to physically torture them but doesn't want to get arrested or something. He is such a creep sometimes."

Apparently, my teacher acting like a child predator should make someone laugh, because that's what Quentin did. He started laughing and wouldn't stop. "It's bullshit!" I continued, "Complete and utter bullshit! He just sits there and watches us as we kill ourselves running back and forth in the gym." Quentin continued to laugh, beginning to hold his stomach and his cheeks bright red. I let out a little chuckle at how stupid he looked. "What is wrong with you?"

In between breaths he sputtered out words. "I was just staring at your face and I thought it was funny, and then I needed to laugh. Sometimes we all need to laugh."

"Okay Q. If you say so," I said while looking at him shaking silently with laughter, tears appearing in the corners of his eyes and rolling down his cheeks. If I didn't know any better, I would have thought he had just gotten stabbed by how he gripped his stomach. "Take a deep breath," I said, placing my hand calmly and awkwardly on his back.

It took him a while to finally collect himself and when he did, I didn't want to risk him laughing again, so I quietly got up from the bench, not saying a single word. We walked back down the city streets, Quentin with an idiotically huge grin across his face, me with an annoyed look on mine.

I crossed my arms and moved closer into Quentin as we weaved our way through the increasingly crowded sidewalks. I stood close enough to him so that strangers didn't try to walk between us, but didn't look at us as if we were adorable teenagers on a date. I observed the way some people watched us carefully and some just glanced in our direction or did not pay any attention to us because they had way too much on their minds. Others let their gaze linger on us just moments longer than natural, trying to figure us out, which at first made me scoot closer to Quentin for safety. Then I remembered how earlier that day we had stared at people and made up their stories. One man in particular had a gaze that churned the pit of my stomach. He looked about 30, had a nice button-down shirt, a suit jacket that was too big on him, an unkempt beard, milky skin, and a look in his eyes like the world wasn't good enough for him, far away but also focused. He let his gaze linger on my body way too long, not paying any attention to Quentin or the other people around us. His distant eyes pull at me, fixated. I pulled my arms tighter around my stomach.

As he passed us, he looked me up and down and moved close to me. "Ey, looking good today sweetie," he said in a loud whisper.

I jumped into Quentin and grabbed his elbow, but immediately pushed him away. My heart beat so fast it felt like it wanted to break away from me. I couldn't think about anything besides how each breath got stuck in my chest and the lump at the top of my throat made it difficult to swallow.

Of course, Quentin made me laugh when he yelled back at the man, "Fuck you! You leave her alone! We are kids!" Then he turned back to me and muttered under his breath, "What a creep."

I looked at Quentin and my heart started to slow and settle back into my chest. I smiled at the adorably angry look on his face. I put my hand back on his elbow and laughed a little at him, shakily. "Why don't we just go to your dad's house now?"

"TORI! IT'S SO GOOD to see you, we hear about you too much, but I feel like I don't get to see my son's best friend enough!" Saul greeted us with a toothy smile and open arms. "Riya just started making homemade ravioli for dinner. You all got here just in time to help us! Come in! Put your things over there! And come join us in the kitchen." He shut the door behind us.

Quentin and I both looked at each other, remembering what had happened the last time we had made ravioli. "Yeah, maybe we won't help with that."

"What, why?" Saul looked so disappointed.

Quentin grimaced, "The last time we made ravioli together turned out pretty terrible."

"We don't need to test our bad luck," I added.

Saul frowned, "Aw c'mon it couldn't have been that bad!"

"Last time we made ravioli my dad had a heart attack and ended up needing emergency surgery with major complications. He's fine now."

"No need to risk your life, right Dad?" finished Quentin.

Saul looked stunned and nodded, "Well, you two can hang out with Peter instead."

"Sounds like a plan," I smiled.

We walked through the kitchen to get to the family room. I waved happily at Riya as she cooked and Quentin walked over to her. He placed his hand on her swollen belly. "Hey there little sister," he whispered.

She swatted him away, "Why don't you concentrate on your little brother and get out of the way."

Peter sat on the family room floor with his legs tucked under him, playing with toy trains on a wooden train track he had pieced together. "Hey little man!" I said and plopped down on the floor next to him. I pushed one of the trains along the track. "Do your trains have names?" I asked him. I waited for a response, but he never gave one, so I just kept pushing the train back and forth on the track. I looked up at Quentin, "He has gotten so much bigger since I last saw him. He is almost four now?"

"I am three and three quarters!" Peter yelled.

Quentin laughed and shrugged his shoulders, "Maybe you should ask the man himself."

Peter stood up and put his hands on his hips. He frowned at us, "Quentin, you have to help me put the trains together.

"Tori can help you," Quentin responded.

Peter sat down on the ground and crossed his arms. "I don't want her! I want you! You never play with me anymore," Peter whined.

Quentin stepped over the train tracks towards Peter, "Well I guess we will have to change that!" He lunged at Peter and started to tickle his belly.

Peter screamed with laughter, rolling around on his back and squirming away from Quentin. He laughed so hard but none of Peter's kicking and flailing moved Quentin so much as one inch. "No fair!" he screamed.

Quentin chuckled, "You asked for it, little brother."

Saul walked into the room, wiping flour from his hands on a towel. "I thought there might be a murder taking place in here," he chuckled.

"Quentin is trying to kill me!" Peter pushed out between screams and bursts of laughter. Quentin let up tickling Peter and sprawled his entire body over his little brother so he covered Peter like a blanket, with only his little head sticking out. Peter took a shallow breath and then let it out, "I can't breathe," he said using all his might.

Quentin laughed and rolled off of his little brother. Peter took dramatically deep breaths, pretending that

Quentin had almost killed him. I laid down on the ground next to Peter and mimicked the way he breathed. He sat up and looked at me angrily. "Stop it!" he whined and pushed me with both of his hands.

Quentin, Saul, and I all laughed at him as he crossed his arms indignantly. Glad to no longer be the one who was being laughed at, I resisted the urge to tell Peter he would grow out of being the joke and just laughed along with Quentin and Saul.

Saul left and, much to his delight, we indulged ourselves in Peter's trains. The whole time we were building the tracks, I watched the way Peter watched Quentin and remembered how I noticed Cole looking at me that way when we were younger. Peter was utterly amazed at every movement Quentin made, trying to make his body move the exact same way, and getting frustrated that he could not be exactly like his older brother. After a while, Riya called us in to come help set the table and get ready for dinner. I left happily, allowing Quentin to continue to play trains with Peter.

"He really looks up to Quentin," I said to Riya as I set forks out on every napkin.

She nodded and poured a glass of water. "I am so glad Saul decided to come back here and that this has all worked out so well." She placed her hand on her belly. "Even though he is going to have this one, I am glad that they will both have Quentin. Even as an adult, my siblings have been some of my best friends and role models. It's comforting to know they will have such a good role model."

A smile warmed my face. I was glad that Quentin could finally feel included in Saul's family instead of replaced. "When is the baby due?" I asked.

"Two weeks," Riya grinned, "it feels so unreal. She is kicking, you want to feel?" Riya took my hand and placed it on her belly. "Do you feel that?"

I concentrated. At first I felt nothing but then the baby kicked against the palm of my hand. It felt much more obvious than I thought it would be, pushing at the walls of her belly. This tiny human who still lived inside her mother would one day be a whole human, a living, breathing, feeling human being. I imagined seeing her grow up with Quentin as her older brother and getting to meet her years later and seeing him in her just the same way I saw Quentin in Peter. Maybe she would laugh the same way as him with her head tilted just the tiniest bit to the side and one corner of her upper lip curled up more than the other. I wished to see her copy the way her brother spoke just like Peter copied Quentin and Cole copied me when we were younger. Maybe there would be the same glint of mischief in her eyes before she made a joke just like Saul and Quentin.

I nodded at Riya, "It's so amazing. She is going to grow up and have her own life someday."

"Woah there. Slow down, I'm not quite ready to think about my babies growing up!"

I laughed and placed the last fork on the table. "Table is all set," I told Riya.

"Boys! Dinner!" Riya yelled into the family room.

We all served ourselves ravioli and sat down at the table. "So, Tori, are you ready for high school?"

"Mrhm," I mumbled. "Well, I already hate middle school so much, how much worse could high school be?"

"In my experience I liked high school much better," Riya reassured me. "Preteens are mean and everything in middle school is just not fun. I wouldn't let Peter near a middle school if I had the choice. High school was calmer, we got to choose our classes, and there was so much less social pressure. I enjoyed that a lot."

My palms were sweating, I rubbed the heel of my hand against my jeans over and over again. The pit of my stomach felt deep. I didn't usually notice how the pit of my stomach felt. Deep. Wishy-washy. Like the bottom of the ocean, perhaps. Dark and far away. Maybe like a well. Echoing back at me everything I was yelling at myself.

"Really?" Saul asked. "I hated high school. I had so much more work, and don't even get me started about applying to college. Not to mention in my last year I was very preoccupied with your mother, Quentin."

"Dad! I don't need that image in my head!" Quentin scrunched up his face in disgust.

Saul put his hands in the air, "I'm sorry. You might get a girlfriend of your own soon enough, if you play your cards right." The top of Quentin's ears turned red and he shoved two raviolis into his mouth at the same time. "So, tell me Tori, has this young man had any girlfriends yet?"

I laughed and opened my mouth to tell Saul all about Hally, but Quentin reached both of his arms out to me and batted at my mouth, trying pathetically to cover it. "Don't you dare or I will never hear the end of it."

"So, you have had girlfriends!" Saul boomed.

"Quentin has girlfriends!" piped Peter.

"It's not true," defended Quentin.

I agreed, "It isn't, there has only been one."

Quentin's face turned bright red and he slid down in his chair. If he had drawn the scene in one of his comics there would have been steam coming out of his ears. "Oh! One girl," Saul teased. "Tell me Tori, what's this girl's name?"

"Hally. They dated the summer after sixth grade and they are probably dating again now, but everything is very unofficial these days," I told them. "He could have had many other girlfriends, all the girls at school seem to like him a lot."

"A real ladies man. Just like his father back in the good old days."

"Why is it that all old people always say, 'back in the good old days?" Quentin asked, looking down at his hands that he was shuffling in his lap.

"Because as soon as you have to pay taxes, childhood seems like the greatest thing ever," Saul explained. "But did you just call me old?"

Quentin pursed his lips with a smile and looked up at the ceiling. "No?"

"What about you Tori, any girlfriends?" He chuckled, "Boyfriends?"

I rubbed my hand on my jeans over and over. "No," I forced a smile, but pressure built behind my ears.

Saul laughed, "Well there's plenty of time for the both of you to have girls or whoever."

My breath stuck in my throat and my forearms tensed. Had he only said girlfriends that time? Did he assume I liked girls? Or did he just say that because it went along with the joke about Quentin having girlfriends? My parents would have never said something like that. Was it really that obvious? "I'm sorry, where is the bathroom?"

"Past the kitchen and to the right," Riya told me.

I rose abruptly from my chair and made my way to the bathroom, rubbing my forehead which had begun to sweat too. A sort of dizziness encompassed me and I stumbled through the bathroom door. I clutched the sides of the sink to hold myself up and let the porcelain cool off my sweaty hands. The pressure in the back of my head spread all over my body and squeezed my lungs. I struggled to even take a breath.

I seized the soap dish and slung it at the ground and then a glass of water that sat on the edge of the sink. I slammed my palms against the sink and resisted the urge to scream. I sunk to the ground in the middle of ceramic and glass shards. A large shard of glass glinted in the fluorescent bathroom light; I picked it up and grasped it tightly in my hand. Blood began to drip out the side of my palm. The air smelled pungently of metal and chamomile soap.

Someone knocked on the bathroom door, which I forgot to close all the way. I quickly put my hand behind my back. But Riya walked in, not Quentin.

"Sorry about the mess, it was an accident. I can replace it if you need me to," I took a deep breath.

"No, no, it's alright. Things break all the time when you have a four-year-old, we know not to buy anything expensive. I can just glue the soap dish back together." She walked over to the other side of the bathroom and sat down across from me. "I just wanted to check on you."

"I'm fine it really was an accident."

"Look, I know how hard break ups can be, especially in middle school."

"Who told you?"

She smiled, "No one had to tell me." She reached out to me. I gave her my casted hand. "I know it sometimes feels like you won't get through this, but you will, okay?"

A tear rolled down my cheek and I pulled my hand away quickly to wipe it off. "I just want to feel better!" I said with a quiet sob.

She took my hand back and squeezed it, "This offer might sound strange to you, but if you ever need to talk to someone, I can give you my number. And I'm sure Leah would also be happy to talk to you. It is important that you stay safe."

I nodded and gave her a soft smile. "Thanks," I told her, even though I knew I would never follow up on her offer.

"I'll give you a second, come back when you are ready. Don't bother cleaning it up. I'll piece it together later." She left me alone in the bathroom again.

I looked down at my bloody hand and quickly walked to the sink, making sure the blood didn't get anywhere. I rinsed off my hand, running it under the water until the bleeding stopped. I scrubbed the piece of glass clean and placed it on the ground with all the other shards.

I tucked my hand in my pocket and walked back to the dining room. "Hi sorry about that." I sat down gingerly and folded my hands in my lap.

"Quentin was just telling us about how River escaped into the neighbor's backyard!" Saul roared.

I LAID WITH MY FEET on Quentin's bed and my back on the floor. I had flung my hands up above my head, one clenched tightly in a fist and the other one heavy with the weight of my cast. My eyes wandered through the crevasses in the dry wall of his ceiling.

"Why did you have to tell my dad and Riya about Hally?"

"Don't forget about Peter, he would hate you for that," I avoided the question.

"Tori!"

"Peter really needs your attention."

Quentin took in an exasperated breath. "Just answer the goddamn question, Tori!"

I really didn't feel like fighting with him, "I just thought it would be funny, Saul and Riya are cool."

"Why are you being so difficult?"

"I'm sorry. I just don't want to fight about this," I bit down on my bottom lip, trying not to explode at him.

An unusual heat rose in his eyes, "I know this week has been hard for you but—"

"Hard for me, Jesus Christ Quentin!" I raised my voice a bit.

"But that's no excuse—" he continued.

"Stop Quentin. I don't want to think about it," I brought my voice back inside me this time and clenched my cut hand into a tighter fist.

"There is no reason you have to be so stubborn and unempathetic all the damn time! If you are gonna let it affect you this much, why don't you just talk to me about it?" he yelled.

I turned my eyes away from his intense glare. "What happened with Harper doesn't matter. I don't want to talk about it."

"You make it so hard for me to be nice to you all the time. You won't listen to what I have to say and you are always angry or hurt or whatever. I just don't get it, this isn't you! What is wrong with you, Tori? *Really*? Where did I go wrong? Where did *you* go wrong? You aren't the same!" He tried to get my eye contact. "Tori! What is wrong with you?"

I rested my head in my casted hand, shielding my quivering lip from Quentin and doing everything in my power to keep the heaviness behind my eyes from turning into tears. I wanted so badly to let it all out, to tell him everything, but every time I wanted to tell him I saw the hopefulness and care in his eyes and I couldn't. "You don't know what the fuck you are talking about."

"I might if you just told me what is wrong!"

He really couldn't listen to what I wanted. "God Quentin! Can't you just leave me alone." I knew that if I had just told him everything, we would be okay. I knew not telling him didn't make anything better, but I just couldn't bring myself to force the words past my lips. I wanted him to understand without having to tell him.

I wanted to be a good friend to him. I wanted to feel anything but what I was feeling then. I didn't want to feel the world closing in on my head every time I opened my eyes. I wanted to know the words in my head, telling me my life meant nothing, were all lies. But I couldn't allow myself to be better. I didn't know myself anymore.

A few tears drew lines down my cheeks.

"God Tori, I don't even know why I try to be your friend anymore!"

His words stung my already aching heart and forced more tears out of my eyes. I lay down on my blow-up mattress and turned away from him. I wiped my eyes, with my still clenched fist, then pushed myself up and looked him straight in the face. "DON'T!" I sobbed and slammed the side of my cast into his bed frame. Before I could see the look on his face I turned over and collapsed into the mattress.

Sixteen

"I LOVE IT HERE!" I threw myself across Quentin's bed. "Let's never go back."

He lay down next to me, "It sucks that we only have a week left."

Quentin's eighth grade teacher knew someone that ran this two-week United Nations program over the summer for high schoolers and convinced Quentin he would be a perfect fit. That teacher loved Quentin, although Quentin was loved by all, but that teacher was not so keen on me. Nevertheless, Quentin practically jumped up and down with excitement while asking me to join the program and assured me that my Social Studies grade would have no impact (he had an A, while I had a B-). Now we were in the thick of the program.

"Calla says there is this really good dumpling restaurant down the street. You want to come with us?"

Quentin shook his head, "Josué and I were going to get pizza with some of his friends from his program area."

"Oh okay," I said. "Well, I will see you after dinner?"

"Yeah, can you and Calla come to our room?"

I nodded, "Okay."

 I panted.
"Wait, so you two have been friends since you were in second grade?" Calla asked.
"Yes! I've told you that 10 million times."
"Okay, come on. I want to meet him."
I collapsed on the stairs, "Why?"
"Come on!" She grabbed my hand and tried to drag me up the stairs.
I pulled back on her, "Can't you just stay with me? The boys are just going to be stupid."
She sat down next to me, not letting go of my hand. "All you talk about is Quentin. I want to meet him."
My arm tingled, pressed against hers. I didn't want to give up our aloneness, but I couldn't say no to her. "Fine," I said and got up from the stairs.
She let go of my hand, but let it linger next to mine. She flicked it away and ran up the rest of the four flights of stairs. I trudged up behind her and when I got to Quentin's floor Calla already stood in front of his hotel door waiting for me. She knocked enthusiastically when she saw me. The door clicked open. "You are Calla?" Josué's accent flowed from the other side of the door.
"You are Quentin's roommate, unless Tori didn't tell me Quentin has a French accent."
"I'm Josué." He stuck out his hand to her.
I walked up behind her and pushed my way into the room. "Hi Josué."
"So where are you from?" Josué asked Calla.
"Arizona. You?"

"I used to live in Northern France in a town called Calais, but now I live in Maryland," he responded. "Did you two eat in the dining hall tonight?"

Calla shook her head, "We decided to go to a dumpling restaurant."

"That sounds nice. I had a session late so I just went to the dining hall."

Quentin shrank next to me. I looked at him for a moment, then sighed. "Do you all want to play cards?" I asked.

"I don't know very many games," Josué said. "But my friend Drew told me about one game called, Bullshit?"

"Yes!" Quentin smiled. "Let's play." He hopped off the bed and onto the ground. He motioned for me to give him the cards. I reached into my pocket, pulled out the tattered deck and slapped it into his hand.

We played cards for a while. I noticed Josué staring at me a lot and Quentin deliberately avoiding looking at me. So instead of looking at the boys I watched closely as Calla placed cards down with her slender fingers. When she lied about her cards, the left corner of her mouth turned down just the tiniest bit but I never called her on it. Her fingers tapped the beat of a waltz on the back of the cards before she played as she sat perfectly upright with her legs crossed. When she played her cards, sheets of her long black hair would fall forwards. The hair would start to bother her and she would sweep it all behind her shoulder with one smooth motion.

After we played in silence for a while, except for the occasional, "Bullshit," Josué tried to make conversation. "What is your specialization program area, Victoria?"

"I'm working in an NGO," I told him. "On an access to clean water proposal for the Dominican Republic."

"What's your program area, Quentin?" Calla asked.

"Security Council," he muttered.

"Yeah! We're both on the Security Council," Josué chimed in. "There aren't very many people in the Security Council because only a few countries get a seat! Most of us have special scholarships."

Calla nodded. "What country are you, Quentin?"

"Germany."

"And I'm France!" Josué laughed. "Isn't that funny. I don't think they did it on purpose!"

Calla and I nodded. Quentin just stared at his cards and made his next move.

When the program advisors, who acted like camp counselors, finally knocked on the door and told Calla and me that we had to go back to our room, we were out in a flash. I scooped up all the cards, shoved them messily into the box and scrambled out the door as fast as I could, dragging Calla behind me, with only a, "Goodnight, Q."

"Well, that was awkward," Calla said when we were safely in the hall.

"No better word for it," I responded.

"Quentin was not..." her voice trailed off.

"Anything like I described him?" I finished.

"Yes," she laughed.

I shrugged, "He has been acting really weird lately."

"How so?"

"I guess I always thought high school would change our friendship, but goddamn Quentin, we aren't even in high school yet," I said, not to Calla, but to the air around us as if Quentin would feel my frustration.

"What's changed?"

"We used to be inseparable and now it feels like we are anything but that. He is fine when it is just us, except that we don't really talk like we used to, it's all facts and no thoughts, but we are still us when we are alone. When we are with other people it's different though, it doesn't feel like he is there with me even though he is sitting next to me."

"I know what you mean."

Calla's responses were simple and meaningless, but to me at the time they meant everything. I desperately wanted her to care about me and she understood me like it seemed no one else did. I had told myself after Harper I would be more careful with my heart, but I forgot all about that when I met Calla. I wondered how I had ever survived without her and worried constantly about losing her when we went home.

We spent every night lying in our beds and talking until we couldn't keep ourselves awake anymore. My connection with Calla felt immediate, we spent all of 10 minutes talking about superficial things, then spent the rest of our days sharing things about our lives that we didn't expect to share with another person ever. It was easy with her. I didn't worry about sharing the burden of my pain with her like I did with Quentin. Having her in my life felt like a necessity after just a couple days of knowing her. I could breathe again and the normal of the past few years, the pain in my chest, was completely gone and I was more than terrified to go back to living like that. Was Calla the only thing that had changed? It seemed like the answer was yes. So how could I go back to living without her?

"I don't want to think about it. He's confusing me too much and I don't know how to fix it or whether it is even worth it," I explained.

"I get it, but you talk about him so much."

"And?" I said gruffly.

"I think you know."

For the first time with her a flame burned in my chest and I let out a sharp breath. "You aren't my fucking therapist Calla, why don't you just tell me what you think?"

"I think it's not my place. I think I've known you for all of five days and despite how much I know about you, Quentin knows you better and maybe you should talk to him about this."

I huffed, "Talk to him about why I feel weird about him?"

"Yes, exactly," Calla prompted, waiting for me to understand better. But we arrived at our room, which I unlocked and walked away from Calla. I slipped my shoes off next to my bed and lay down on my back.

"Calla, did you know your name means beautiful?"

She sat down on the foot of my bed, "I did."

"I think it suits you."

"What are you trying to do?" She leaned over me.

"What do you mean?" I sat up, so we were sitting with our legs parallel to each other and our bodies less than a foot apart.

She moved away. "We were talking about Quentin. You are dodging the subject." She avoided my eyes.

I threw myself back onto my bed, "Teenage boys are so annoying."

"And teenage girls are so confusing and dramatic."

"What?"

"I'm just saying, you have no idea what he is thinking. Why don't you just talk to him?"

"I'm tired. I'm going to put on my pajamas." I got up from my bed and walked over to the drawers.

"What is it that you said about him?"

"I said a lot of things."

"And you meant them all."

"You don't know that. You aren't a mind reader." I pulled my shirt over my head and undid my bra. I quickly replaced them with my nightshirt.

"Oh, I'm not?"

"Well, if you are, tell me what I'm thinking."

"You are terrified and angry because doing nothing scares you and doing something scares you even more. You love him and don't want to hurt him, but you also don't want to screw up his image of you. Wake up! He knows already. You care about him a lot and don't want to screw things up, so you are leaving things on the edge. And they are gonna fall off eventually because you clearly don't have a grip on what's going on."

I didn't respond, just put on my pajama bottoms and went to the bathroom to brush my teeth. When I came back into the room Calla had changed into her pajamas and sat on her bed waiting for me. "Victoria, I think it might do you some good to discuss it at least."

"I already did that," I said and climbed into my bed, pulled the blankets over myself and laid my head on my hands. "And you got one thing wrong: I care nothing about what Quentin thinks of me. I care if I hurt him."

"Can I ask you something?" Quentin asked.

"Mhmm," I replied while moving a gluey chunk of dining hall pizza crust from one cheek to the other.

"Do you like Calla?"

"I mean I probably would be complaining about her a lot more if I didn't. I am living in the same room as her," I said with my mouth full.

"No, do you *like* her?"

"No." Yes. Of course I liked her, but I couldn't tell him that. If I told anyone she could find out and that might be worse than leaving the program, which I had accepted was inevitable. She might never talk to me afterward and that petrified me, especially because I couldn't read how she felt about me. "Why?"

"Well, I just wanted to make sure, it seemed like you might."

"She's my roommate, Q."

"And that doesn't mean you can't like her."

"Why did you want to make sure I didn't like her?"

"Well," he paused. "I wanted to know if I could ask her to the dance on Saturday."

"The dance?"

"Yeah, there is a dance on the last night, didn't any-one tell you?"

I shoved more pizza in my mouth. "And you have to ask my roommate?"

"Well, I haven't exactly made friends with many girls here. And I know how you would feel if I asked you."

I sucked in my breath sharply. "You barely even know Calla, why do you have to ask her?"

"Well, I wanted to. And Josué wanted to ask you to go with him, too. We could do like a double date?" Quentin asked nervously.

"Me? And Josué?" I almost laughed, but stopped myself just in case Quentin didn't find it as funny as me.

Quentin smiled with his eyes and let out a small laugh, "Please, just do it for me? I know Josué isn't your ideal date, but for me?"

I should have said no. My whole body screamed at me to say no, to ask Calla to go with me. To hold her hand. To kiss her and not look back. I pictured the look on the boys' face when they saw us all dressed up and walking hand in hand to the dance. I would hold her around the waist and put my head on her shoulder and we would stand in the middle of the dance floor. Everyone would marvel at our confidence and they wouldn't care that we were both girls. I wouldn't have to listen to Josué ramble about the Security Council all night. Instead, Calla and I would slip out of the dance early and run the whole way back to our room where we would spend the whole night awake, before the dreaded moment when we had to say goodbye.

"Fine," I muttered.

"What's wrong?"

"Nothing, I'm just hungry," I said and shoved more of the cardboard pizza in my mouth, but the crumbs got caught in the back of my throat and made me cough.

Quentin laughed, trying to hold himself back but only succeeding in turning his face bright red. I swallowed the huge lump of pizza, then smiled at his red face and laughed along with him. "I don't know how it is legal for them to feed us this shit," I gagged.

"I don't know why you are eating that shit," Quentin chuckled and popped a baby carrot into his mouth.

"I'm hungry! You are barely eating, and I am running out of money so what other options are there?"

He shrugged, "I choose starvation."

"You ready?" I asked Calla.

"Almost."

I looked at myself in the tiny mirror and adjusted the straps of the slip dress. I twisted around to see how the navy satin of the dress I stole from Calla puckered at my thighs. I sighed and turned back around to look at the cowl neckline and adjust its folds. I touched my scar lightly, then turned back to the front and flattened the dress on my body.

"Let's go Calla," I complained, "The boys are waiting for us."

When we finally got out of our room a few minutes later, there the boys were, impatiently waiting for us. Josué saw us first and stood up a little straighter. "You look very nice, Victoria," Josué said to me.

I nodded at his outfit, a button-down white shirt and black pants with a plain red tie, very him. "You too."

Quentin had already walked over to Calla, who wore a short velvet dress with long sleeves and a mock neck. Its dark burgundy color complemented her golden skin and dark hair like the colors of an autumn sunset bleeding into the night sky. She had complained earlier that it didn't work for the summer, but I assured her that she looked beautiful. She did. I had to force myself to look away from her when we were getting ready and then as she spent the rest of the night joking around with Quentin, but I still remember exactly what she looked like. Her long dark hair lay down her back, except for two pieces from the front that she pinned to the side of her head. The dress fit her perfectly, tight on the top and looser on the bottom, fitting her like it would have on a model. She had put on a perfect amount of eyeliner, making the fluttering of her eyes look like that of a swallowtail butterfly, and applied lipstick before deciding that it looked weird and removing it, leaving her lips just the right shade of deep pink.

The four of us walked over to the dance, but we didn't really walk together. Quentin and Calla walked ahead of Josué and me. I watched them angrily as they leaned into each other and laughed and I stood as far away from Josué as I could. He chattered about his program area, but I didn't pay attention or respond. He didn't even seem to notice or care.

I stared at the back of Quentin's head as if my eyes were lasers and I could burn holes in the back of his head. His wavy hair looked less unkempt than normal and it seemed like he ironed his dress shirt. I imagined singeing his hair with my eyes and burning holes through his shirt. Not to hurt him, just to ruin the moment he was having.

"Your eyes are very pretty," Josué said.

I almost laughed; my eyes are the plainest shade of dirt brown I have ever seen. "They're just brown," I stated.

"Yes, but they have so much emotion."

I turned towards him, surprised. "What?"

"I think it is beautiful when I can see emotion in someone's eyes. And your eyes are not just brown, they have a deep color that is mixed in with the brown."

I felt my face blush. "Thanks, Josué."

The rest of the night I sat on the side of the room with Josué and we talked about the program and our lives. Somehow, I didn't get annoyed by him in the first five minutes, he had a lot of interesting stories about his family. He had three older siblings and a lot to say about them. They were his best friends. I wanted to give him a hug and laugh at his stories all at once.

Talking to him kept my mind off my anger at Quentin, but not off of Calla. And the next day when we had to say goodbye, I felt my first tears for months welling up in my eyes. The few tears that ran down my cheeks felt strange.

"Thank you for last night Josué, and you have to text me, okay?"

"Yes, okay," he agreed. He did text me the following day and after that Quentin and I would video call him all the time when we were together. I still talk to Josué almost every month. He even took it well when I told him I didn't like him the same way he liked me. He told me that not many girls would even talk to him, which just made me feel worse for not liking him back.

Then the time came for Quentin and I to board our flight, the dreaded moment with Calla. I gave her a hug and held back the tears that were brewing behind my eyes. "I don't want things to change," I whispered into her neck.

"Things are only temporary, Victoria."

"You have to call me. I need you, Calla."

She pulled away from me and looked me straight in the eyes, "No you don't. You are strong without me and I know you have found that part of yourself, you just have to find a way to let her out when I'm not there, okay?"

I wrapped my arms around her again, "I am going to miss you so much."

She pulled away from me again and held onto me by my elbows, "I know, and I will miss you." Her calm only made me want to punch her, but I hugged her again instead.

"Tori, we gotta go," Quentin called to me from the front of the boarding line.

I quickly gave Calla one last hug and ran to get in line with Quentin. I stood close to him and gripped my boarding pass tightly with both hands. I handed the crinkled boarding pass to the person checking it while looking up, trying to keep my eyes dry. Tears were something that usually came to me in frustration and in fear. They hadn't come to me for months because it seemed with the pain I was in, I couldn't let myself feel it anymore. But when we were standing in the tunnel waiting to get on the airplane, streams of silent tears rolled down my cheeks.

I felt Quentin's hand on my shoulder, a familiar touch, that only made things worse. "Are you okay?" he asked.

I shook my head "no," and turned away from him to hide my tear-soaked face. He grabbed onto my elbow and turned me back towards him. He gazed into my eyes and allowed me to come undone in his arms.

He held me there in the airplane tunnel as I shook from the fear of losing everything I had with Calla. And I held back a scream imagining having to return to my house and our tiny confined town where I wouldn't be able to be me the way I wanted to be.

When we got on the plane, I rested my head on Quentin's shoulder for the entirety of the short flight and let the few tears I had left roll from my eyes and soak into Quentin's sweatshirt. He didn't say anything the whole plane ride, he just held me and stayed with me, just like he always did.

When we got home Calla texted me maybe two or three times, but nothing felt the same. Calla tried to tell me it wouldn't be the same after we left, but I refused to believe she could be telling the truth. I still wonder whether she cut me off on purpose. Maybe the distance broke us, but I doubt if I ever saw her again anything would be the same, because just like that, she disappeared from my life, almost as fast as she entered it.

The thing that scared me the most was that after a few days I didn't care. Things didn't last forever. Calla had helped me. Yes. It had been exactly what I needed, but now it was too much trouble to preserve the relationship. Why was it worth it to save a relationship that wasn't going to give either of us joy the way it was? Why was it worth it to try to save anything when I could just live?

HIGH SCHOOL

"Love does not begin and end the way
we seem to think it does. Love is a battle,
love is war; love is a growing up."

James Baldwin

Seventeen

"FIRST DAY OF HIGH SCHOOL!" I shouted as I rode up to Quentin's house on my bike.

"Go Rams!" Leah shouted back with her fist in the air.

Quentin swung his leg over his bike, "Bye, Mom," he said in his new deeper-sounding voice.

"You excited?" I asked Quentin as we rode out of his driveway.

"No, I've decided we should probably just go back to this summer."

"Yes!" I agreed, "And just do Model UN again."

"What would happen if we just didn't go?" Quentin asked.

"Like to school?"

"Yes."

"At all?"

"Yes."

"You can't be serious," I laughed.

"Why don't we just ride to the clearing instead of going to school? It would be nice, just us and no school.

We wouldn't go at all; they would just think we moved or something. Why not?"

"Umm, wouldn't they call our parents and eventually call the police? Not to mention our futures and being able to get a good job ever?"

"Okay fine, we will go," he relented. "What do you have after lunch?"

"Band and then biology, I think?"

"Let's go at lunch then? Band isn't important and you can just tell your parents you couldn't find the class and the teacher accidentally marked you absent."

"I don't know, Q. On the first day of school?"

"C'mon! Just us again."

I couldn't deny his begging. "Fine," I said, "but we are not going to miss any of sixth period."

We arrived at school and pulled up to the bike racks. Quentin smiled, "Meet me here after fourth period."

"I don't know Quentin, the school is so small, maybe if we went to a bigger school, but it feels like they are watching us all the time."

"No, you are not backing out now, you already said yes."

"Tori!" Quentin hissed at me from the bike racks.

I laughed, "No one is watching us, they don't care. I forgot the juniors and seniors have off campus lunch."

"Oh yeah. Well let's go then."

We jumped on our bikes and rode off campus with our heads down, just in case someone realized we were freshmen. We rode out of town and found our trail just with muscle memory even though we had only gone to the clearing a few times that summer. When we got to the clearing, I dropped my bike on the ground and held my arms up to the sky with joy.

The summer had begun to wash away, but the heat still beat down on my tanned and Quentin's freckled summer skin. A breeze drifted lazily by and cooled us down just the perfect amount so that I didn't sweat in my shorts and tank top. Quentin walked over to the shade and sat down against the giant hemlock tree. I went over to him and placed my backpack down on the ground between us.

"Do you like high school?" he asked.

I thought for a second, "I mean it's only been a few periods, but I think I do. Middle school didn't make me ever want to go to school ever again, but I think high school is better. Calmer."

"I guess so."

I sat down next to Quentin and leaned up against the hemlock. "None of my teachers seem to care about us very much, and I haven't decided if that is a good or bad thing."

"What do you mean?"

"It's just that in middle school most of the teachers seemed so excited to get to know us and then start teaching, but most of my teachers just got straight to the point and started doing lessons this year."

"Mine did too. I already have more homework than I did most days in middle school," he told me and took a deep breath.

"You are going to do fine, Q. You have a much better work ethic than pretty much anyone our age."

He wiggled his eyebrows at me and gave me a fake smile. "Why, thank you."

I laughed, "You're so annoying!"

He put his hand on his chest, "Me? Annoying? Impossible."

I pushed him, "Yes you!"

He pushed himself off the ground and dusted the dirt off his elbow. "You will never guess who decided to hang out with me during P.E. today."

"Who?"

"Guess!" he grinned with his whole face.

"Why do you look so happy?"

He looked up at the sky and shrugged, "Guess."

"If you told me I would never guess then how is guessing going to be very productive?" I argued.

He made a face at me, "It's a figure of speech, Tori."

"Okay," I grumbled.

"Do you even care?"

"Sure I do, Q."

"It doesn't seem like you do." His finger tapped on his thigh.

"Do we really have to argue about this?" I calmed my tone.

"I'm not arguing," he crossed his arms over his chest like a little kid.

"Just tell me."

He grinned again, "Hally."

"Hally?" I asked, trying not to exhibit any emotion. Was this his way of telling me there was something between them again? It wasn't like I didn't know. I felt him sneaking around in eighth grade. Why did he have to bring it up like this?

"Yes. Do you have a problem with me being friends with her again?"

I wanted to just tell him yes and not to go down that rabbit hole again and that she never actually cared about him and *why is he trying to ruin his life?* "Don't you remember the first day of sixth grade?"

"Not really."

"You were so excited that Hally wanted to be friends with you. Do you remember what happened the rest of sixth grade?"

"Yes, of course I do. And who says it's a bad thing if that happens again."

"Didn't you break up with her for a reason?"

"I seem to recall that I broke up with her because you didn't like her."

"That's not true. You broke up with her because she annoyed you and you didn't like her anymore."

"That's what I told you."

I tilted my head, "What? Are you trying to tell me that it wasn't true?"

"Yes!" he exploded. "I *am* trying to tell you that isn't true! You always hated her and when we were dating you were always so mean about her. And I cared about your opinion so much that I finally broke up with her."

I stood up and paced back and forth in front of him. "So, you are trying to make this my fault? I never told you to break up with her! That was your fucking choice, Quentin!"

He took in a sharp breath. "Why can't you just give me your damn support for once, Tori!"

I pulled my hair out of the folded over ponytail I had carefully placed it in that morning and ran my hand through it. "Q, you know I love you whatever you do."

"It doesn't really feel like that's what matters! All I want is your goddamn support! Is that so impossible?"

"Maybe I'm not giving it to you because I care about you."

"But you don't respect me!" He shrunk back from me as he said it.

"Quentin," I reached out to him, but he moved away from me.

He stalked over to his bike and picked it up from the ground, "If you aren't going to respect who I chose to be friends with then I guess I just won't listen to your opinion at all." He swung his leg over his bike and started to pedal.

I ran up to him, "Can we just talk about this?"

"I've heard all I need to hear." He tried to pedal again, but I grabbed his sweatshirt.

"Quentin, that's not fair, hear me out."

He jerked away from me. "Life isn't fair Tori, is it?"

"Quentin, will you please stop acting like this isn't real life and just talk to me like a regular human being?"

"You are the one who is acting like this isn't real life," he retorted. "Most people who don't support their friends realize the consequences."

I stopped breathing for a moment, my mind running through the outcomes of this situation. "Q," I pleaded, "just talk to me, this is out of nowhere, just give it some time." I bit my lip at my lie, but I had to. We had been arguing about Hally for years. All of our arguments went unresolved. We both knew what the other person thought and knew we couldn't change their mind.

"Leave it alone, Tori," he said, and rode off along the trail.

I kicked the earth in front of me, pebbles skipping after Quentin. I couldn't take it; she was horrible for him. She was horrible.

"I CAN'T BELIEVE THIS is the last season," I said and settled into the couch.

"I can't believe we have been watching this damn show since we were in third grade," Quentin said and sat down next to me, bowl of cheese puffs in his hands.

I pet the top of River's head, "That accident did bring us some good, didn't it?"

"I'm not sure if this outweighs the entire summer we lost."

"We? I was the one on bed rest," I laughed.

"Okay, the summer you lost. But I lost it in sympathy with you."

"Sure," I said and pressed play on the remote controller. Finally.

We sat there on the couch, the same couch from when we first found our show, and watched TV, on the same TV, and laughed about it still. It made me feel like we were back in third grade when it didn't seem like our little world was falling apart piece by piece, almost slow enough that I didn't notice. Finally, Quentin and I were there together like we had always been.

When the show ended, we went into Quentin's room. He sprawled himself across his bed and I took my usual position, laying on the ground. "How's Abigail?" I asked.

"She's good, I guess. She is so tiny, it is insane. I mean obviously, she has grown a lot since she was born, but she is so small. And it is so crazy looking at her because she looks so much like Saul," he said with wonder.

I laughed, "Is that a good thing?"

"Well, I mean, she might get bullied if she looks like a thirty-five-year-old man her whole life."

"If she looks like Saul, then she probably looks like you, doesn't she?" Peter looked nothing like Quentin, understandably because Riya's darker complexion and distinctive features dominated Peter's face. I would have been surprised that Abigail looked anything like Saul, except for the fact that his genes completely took over in the making of Quentin.

"A little." A soft smile took over his face that he didn't know I saw. "I can't believe they named her Abigail."

"Why?" I asked.

He chuckled, "Saul didn't get the Jewish name in with Peter or me, so he had to pick such a generic name, maybe not just for Jewish people, but it's pretty common. I swear there were four Abigail's in my Hebrew School. At least he didn't pick Rebecca or Rachel or Sarah," he sat up and laughed, "or Miriam!"

"What are you talking about? Those are perfectly normal names."

"Those are all very Jewish names. Like Jacob or Ben for boys. If you go to any Jewish gathering, there will be at least a few people with those names," he explained.

"Hmm," I replied.

I held my phone above my head and scrolled through it for a while in silence. Quentin just laid on the bed. I felt him watching me but I didn't look back at him. I wanted to just lay there and not do anything. I didn't want any arguments, just the peace of Quentin's presence beside me.

"Do you want to do something?" Quentin interrupted the silence.

I rolled over on my side and looked at him, "Like what?"

"I don't know? Go somewhere?"

"Where?"

"Let's just go downtown," he decided.

I pushed myself off the ground, "Okay, let's bring River with us."

When we got to our town's few blocks of commercial area, we sat down at a table in front of The Dimond. I pulled my jacket around me tightly, shivering from the cold of late October. "Do you want anything from the cafe?" Quentin asked.

"Can you get me hot chocolate? I'm freezing."

He laughed, "Sure."

I handed him three dollars with a shaky hand, "Why are we here again. It's so cold!"

"Because it is better than sitting in my house," he said and left me outside clutching tightly onto River's leash.

"Victoria!" A sharp voice yelled from behind me. I turned around and much to my dismay Hally stood there. "Is that your dog?" She came and sat across from me in the seat Quentin had just been sitting in. "What's his name?"

"River." I gritted my teeth, resisting baring them at her like a predator, in a growl. I wished River would do it for me.

She scratched the top of his head and made cooing noises at him, "He's such a beautiful boy! When did you get him? I didn't know you had a dog! He does look familiar though."

"I don't."

Ignoring me completely, "Yes, you are a good boy aren't you!" She let River lick her on the face and I pulled him away from her, annoyed that he even liked her. "What are you two doing out here all alone in this cold?" she asked River.

"I don't know, what are we doing?" I mumbled.

She completely ignored my response again. "So, Victoria, you have Mr. Stein, right?"

I nodded, "Third period."

"I was wondering what you were doing for that project we got assigned on Friday?" She asked me as if she had scoured through all of town just to ask me a question about a school project, she didn't even know the name of.

"Mr. Stein said he's assigning the topics tomorrow."

She put on a fake confused face, "Oh, he gave us our topics today."

I shrugged, "Maybe he just did that for your class."

"Are you sure he didn't just give your class the topics and you weren't there?"

"I'm pretty sure I know where I was today." I couldn't let her be right.

"Are you sure? Because you weren't in second period, I remember."

"And why are you keeping track of every period I miss," I snarled at her. River pressed his head against my leg and looked up at me with his big eyes.

Quentin came up behind Hally and handed me my hot chocolate, "You weren't in second period today?"

"Quentin!" Hally jumped up when she saw him. "It's so good to see you!" She wrapped her arms around his neck, crushing his arms between them. "That's River, isn't it? No wonder he looked so familiar!"

"Don't you two have third period together? You saw each other earlier today." Her excitement seemed completely ridiculous, unless my suspicions were correct and all my warnings to Quentin were in vain.

Quentin pulled awkwardly out of her hug. "Why weren't you in second period today?" Quentin asked.

"No reason."

"So why weren't you there?"

"I just told you."

"If there was no reason you couldn't be there, then why didn't you go?"

"You aren't my dad, Quentin."

"That's right, I'm not your dad, your dad wouldn't even notice that you were ditching school, but still expects you to be perfect anyway. I don't do either of those things."

I scoffed, "That's not true."

"I should give you my chair Quentin," Hally interrupted.

Quentin looked over to Hally and said in a calm tone, "No, I'll get one, it's okay."

I stood up. "Actually, it's okay, he can have mine. I am going to take River for a walk and leave you two alone."

"Tori just sit down," ordered Quentin.

"Why should I listen to you?"

"Fine, if you are going to go, give me the damn dog." He reached for the leash in my hand, but I wouldn't let go. He pulled on it, but I held on tightly, staring him down. He tugged on the leash again and pulled me a step with it.

River barked. "Will you two please stop! You sound like my parents," Hally yelled.

Quentin moved towards Hally and I took the opportunity to yank the leash out of his hand and began to walk away. I turned around to see Quentin's eyes plastered to my back and his mouth pursed in a line. "I'll drop the dog off at your house!" I yelled at Quentin.

"Okay, do that!" he bellowed back.

I left Quentin and Hally to do whatever their hearts desired, completely forgetting my hot chocolate. Maybe Hally would drink it and Quentin would pretend that he saw her talking to me and bought it just for her. I walked with River for a while before deciding to drop him off at Quentin's house. By the time I got there, the sun had already begun to set.

I let myself into the house using the spare key they hid on the overhang of their front porch, not sure if anyone would be home yet. "There you all are!" I heard Leah's voice from the kitchen. She walked into the living room in her pajamas. "Where is Quentin?" I stood in the doorway and stared at her and River tugged on the leash to greet her. "What's wrong Tori? Did something happen to him?"

I shook my head solemnly.

"What happened Tori," Leah insisted.

I shrugged, "Here is your dog." I handed her the leash.

"Is this about all the arguments you two have been having?"

"You know about that?"

"You all bicker like an old married couple and aren't exactly quiet about it," she said jokingly, then saw the upset look on my face. "Come sit with me, Tori." I let her guide me to the couch and sat down next to her. "I feel like I don't see you at all anymore, my son is always in these weird moods and when you are here you two always find something to be angry about."

I nodded, "I don't know what to do."

"I can't tell you. I love you Tori, but if you hurt my son, you will never see the light of day again," she laughed.

I smiled, "Do you argue with your friends?"

"Not like that, but I have never had a friend like you and Quentin. All relationships are different and all they need's a little love, work, and maintenance occasionally."

"What do you mean?"

"For example, with me and my boyfriend—"

"You have a boyfriend?" I cut her off.

"Yes, but after I tell you this, forget you ever heard it."

I agreed and placed my hands on my lap, ready to listen.

"So, when Gary and I argue, which we do a lot, it does not mean our relationship is any less good than a couple who doesn't argue, because it is about communication. For some couples they need to argue to communicate and as long as the relationship still feels fulfilling to them, it doesn't matter too much. But, when

Saul and I were together, especially when I was pregnant, we would argue all the time and it wouldn't be the productive sort of arguing, just screaming at each other, insulting each other, and not actually making up afterwards."

I nodded, thinking about what I didn't want to be true, that my arguments with Quentin were more like Leah's with Saul, that their relationship had ended with Saul leaving. "Okay," I said.

Of course, at that moment Quentin burst through the front door, not noticing us sitting on the couch, he had this giddy smile across his face. I wanted to stand up right then and slap him. All he saw in Hally was a girl who needed him, a girl who had made mistakes. He trusted her too completely. He turned and saw us on the couch, immediately the smile slid off his face. "What are you doing here?" he asked me.

I got up from the couch, "Returning your damn dog'," I said, mocking his tone from earlier. I just walked out the door to leave him to mull over his options, silently telling him to choose her or me.

Eighteen

I WALKED INTO THE CAFETERIA, searching for a place to sit. I thought figuring out where to sit in the cafeteria wouldn't be a problem in high school. Over the summer, Calla told me that her school let all the grades have off-campus lunch. I guess because of the heat where she lived in Arizona, they didn't have the problem of the entire school being stuck in the stuffy cafeteria during winter time.

I scanned the tops of the heads of my peers, hoping to spot Oda or Spencer or someone from the soccer team. My eyes came to Quentin, who seemed to be sitting alone. I thought I might as well be peaceful and eat lunch with him. I walked over to him and he smiled when he saw me. I sat down next to him, "Hey, stranger," I said.

"Hi Tori," he smiled.

"So how is everything?"

"Okay. My mom has a boyfriend named Gary."

I laughed and gave him a grin, "I know."

"What?"

"She told me."

A smile spread across his face, "Goddamn it! I always knew you were her favorite!"

"That's not true! You are perfect!"

"That is also not true, but she doesn't spend as much time with you so she doesn't know all of your weird quirks!" he laughed at himself.

I shook my head, "You are perfect. You're nice to everyone, perfect grades, perfect set of extra curriculars. Plus, you like your mom. That is very rare."

"Okay, okay, you have a point."

"Oh, and he's humble too."

Quentin scrunched his face together and pulled up one side of his mouth, "Thank you, thank you very much."

"So... what were those weird quirks you were talking about?" I pestered.

"Well, there are just too many to say..." he shrugged.

I hit his shoulder, "Shut up!"

"There is the way you always lay on the ground, I don't get it. And the way you bite off the tops of strawberries before eating them and you call soda 'pop', which I can't seem to train out of you. And you used to call fireflies 'lightning bugs' before I trained that one out of you! And when you cook you make the biggest mess I have ever seen. And how you—"

"Victoria!" Hally came up behind Quentin with a tray from the school lunch line. "How are you, it's been too long since we've talked!"

"It's been since second period, Hally."

"Yeah, but that is talking in class, it is so different than actually talking."

I touched Quentin on the arm and stood up. "Tell Leah that I want to meet Gary sometime."

"But, Victoria! I just got here."

"I know." I took an excruciatingly long pause, "I just remembered I have to give Oda something, so I better find her."

I got up and walked around the cafeteria. Despite the snow outside, the cafeteria was so stuffy it was hard to breathe. The smell of teenagers packed together in a too-small room punched at my nose. I finally spotted Oda sitting with a few other people and slid into a small space next to her.

"I saw you talking to Quentin, how did that go?"

I shrugged, "Good I guess."

"Then why are you talking to me?"

"Because I like you and you are my friend."

"Tori," she said sternly, "we all need you to make up with Quentin, for the good of society."

"There really isn't anything wrong!" Oda gave me another stern look. "I just want to live life as it takes me Oda. Be happy, not give a fuck about anything. Quentin and I are fine. I'll do whatever I want." I waved my hands in the air, "Be a *normal* teenager! Have fun, maybe get a boyfriend! Everything is fine."

"Then why did you leave?"

"Hally."

Oda rolled her eyes, "You do have a problem."

"I don't want any problems with anyone. Quentin and I are good, okay?"

"Fine," she put her hands up.

I put my head on my arms, "Ach! I have to do a presentation in French today."

"Don't you have like an F in French?" Oda asked me.

"It's actually a C minus," I defended myself.

"Your parents must be really happy with you," Oda joked.

I nodded, "So happy!"

"At least you don't have an older sibling for them to compare you to."

"At least they will have extremely low expectations for Cole."

Oda laughed, "No! Cole will be their only hope. He must be perfect enough for you both, so they can have a child to brag about when people ask them about their failure of a daughter."

"Hey!" Spencer said from behind me, holding a tray of school lunch.

I scooted into Oda, making as much room for him as I could. Spencer sat down and his friend Brayden sat down in between us. Brayden and I had been going to school together since preschool, like most of the people in my school had, but we had never really been friends. I never even thought much about him, except in fourth grade when I had a brief childhood crush on him. And then suddenly he sat uncomfortably close to me in the stuffy cafeteria on some random winter day and I couldn't stop staring at him.

"Hey," Brayden said.

My stomach did a flip. "Hey," I said to Brayden

"Hey," Oda said and leaned into me, pushing me further into Brayden and consequently, Spencer.

Spencer looked between us all, "Umm, okay?"

Brayden straightened himself out and looked me over carefully, like he saw a new person in me. "We have math together, right Victoria?"

"Yeah, with Mrs. Hayward," I smiled.

Brayden laughed, "'The only way to learn mathematics...'"

"'Is to do mathematics.'" I finished our teacher's saying with a grin at Brayden.

"Paul Halmos." Brayden said.

I nod, "How many times do you think she has said that this year?"

"Oh, at least three times a week, which would calculate out to..." he gave me a joking smile.

"You know what Mrs. Hayward would say."

Spencer frowned at us, "Are you intentionally making fun of my mother in front of me or is she actually that bad?"

"Neither," Oda chimed in. "They are just looking for a way to casually flirt with each other."

My cheeks rushed with heat and I turned away from Brayden to hide my pink cheeks. "Oda! Stop making unreasonable accusations!"

"None of my accusations are unreasonable, you just won't admit that they are true," she said smugly.

I looked back at him and found myself caught in the brightness of his deep brown eyes staring back at me. He grinned, revealing a space between his second tooth and canine, unusual in his otherwise perfectly straight teeth. He pressed his tongue against the space between his teeth and pursed his lips into a sideways smile.

COME MY BIRTHDAY in March, the cafeteria had emptied out a little, the conditions mild enough for the upperclassmen to make their way out into the bitter air just to avoid the cafeteria. I scanned the cafeteria to find my friends and my eyes immediately landed on Oda's brightly colored sleeve waving at me. I smiled and ran over to them. My heart sank when I didn't see Quentin sitting at the table with them. I had been wishing with everything I had that whatever had been going on between us would just end, we would just make up and be our normal selves again. Or maybe he would just let it go for my birthday.

I know I had to let go. I had been in a downward spiral for so long, I didn't easily decide to just let myself live without the weight of expectations. But I thought that not caring must be my answer to happiness.

I hated that I knew I was lying to myself, so I pushed it deep inside me and tried to embody the girl I wanted to be, which was a girl who didn't need to go to class, who didn't need to be careful about the things she tried, who didn't need to worry about other people's feelings, who didn't need her best friend. She didn't need anyone but herself. But when I looked at all my friends who were waiting for me on my birthday and Quentin wasn't there, my heart still broke into a million pieces and I had to hold back tears as I smiled gracefully at all the people who still did love me.

I sat down next to Brayden, he wrapped his arm around me and gave me a kiss. "Happy Birthday," he whispered to me as he pulled away from our kiss.

"Spencer and I made you a cake!" Oda informed me.

I forced another smile, "Thanks Oda."

I leaned into Brayden and put my head on his shoulder. "What's wrong?" Brayden asked me in a hushed voice.

I sat up a little, "Nothing. I'm all good." I composed myself and held my face in a smile. "Let's eat cake!"

Spencer pulled out a container full of cut up pieces of cake and plopped it on the table. "Let them eat cake!" he said with a flourish of his hand and pulled off the top of the box. "Sorry, we didn't have one of those fancy cake boxes, so we kind of shoved it in here."

I laughed, my heart lifting a bit, "It's amazing... ly disgusting."

Spencer took a mini bow in his seat, "My pleasure."

Brayden reached into the box of cake and grabbed the biggest piece, "For the birthday girl." He offered it to me.

"I'm not touching that. Look, your hands already have frosting all over them!"

A sly look came over his face, "I guess I will just have to feed you it then."

"I'm not sure I trust you," I scoffed with a joking smile.

"Open wide!" Brayden said and shoved the piece of cake in my direction. I opened my mouth just in time so the piece of cake didn't just smash all over my face. I coughed with the dry crumbs that congregated in my throat, my mouth too full of cake to swallow.

"Ahhh," I tried to say, but just spewed crumbs everywhere.

As soon as I finally could get the piece of cake down, Brayden laughed and kissed me, preventing me from catching my breath.

"Stop!" Quentin said with a disgusted look on his face. "No one needs to see that."

I looked up to see Quentin standing behind Oda. A huge smile grew across my face and my heart pieced itself back together once again.

"Quentin!" I beamed at him.

"Hey, what's up?" He sunk back a little.

I saw him pulling away from me and I got up from my seat next to Brayden. "You want to go outside?"

His face turned red and he shrunk away from me again. He shrugged, "Sure."

I walked over to him and we weaved our way around the tables in the cafeteria. I stopped when we got to the entrance, "Hey," I said cautiously.

"Happy birthday!" he said, like our awkward interaction in the cafeteria hadn't happened.

"Thanks, Q." I used his nickname tentatively, but when he didn't react, I relaxed a little bit.

"How are you?" he smiled.

I grinned back at him, "I'm good. How are you?"

His face dropped a bit and I felt him sink away from me again. "Do you want to come to my house today? My mom says she misses you."

"Yes!" I said before he could take it back. "I miss her too." I could hear my voice saying *I miss you* but it didn't come out.

"She'll be happy to see you, and so will Gary!"

"I get to meet Gary?"

Quentin nodded, "Maybe. I'm not sure if he is working today."

"Well now that I know that I will come for sure!"

"You were considering not coming if you didn't get to meet Gary?"

I laughed, "And I might have to leave if he isn't"

Quentin chuckled and looked down at his hands.

"Do you want to come sit with us? Spencer and Oda made cake, it's pretty squashed, but good."

He gave me an enthusiastic nod. "I'm always up for cake, but you might have to tone down the PDA."

I stuck my hand out, "Deal."

He took my hand, "Are you going to remember this deal when we get to the table?"

I looked away from him jokingly. "Maybe," I drew out the word.

"Let's go then. I need some cake."

We weaved our way back to the table and were greeted with a happy, "Quentin!" From Oda and Spencer. I took my place next to Brayden and Quentin sat across from me. Brayden wrapped his arm around me and leaned in to kiss me, but I turned my head away and gave Quentin a smile.

My last few classes of that day were as excruciating as ever. For some reason no one in band could get their parts right and the whole time my ears rung with the screeching noises. I discovered Quentin leaning on the wall outside of the band room when I finally got out of class.

"Oh, thank God!" I sighed. "Relief from that agony."

He shrugged, "Would sound even worse if I still had my trumpet."

"You're right. We should be glad you quit," I laughed.

"Thanks for the vote of confidence," he chuckled.

"Let's go, let's go," I urged him.

"Alright."

"I gotta meet Gary!"

"Wow. I see how it is."

I made my way through the crowd leaving school and out the front door. We took our time walking to his house. Making small talk about class and walking in silence. When we got to the intersection where our accident happened, I looked down the hill and laughed. "Wow, it really doesn't seem as steep as it used to."

He grinned, "It used to feel like a mountain. We could barely get up it."

I stabbed him in the middle of the chest with my index finger. "You mean you couldn't get up it, you with your sickly body."

"Hey, you hate Hally forever for making fun of me, but you're allowed to?" he laughed.

I looked away. "That's different."

A pebble he kicked while shuffling his feet went rolling down the hill.

"Hey c'mon," I smiled and grabbed his hand. I ran down the hill while dragging him along behind me.

"What are you doing?" his voice echoed around the street.

My jaw bumped up and down with each step, "Running!" I let go of his hand and took a huge leap with each step. Soaring down the hill. When I got to the next street I slammed my feet down, bracing myself to fall. But I didn't. I jumped around and looked over at Quentin who slowed himself with his heels so his momentum wouldn't bring him crashing into me. I ran back up at him, laughing, and caught his hands with mine.

"Don't you love days like this?"

"What? Your birthday?"

I shrugged. The calm of the mid-afternoon didn't bring a single sound from the street around us. I could only hear Quentin's strained breaths next to me. A ray of sunlight warmed my forehead, but couldn't reach my shivering arms bundled in coats. I sniffed and pinched the tip of my nose. "It's just a nice day."

We got to Quentin's house to find Leah sitting on the couch. "Hi Mom. Is Gary coming?" Quentin asked.

She didn't look up from the book she held, "No, he had to do something for work."

"Well, I guess I'm just going to have to go then." I turned around to walk out the door.

Quentin grabbed my arm, "Ha-ha, so funny."

Leah jerked her head up from her book. She made eye contact with me, biting her lip so she wouldn't grin too widely. "Tori!"

"Hi Leah," I said as Quentin dragged me into his room.

I sat down on the floor and stuck my feet out in front of me. I dug my fingers into the carpet. I pinched one of the worn-down fibers between my fingers. It was called triexta. I had looked it up one day out of curiosity when Quentin and I lay in his room not saying anything. I thought it sounded like a name some crazy parents would name their kids. I liked the way my mouth felt when I said it. My lips stretched to the side when I said the "x" and my tongue pressed against the back of my mouth and then clicked in the front with the "t." I liked to say words like this aloud and feel them in my mouth. They felt so figurative, just some letters randomly associated with something in our minds, but when you said them aloud, they laid themselves in front of you and were figurative no longer.

"What are you thinking about?" Quentin asked me.

"Triexta."

He furrowed his brow at me. "I have no idea what that means."

"It's the carpet."

"Hmm." He looked down at his hands. "Tori?"

"Don't you like how it feels when you say it? Triexta. Tri-ex-tah," I sounded out.

"Tori?" Quentin tapped his finger up and down on his knee.

"Triexta."

"Can I talk to you about something?"

I raised one eyebrow at him with a grin. "Is it serious?" I joked.

He shrugged, "I just wanted to talk about something."

"Aw c'mon. Don't kill the mood. This is a happy day!" I grabbed his arm and pulled him off the bed. "I want to go talk to your mom!"

I pushed my way out of his room and flopped down on the couch next to Leah. "So how is Gary?"

"He's good," she laughed, while still looking down at her book. "Hold on, I'm in an important part... I just have to finish this chapter."

"All of you are a bore! And I can't believe Gary isn't here!"

Quentin placed himself between Leah and me. "We still have a lot of episodes to catch up on! Unless you have been watching them without me!"

"How could I do that! That would be the ultimate betrayal." I laughed. "I would never!" I punched him in the shoulder, "Have you been watching them without me?"

"No! That's why I asked you."

"Unless you were asking me to cover up the fact that you were actually doing it."

"If I was actually doing it, why would I draw attention to the subject?"

"Because you were trying to be a criminal mastermind and trick me," I tapped my head, "but nothing gets past this noggin."

"You're crazy."

I contorted my face in as many ways as I could. "Really?"

He chuckled and turned on the TV.

After about four episodes I finally peeled myself off the couch and forced myself to go home. I had a pile of homework in my backpack screaming at me that it had to be done and I assumed it was my obligation to be home for dinner on my birthday.

"Bye!' I groaned as I walked out the door.

Quentin laughed at me, "Go!"

I pushed the door shut until I felt it click into place. I stood on the porch and waited until I could force my fect to leave. I knew how my birthdays always went at home and I always dreaded it. I had to make fake conversation about how my day went. Even if it went well and I didn't have to lie, I always lied about what I had done. After that I had to sit through whatever terrible meal my mom had decided was my favorite food that year with a "remember sweetie, when we ate this with the MacGregors, you said you liked it?" I guess it was admirable that my mom even remembered me complimenting her meals when we had guests over, although I don't ever remember making those comments and I didn't know if I had actually made them. I always had to sit and talk to my grandparents while my dad watched the news and made comments to my grandfather about politics. I never enjoyed it, but Cole and I suffered through it every birthday.

When I heaved open our front door, my eyes were met with the sight of Cole sitting in a chair in the entryway. "Happy birthday!" he exclaimed.

I tilted my head at him, "How long have you been sitting there?"

"Only a couple minutes."

"How did you know when I would be home?"

He lifted up his phone, "I tracked you."

"Remind me to turn off my location on that app."

"Happy birthday!" he said again.

"Thanks, Cole. Are Mom and Dad home yet?"

"No."

I started taking off my layers. "Did Mom tell you when she was going to be home?"

"Not really."

I walked past him and into the kitchen which smelled like soy sauce and something else I couldn't place my finger on. "What are you doing?" I said, referring to the mess that covered the entire counter and kitchen table.

"Just trying to make us dinner."

"Why? Doesn't Mom have some awful meal planned?"

"No."

I sighed and knew exactly what had been causing him to act so weird. "They aren't coming?"

He shook his head. "Mom said they would be home late."

I shrugged it off, "So what are you making?"

"Are you okay, Tori?"

"Yeah, it's fine. It will be better without them anyways."

"I'm sorry."

"Don't be! They created you, not the other way around! You are much better than them." I picked a carrot up off the cutting board and popped it into my mouth. "So, what is it that we're making?"

He laughed and pushed me away from the food. "You mean me. You are not going to get anywhere near this unless you want to kill us. And it's stir-fry."

I laughed and went over to sit on one of the kitchen stools.

Cole and I ate our stir fry while sitting on the living room rug and watching a movie. By the time my parents got home, I had done most of my homework and I sat at my desk listening to music.

My mom stuck her head in my room from the dark hallway. "Happy birthday, Victoria. Sorry we were late."

"Yeah, whatever."

"We can call your grandparents tomorrow."

"Great," I muttered.

"Don't talk to me with that tone," she scolded.

I threw my arms in the air, "You missed my birthday and I'm not allowed to be upset?"

"I apologized and said we can do it tomorrow, is that not enough for you?"

"No! I thought I could at least expect my parents to be here on my birthday! And all you're gonna give me is an apology?"

"Oh *please*," she growled, "we give you *everything*. Look at this house, look at your room, and your clothes, and that computer you are doing your homework on. Your father and I *worked* for that and you sit there ungrateful and use it all without questions."

"You don't give me everything." *You don't give me love*, my brain screamed at her. "I don't even care about this house or this fucking computer. I don't care how many hours you worked for it. You didn't even have to do anything to get there. You were destined to have this life from the day you were born into a rich family and married your perfect rich husband just like they wanted to. You didn't work for this, you got it handed to you on a silver platter." I slammed my fist down on my desk.

"Watch your language young lady," she hissed. "You should be grateful to have your life set up for you like it is."

"I don't want your perfect *fucking* life," I looked her straight in the eyes. "I don't want your money. I don't want anything to do with you after I can leave here. I don't want any of it. It's poison." The word slid off my tongue and through my room. "Get out."

In April, during the height of my springtime allergies, the juniors and seniors could finally eat outside again, so us freshmen had the space to spread ourselves out in the cafeteria. I had told Quentin I would go to the clearing with him that day, but then realized I couldn't. I had a band rehearsal for our spring concert and I didn't want to risk being late. I had already been late to band too many times, sneaking off campus with Brayden during lunchtime and losing track of time together.

I sat down next to Oda and sneezed.

"Gesundheit," Oda said.

"I was the one that sneezed, you don't have to mock me," I chuckled.

Oda laughed at me, "Have you seriously never heard that before? It's like saying 'bless you' in German."

I shook my head and sneezed again.

"Jesus," Spencer said, "Get a hold of yourself."

I wiped a tear from my eye, "I can't. I'm allergic to the air!"

Brayden walked over to us and sat down next to me. "I thought you were having lunch with Quentin today."

"I have a band rehearsal," I poked him, "and you have already made me miss too many band rehearsals."

He shrugged, "What can I say? I like spending time with you and your parents just don't work enough."

I gave him a knowing smile, "My parents work all the time."

"Yes, but your mom works from home too much," he gave me the same knowing smile and leaned in to kiss me.

"We don't need a demonstration!" Oda interrupted.

Brayden pulled away from me and put his hands in the air, "Okay, okay!" He gave Oda a second without touching me, then leaned back in, "but there just isn't enough time. Never bail on me."

I grinned at him, "I won't."

Quentin walked into the cafeteria, an annoyed look across his face. He looked over to us and I turned my gaze to Brayden, pretending I didn't see him, not wanting to make a scene in front of all our friends. Oda lifted her arm to wave him over to us, but he turned away, pretending not to have seen her and walked over to a mostly empty table, except for a girl who ate her lunch silently and Hally who seemed to be doing her homework.

I stared as Quentin walked up behind Hally and tapped her on the shoulder. She jumped a little, then turned around and grinned. Hally jumped up in excitement and quickly wrapped her arms around his neck. He stood there stiffly while she touched his face and chattered about something. He took the seat next to her and listened to her talk with a blank look across his face.

After a few minutes of Hally flitting around him, she gave him a concerned look and took his hand which rested on the table next to her. She asked him a question and he gave her a half smile and a shrug. Hally got a disappointed look across her face and pulled him into a tight hug, but this time he leaned into it and wrapped his arms around her. When she pulled away from him, Hally gave Quentin a warm smile and continued to hold onto his hand. He smiled back at her and the blank look across his face turned into more of a content one.

Quentin started to talk about something, while Hally nodded and responded occasionally and continued to work on her homework. Hally looked up from her homework once and noticed my unwavering gaze on them, she smiled at me awkwardly and whispered something to Quentin. As he looked over to me, I turned away and looked at Brayden, then gave him a kiss on the lips for good measure.

"What was that for?" he laughed.

I shrugged, "Because I like you."

I looked back at Quentin who tilted his head as he leaned over Hally's homework and pointed at something on the piece of paper. He sat back and looked my way, this time I didn't look away from him. Instead of letting our eye contact linger Quentin broke it to look at Hally. She furrowed her brow at him, then he leaned into her and gave her a light peck on the lips. She leaned back into him with her hand pressed up against his chest, then she pulled away from him, with a mix of confusion and joy strewn across her face. Hally asked him something and he nodded in response with a giddy half smile.

"Are Quentin and Hally dating?" Oda asked me, baffled.

I shrugged, "When weren't they dating?"

"Yesterday. Are you trying to tell me they have been dating this whole time?"

"But neither of them said it or acted on it."

"That doesn't make any sense," Oda laughed.

I shrugged, "They just can't stay away from each other, can they?"

Nineteen

THE SUMMER BEFORE tenth grade was my second summer without Quentin for as long as I'd known him. No riding bikes at sunrise and sunset on the same day or laying in the clearing, getting sunburned, and discussing life and the universe. No eating popsicles at Oda's house or avoiding going to the pool and seeing anyone from school. No evening picnics with my family catching fireflies or hikes with Leah and River. No Quentin and me.

But it didn't really concern me at that point, even though now I regret not having that summer with him, and can't stop thinking about what it could've been.

Then, I just wanted to spend the summer with Brayden. It would have been our first summer of many, I hoped. I planned out every moment with him. I wanted to sneak him into my room on the hot days where my mom was working and we would lay there together, doing things I knew my mom certainly wouldn't approve of and doing everything we could do to cool down, or not. Then we would sneak out of my house as soon as my mom got home. We would keep each other warm in our shorts and t-shirts, sitting outside on the cool summer nights. We would lay in a field of grass, holding each other tightly and looking up at the stars.

Happily, my mom decided that I did not get to have any of it that summer. My grades had been plummeting during my freshman year and my parents decided they would take action. It was time for another correctional summer with my grandparents at the lake house. Cole and I were shipped off this time for the entire summer, leaving us just one week at home before school started.

Cole complained incessantly about how he didn't deserve to be sent away during the seven-hour drive to a lake on the outskirts of Monticello, Indiana, where I was born and both my parents grew up. My parents spent one night at the lake house before leaving Cole and me bright and early the next morning to begin their trek back home.

I agreed that Cole didn't deserve to be there. He was pretty much as close to perfect as my parents could ask for. He was sweet and polite, he never talked back to them or complained about their rules. He actually spent time with them whenever he could and he got straight A's. He was loving and shy, but good at talking to adults. The best brother and best child my family could ask for.

My grandparents almost completely ignored us during the day, my grandma continuing with her regular schedule and my grandpa only occasionally taking Cole on fishing trips in the mornings. So during the day Cole and I found ways to entertain ourselves, usually hanging out at the lake or going into town. Cole made a few friends that were his age, but there seemed to be no kids around that were my age.

"So, Cole, do you like that girl from the lake?" I asked him one day when we were on a walk.

He kicked a stick along the path. "Which one?"

"You know which one I am talking about! The one with the red dye in her hair!"

He kicked a couple more sticks, "I don't know."

I punched his shoulder with a smile, "You like her! My little brother is growing up so fast!"

He gave me a look, "You act like you didn't have real feelings when you were my age. I'm only two years younger than you."

"Two years that I don't wish on anyone."

He frowned at me, "What?"

"It's just that the last two years of my life have kind of sucked," I admitted to him. "And I could never wish that on you." I rubbed my knuckles into the top of his head. "I want my little bro to stay young and happy forever!"

"This year couldn't have sucked that much!"

I shrugged, "Not as much as last year. Why?"

"Well, you got that boyfriend of yours!"

I turned to him, shocked. "You know about Brayden?"

"You check to see if mom is home, but you never check to see if I am home."

My face immediately turned bright red, "Oh my God. Cole, I am so sorry!"

He laughed, "It only happened twice. And after the first time, I knew to make my way out of the house A.S.A.P."

I covered my face with my hands and looked at him through my fingers. "I'm sorry," I whispered.

"Can I ask you something?"

"Yeah, sure."

He cracked his knuckles a few times, "Okay, can you just listen for a second. Just don't say anything."

I nodded in agreement and we kept walking down the path.

"Were you and Quentin dating or something? Because you two were always together before and spent a lot of time with me. I feel like after Dad's heart attack things were different and then you stopped hanging out with him very much and you started skipping class and dating that guy. And you were just happier whcn you were with him, so what happened?" He took a deep breath, then looked up at me with big eyes.

"Cole," I started.

"Oh, it's something else. It's okay, you don't have to answer if you don't want to," he blurted.

I grabbed his upper arm, "Cole. It's okay." I laughed, "This is what I was talking about, middle school sucked." He relaxed a bit in my grip and I let go of him. "I was never dating Quentin, but I won't deny that he did like me for a while." I raised one eyebrow at him with a grin. "I ended that, but that isn't what changed our friendship and neither is Brayden. It's just a whole mix of things. I gucss it's called growing up. You know what I mean."

He gave me a smile, "I think that I do."

"And as for me acting differently after what happened with Dad, well, just everything felt harder after that. And I was," I corrected myself, "am dealing with some things about myself, that I may be dealing

with my whole life, but who knows, we are still young!"
I told him cheerfully.

He refused to accept my light-hearted attitude,
"What things?"

I sighed, "You can't tell Mom and Dad, okay?"

"It's not like we tell them anything anyway."

I laughed in agreement. "Well, here is the thing: I am
bisexual. I like boys and girls," I explained.

He tilted his head at me, "Have you dated a girl
before?"

I shook my head 'yes,' with pursed lips, waiting for
his disapproval.

"You can't tell Mom and Dad," he said harshly.

My heart sank. "I wasn't planning on it," I retorted
in the same harsh tone.

His face softened, "I mean you can't tell them
because I need you. I can't deal with them on my own. I
love you, Tori."

I pulled him into a sideways hug as we walked. "You
too, little brother."

He got a concerned look across his face, "Is that
why you and Quentin aren't friends anymore?"

"We are still friends. He is still my best friend and
maybe we just need some time to become ourselves.
And anyway, Quentin would never not be friends with
me because of that. Leah raised us to be good liberals
like herself," I joked.

"People at home don't like liberals very much.
People here don't like liberals very much."

I shrugged, "That's not really my home. As soon as I
graduate, I am moving to Montana and becoming an

author. I don't want to spend a second longer in that place than I have to."

"If home isn't your home, then where is?" Cole inquired.

"I guess I don't have one. People I care about are my home. You are my home." I squeezed him tightly with my arm. "But not Mom and Dad," I added.

He loosened himself from my grip, "Thanks Tori, but I like home."

We spent most of the days that summer walking and hanging out at the lake. And most of the evenings convincing my grandmother that we were civilized enough and that I wouldn't be skipping classes anymore. I spent the nights on the phone talking to my friends and wishing myself back to Pennsylvania.

On the last day that we were in Indiana, I stared at the grass in the park where we brought our lunch, "Does the grass look greener here?"

Cole laughed, "What are you talking about?"

My eyes flickered around on the grass. The grass looked neon, but with the iridescence taken away. The color kept bringing my eyes back to the tiny blades and their defined tips. Triangular, with the flat cutting edge of a butcher's kitchen knife. I looked up at the sky, which didn't have a single cloud; its blue looked bluer. And the pink of flowers on a bush nearby looked pinker. And Cole's eyes looked a more vibrant brown. "Everything is just more."

"Have you not been wearing your contacts or something?" He raised his eyebrow at me. "Everything seems normal to me."

I swallowed hard and then blinked several times, "Hmm."

"Tori, is eighth grade really gonna be that terrible?"

I frowned. "Not if you don't let it."

He rubbed his palms together over and over again, "It's just you said—"

"Don't listen to everything I say, you aren't me."

"But—"

"Cole," I reached my hand out to him, "Take my hand."

He looked down at my hand and pointed at the thin scar that crossed my palm. "I never noticed that before."

I balled my hand up into a fist and placed it back in my lap, "I just fell, umm, on a hike and I hit my hand on a rock when I caught myself."

"That must have hurt! And it must have been a very long rock."

I nodded, "Yeah, yeah it did." I looked back at him. He held so much tension between his hands as he rubbed them together. I hadn't seen his anxiety creep up for years. It had been a constant problem for him when we were little, a problem no one in my family ever mentioned. I grabbed one of his hands and pulled it towards me. "Cole, now listen to me about this because I know I am right. You are the best brother ever. You are kind and caring, more than I ever have been. And you are smart and very handsome. You are perfect, okay." I squeezed his hand. "Perfect. My favorite brother. And if you ever need anyone to talk to, I'm just in the next room over." I gave him a soft smile.

He gazed up at me, "Yeah, okay." Then he gave my hand a little squeeze.

Cole spent the days when we got back trying to make up for all the summer he missed, hanging out with his friends at the pool and walking around town like all the other teenagers, pissing off the senior citizens.

I spent the majority of the days we got back before school started making up for the time I lost with Brayden who had ever so much to share with me about his fantastic summer. We spent most of each day just sitting outside, talking, and finding places to make out where people in town couldn't find us. We did this until the few days we had together ran out and were forced back into the world of school, our other friends, and the complications of life we had so gladly pushed away in our short time together.

On the first day of tenth grade, I saw people I hadn't seen since we got out of school in June. Oda threw a giant hug my way when I sat down next to her at lunch, which I gratuitously received, but besides her and Brayden, I hadn't minded not seeing anyone else from school for 10 weeks.

"Do any of you all have Mr. O'Connell?" Oda asked while taking a huge bite of her sandwich.

I shook my head, "No. Good or bad?"

"I haven't decided yet. He seems kind of crazy, but I am not sure if it is good crazy, or bad crazy," she laughed.

I nodded and started to ask what subject he taught when I saw Quentin approaching us tentatively. He walked up behind Oda, clutching his huge World History textbook in his arms. He tapped Oda on the shoulder, without making eye contact with me, "Scoot over?" he asked her.

When she looked up at him a huge smile spread across her face, "Of course! Anything for Quentin Flasch!"

Spencer looked up from his phone, "Flasch!" He gave Quentin a fist bump across the table.

"How was the summer training? A few of my friends told me that coach fucked you all up," Brayden said.

Quentin laughed, "His expectations were way too high. Half the team had injuries by the end of the first week," he exaggerated.

"But not Quentin! The Flasch," Spencer added.

Brayden raised his eyebrow at Spencer, "And you? Hayward?"

He made a tough face and flexed his arm muscle, "Us Haywards are made of steel."

"Spencer pulled his quad two weeks in," Quentin contradicted. "Do you have summer training for basketball?"

"No, but I did do some coaching for the elementary schoolers basketball camp," Brayden responded.

Oda leaned into her hands until she slid out of them and her head bumped the table, "So Victoria, what did you do this summer?" She cut off Brayden.

I rolled my eyes at the ceiling, playing along with her. "Well, I spent the whole summer shopping and putting on makeup and brushing my hair!" I said, making my voice higher and more sarcastic.

Oda pretended to flip her hair across her shoulder, but she recently had cropped her curls close to her head so she had nothing to flip. "Oh my God! Me too."

Spencer imitated her, "Oh my God! Me too!"

I narrowed my eyes at the boys and made my voice gruff, "I spent the entire summer training for my fall soccer season. I swear, Coach was trying to murder us with all those sprints. And I didn't have any time to fuck my girlfriend!" I said in a whining tone, pulling out all my words. "But I would've if I had the time, I wasn't sore or anything," I added onto the end.

Spencer, trying to hold back a laugh, let out a little snort through pursed lips, looking constipated.

I scrunched my face up at him and showed him my teeth in a fake smile. "Now you know how strange you all sound to us."

Brayden held his hand up, "Okay, okay, but we would never actually say it like that!"

"Roll tape to two minutes ago," Oda said.

Spencer snorted again, "She has a point."

I lifted my finger at him, "We're talking about you too, boy!"

"In our defense," Quentin said, "we didn't say the thing about fucking our girlfriends."

"But I felt the nonverbal communication," I argued. "And I know it's true for this one," I turned to Brayden and gave him a nudge with my shoulder.

"Not my fault," he shrugged and looked away from me, waiting for a reaction. When I didn't give him any and just kept staring at him, he leaned over to me and planted a kiss on my lips.

"No need, no need," Quentin interrupted.

I pulled away and laughed, "Maybe you wouldn't be so grossed out by it if you were with a girlfriend of your own."

"Yeah, where is she anyway?" Oda asked Quentin.

He shrugged, "Who knows."

IN THE RUSH OF everyone pushing through the halls, anxious to get out of school, Quentin caught me on the shoulder just as I left the building. "Tori," he said.

It felt right to hear his voice say Tori again. Everyone was calling me Victoria those days, even my parents because there didn't seem to be a time when they wanted to say my name in a kind way. Even Oda and Spencer had taken to calling me Victoria more often than not. Cole is the only one that seems to call me Tori anymore.

I turned to him. My hands began to sweat at the thought of it being just us after so long. "Quentin," I responded.

He walked away from the people, crowded and buzzing around in the courtyard. "I broke up with her, you know," he told me.

I pretended like I hadn't already figured it out. "Really?" I asked, trying to sound sympathetic.

He pursed his lips, "Yep, about a week ago."

"Why?"

"Wasn't working out, I guess."

Relief washed over me, "Thank God."

"What?"

"I'm just glad you two are finally over. We all knew it wasn't going to work out. I just couldn't watch anymore." I explained with a smile across my face. Honesty at last, I was thinking, finally we were on the same page again.

The expression on his face turned and his fire appeared in his eyes. "We? You mean you knew it wasn't going to work. It's nice to know that my best friend has been rooting against me this whole time."

"Quentin, you know that's not what I mean."

"Isn't it? You didn't want us to be together from the beginning!" He raised his voice.

His anger burned like a crackling fire, soft, and calm. Beautiful, which makes the most dangerous things. Convincing you to want them until you get burned. I couldn't help myself from feeding the fire, it lured me to it, and scorched me so slowly my skin ignored the pain, whispering that I needed it until I couldn't let go, the most beautiful danger of all.

I thrust my arms up in the air to exaggerate my point, "And now it is finally over!"

"That's not the point, Tori!" He yelled this time, and a few people from the courtyard turned to look at the noise.

I pulled him farther away from school. "What is your point then?"

"You were against *me!* It doesn't even matter where Hally came into the picture, you didn't respect what I wanted!" Each word getting louder than the previous one, the tension built in the air between us like a ticking time bomb. "You never have!"

"That's just not true. I have always cared about what you want, but what I wanted was what was best for you and you might not see that now, but you will eventually."

"What's best for me is a friend who can respect what I want!" he fumed.

"You don't even want Hally now, so why can't you just admit that I am right and we move on? Why do we have to keep fighting, Q?" I pleaded with him.

"You're not always right, Tori! You don't have to save me, just support me!" He ran his hand through his hair violently and paced back and forth a few times. He tapped his fingers on his jeans, struggling to make the right words come out of his mouth. "We keep fighting because the problem started way before Hally," he said in an even tone. "Hally was never the problem and if you think she is, I don't know where you have been, because these last few years clearly haven't looked the same to the both of us."

The way he spoke in such a calm tone, despite the tapping of his middle finger on his hip, dug under my skin and itched like an insect that I wanted to rip out. My head buzzed as I resisted the urge to just scream at the top of my lungs. "What was the problem then?" I hissed between gritted teeth.

"Us!" He corrected himself, "You! You were the problem. You changed and you stopped caring about us. You are a bad friend, Tori."

In an instant the sensation in my skin changed from itching to numbness. I stood there in shock, staring at him and not knowing what to do. I was the problem? I had always cared about our friendship with everything I had. I never wanted anything to change. I hid the darkness I felt from him to spare him from my pain and somehow that had changed me, but I couldn't believe it changed our friendship. It couldn't have been me. It hadn't been me. That was absolutely impossible. He decided to date his childhood bully and not talk to me about it. He had changed. No, this wasn't my fault. I knew that couldn't be true.

He got antsy with my silence, "God damn it, Tori! You can't even have a fucking conversation with me! Don't you see what I am talking about. This isn't right and I shouldn't be the one trying to fix it. I love you, but you have to fucking talk to me. It isn't enough anymore; this isn't enough anymore!"

I felt tears welling up behind my eyes and I struggled to keep them there. This couldn't be real, none of this could be true. He was *my* Quentin. He had been and always was going to be my best friend. We were made for each other, like two peas in a pod. We were Tori and Quentin. We were us.

He couldn't take it anymore, "See you around, Tori," he said and began to walk in the direction of his house.

"Quentin!" I yelled after him, but he didn't turn around.

Twenty

When I filter memories through my mind, each one has a strong emotion attached to it. When I look at the memories like the day of our first accident, it feels warm and exciting. I see it and I can feel my pure love for Quentin and the open feeling of freedom you can only feel when your mind hasn't been exposed to the world yet. When I look at the memories after the accident, the intense brightness feels a little dimmer, but the innocence is still there and the joy too. Like iridescent white.

When I look at my memories in sixth and seventh grade, they seem muddled, no emotion feels stronger than the others. The innocence is fading and the joy becomes less intense. I start to feel the stress and pressure of growing up, but it isn't dark yet. Muddy brown.

Mid-way through seventh grade the memories darken. The world didn't want me how I was. No matter where I went, I would never feel quite at home. My mind became clouded, I didn't even feel like me anymore. Black, just black. No space, nowhere to go.

After I met Calla, the darkness began to ease up again, replaced by a fog in my head it turned grey and the memories are mixed. Each memory has a different emotion, a lot of them grey and a lot of them blue, but so many were yellow, green, red, and whatever else my brain could come up with.

My relationship with Quentin teetered precariously, perched at the top of a hill, not falling but not staying put.

I think that the fight at the start of tenth grade marks the moment our friendship toppled down that hill.

It also started a period of memories that I can't begin to categorize. They have no color, not white, not black, not even dark at all, just empty. The emotion is gone, my head disconnected from my heart, everything distant and hard to see. I can't file these memories away the way I do other memories because I can't seem to place my thoughts and feelings.

That fall brought ever so many dead leaves for me to hear crunching under my feet as I walked to school alone every day. The new school year brought teachers loading us up with all the homework they could think of. It also brought fun things like homecoming, which my school didn't make a huge deal of but everyone always went to the game.

The homecoming day was the coldest day of the fall so far that year which meant that I sat cuddled up closely with Brayden under a blanket as we watched the game. I occasionally would detach my fingers from Brayden's hand to steal some of Oda's french fries. Spencer sat next to Brayden and they discussed who they thought would be on the soccer team that year, as well as yelling at our football team every time they messed up a play. I talked to Oda about class and she told me all about the boy she had met from the next town over.

"Josh," she looked dreamily up at the dark sky, "he's perfect you know."

I nodded, unconsciously scanning the stands for Quentin. It wasn't until near halftime my eyes caught sight of him sitting in the row above us. He sat on the edge of a group of his cross-country friends, he seemed disengaged from the conversation as he looked off into the distance. I watched him as he stared down at his hands and rubbed them together uncomfortably, despite his warm jacket and hat I saw him shiver. He stood up from his seat and hurried down the bleachers. I caught his eyes as he walked past me and gave him a weak smile. He stared at me for a moment, but then continued quickly down the bleachers. His friends didn't even seem to notice he left.

The frost that year turned the leaves brown before they even had the chance to become the familiar warm tones of fall. The brown, dead leaves were dull, but the grey sky with a slight undertone of the bright blue I loved on summer days always cleared my head in the mornings when I walked to school.

Oda started acting odd around the time when the leaves turned brown. Her lovable, witty self seemed to disappear into the cold wind along with my scarf one day in late October. Talking to her felt like she had put a wall up between us, the same conversations we had about her insane art teacher didn't make her laugh the way they had before.

Around that same time, I remember seeing Quentin and Hally together again. I noticed that Hally hadn't just stopped trying to make amends with me, she had stopped being nice to me all together. Bitterly I embraced her coldness and doubled my own. I guess my stubbornness had finally won out and I had gotten my way. Except this time, I wouldn't have Quentin. It didn't fuel the same anger that usually got me into arguments with him. I started to give up on him, I think.

For Halloween, Cole and I always dressed up together and trick-or-treated, up until seventh grade when we started our tradition of putting on pajamas and watching movies while eating all the candy my mom bought instead of handing it out. My parents had never been the kind of parents to like Halloween very much, so it felt like a gift to both of us to spend that time together.

When Brayden found out that I had never spent a single Halloween away from my little brother he made sure that year would be the first one. Conveniently for him, a family friend of Oda's parents died and they left for three days right on Halloween. We invited a whole bunch of friends and spent the whole night getting drunk while horror movies played in the background.

"Where's that boy of yours Oda?" I lulled.

She lifted her arms in the air, "Who knows? Probably doing some *other* girl!"

"Isn't he *your* boyfriend."

"Yeah, but he wants to, *you know,*" she giggled. "And I told him *no!*" She opened her eyes wide, "He didn't like that very much." A tear rolled down her cheek and she swatted at it as if she was swatting at a horse fly. "Speaking of boys," she threw herself over me drunkenly and pointed towards Brayden, "That one wants to do *you*."

I laughed and lifted her off of me, "It's okay. We do it *all the time*."

"Tori!" she giggled.

I pushed myself off the ground, "My lady, have a good night." I said with a sweeping bow. And then started to make my way over to Brayden, my vision clouded by a heaviness on my brow.

"Not in my bed please!" Oda yelled after me.

I plopped myself down on Brayden's lap, who I interrupted, deep in a very animated discussion with Spencer and who clearly had much less to drink than me. I wrapped my arms around his neck and looked into his eyes, "Let's go to a different room."

A grin came across his face and he looked back at Spencer, "Sorry dude." He said and stood up with my hand clutched in his, grabbing a mysterious bottle of alcohol on the way.

The headaches we all had at school the next day weren't very fun and Oda groaned about hers all through lunch.

About a week after Halloween, I ran into Leah at the grocery store. "So how are you?" she asked me. "It's been too long."

"I know it has been. I'm alright. How are you?"

"Leah, do we want the red or yellow peppers?" A man walked up next to Leah, holding two peppers in his hand, "I know the orange ones are your favorite, but they didn't have any." He looked up curiously at me.

"Gary, this is Tori. You've heard about her." Leah smiled at me, "And Tori, this is Gary, my boyfriend."

Gary put both the peppers in the shopping cart and stuck out his hand to me, "Nice to finally meet you, Tori."

I shook his hand, "You, too."

"I've heard a lot about you, mostly from Leah. It's kind of a touchy subject around Quentin," he chuckled.

Leah hit his arm with the back of her hand, "Gary!" She turned to me, "We miss you."

I stared down at the floor. "Yeah. So how are you two?"

Leah grinned and took Gary's hand, "He is actually moving in with us next week! I mean when he is not traveling for work, which is a lot of the time."

"The house isn't really big enough for all three of us all the time though!"

I turned up the corner of my mouth, "Wow, sounds great!" I didn't ask her about Quentin.

I think that year's Thanksgiving may have been the worst one I have ever had. We went to my grandparents' house, my grandparents who spent the whole time talking about politics and making me uncomfortable as my dad agreed silently with them. My mom got into a huge argument with my grandma and they burned the turkey. After that we had a dinner filled with passive aggressive comments and my mom making sure that Cole and I didn't move a hair out of place. At least when we got back home, I found the town covered in a fresh white blanket of snow.

I refused to let my mom drive me to school, the walks were the only time I had where the emptiness felt right. Even as I shivered uncontrollably in the snow, I loved it. The snow in the winter hides things, just like so many things in our life are hidden, until the snow melts in the spring. It covers the rot with beauty, so many secrets and so few hours in the day to find them.

The leaves in the fall fell so seamlessly, their death a planned cycle. Their colors made us forget that they were dying and as soon as we would start to notice the oranges and yellows fade away, it all became covered in snow. We didn't have to notice the trees' bare branches because snow perched itself on them so carefully. We could forget the death and the dirt that lay underneath the snow because it found itself covered by a layer of simplicity. And that soil would soon bear new life, if only we could make it through the winter.

Still, it made me shiver when the snow soaked in over the tops of my boots and stung my skin. I found warmth in an invitation to Brayden's one Saturday at the end of winter break. Even though he had been ignoring my texts, I ate up every moment I could spend with him. He told me his parents were going to the city and he wanted to watch movies and hang out all day. When he told me this of course I knew what he meant because he had said it so many times before. I would have been happy to oblige until I remembered that I should have started my period the Thursday before. I told him that I would still come over and that we could actually just watch movies together all day.

I got to his house bundled up in my sweater that I wore when I wanted to look nice but didn't want to try too hard. The sun shone brightly off the snow and into my eyes, forcing me to squint as I walked to his house. We first watched *Elf,* which Brayden unsuccessfully tried to get me to watch in October, and then we moved on to *Home Alone.* We snuggled together under a blanket and I looked up at him with a smile on my face. I realized I didn't have my period like I thought so we could do what we originally had planned to do. I leaned up to kiss him and he leaned back into me. I turned my body so I pushed him backwards on the couch and reached for the bottom of his shirt.

I felt his hand stop me, "Victoria, I thought…"

"I know, but I'm not," I sat up on my knees. "I mean my periods are pretty irregular, but I didn't get it last month either which is a bit odd. My mom put me on another one of her diets and I've been using the treadmill a lot ever since the soccer season ended, it's probably just that."

He pushed himself up on his elbows, "Yeah, we're careful, it couldn't be…"

"No, it couldn't be," I laughed and leaned back over him, "We're careful."

He kissed me and then pulled away quickly, "What about the Halloween party?"

"I thought we agreed we used a condom?"

"But I'm not one hundred percent sure… and we were drunk. I could have done any number of things wrong!"

For some reason I stayed so much calmer than Brayden who went into pure panic mode. He had a crazed look in his eyes and he had thrown off the blanket to start pacing around the room. "Brayden it's fine! I think I would be able to tell if I was..." Brayden looked as if he had just been hit by a bus, but my thoughts became occupied with how I had been feeling differently and how I had just placed it all on my mom's new diet. "You know what, I'll just take a test so we can know for sure." I patted the couch next to me, "Sit down."

TWO DAYS AFTER THAT I trudged all the way to the other side of town in the snow to the one drug store in town whose owners didn't know my parents to get a pregnancy test. I walked with my hands gripped around my keys and my coat wrapped tightly around me because the sun had barely risen and the clouds covered most of the light, but my parents both had things to do so I knew they wouldn't bother me.

As I walked, I picked up my phone and dialed Oda. "I have a question," I said when she picked up.

"Yeah?" her voice echoed from the other end.

"Did you ever have sex with Josh?"

She laughed uneasily, "No, I told you I didn't want to."

"So, you didn't?"

"Why?"

"Well," I took a deep breath, "umm... I think I might be..." my voice trailed off.

"Victoria!" she blurted. "Are you pregnant?"

"Shh, Oda!"

She laughed, "No one can hear me."

"I'm late for my period... by like two months," I admitted.

"Umm, well are you gonna do something about that?"

"I'm getting a pregnancy test right now."

"Oh God, Victoria, this is bad."

"I know! But I think it might be fine. I have really bad cramps and I'm nauseous for some reason, and a headache. Maybe, I'm gonna get my period, or maybe..."

"...It's morning sickness," she finished my sentence. "Tori, what are you gonna do if it's positive?"

"Be murdered by my parents."

"Would you keep it?"

"I haven't taken the test yet!" I sighed. "I got to the drug store. Bye Oda!"

"Victoria!" she said as I hung up the phone.

I went into the store and walked around before slipping a pregnancy test into the huge pocket of my winter coat while the store owner checked out the only other person in the store. I grabbed a candy bar, paid for it, and quickly rushed out of the store.

As I walked back to my house I noticed a wetness form on the inside of my legs, which I first mistook for sweating inside my heavy pants until a few blocks later when I recognized the unmistakable feeling of blood. I threw the unopened test in the nearest trash can and walked as fast as I could back to my house.

When I got home, I immediately jumped into the shower to wash off the cold and blood, then I changed into my favorite pajamas. I curled up in my bed with my heating pad because my cramps were already getting to me, worse than ever, and I took a nap. A few hours later when I woke up, I sat up in bed and called Brayden.

"Hey," he said.

"Hey..."

"What's up? How are you?"

"I'm alright," I said weakly.

"Yeah? Did you get the pregnancy test?"

I nodded, "Yep, but I didn't take it."

"Why not? Do you need me to come over and do it with you?"

I laughed, "You can't take a pregnancy test stupid."

"Is something wrong? You sound weird."

I smiled at his concern. "Everything is just fine. I got my period, we're all good." I said the words and for the first time in months the emptiness in my head was joined by a deep heaviness in the bottom of my heart.

He sighed loudly, "Oh that's so great Victoria, you don't even know how relieved I am!"

"No, I don't," I said quietly.

"What did you say?"

"Well, we can't hook up for a while, this period is pretty bad."

"It's okay! You don't even know how scared I was."

"No, I don't," I said again because I didn't. The emotions there inside me didn't make sense. I should have felt a weight lift off me like Brayden did, but I didn't. My body just felt empty, emptier than before.

BEFORE SPRING COULD START, I had to have my sixteenth birthday, which turned out to be rather uneventful. So much for a sweet sixteen. Ever since Oda told me she and Josh broke up, she had been quieter than ever.

Every moment I spent with Brayden had become so awkward that we both started avoiding each other. And overall, I just couldn't have my birthday without Quentin, who still gave me smiles in the hallway sometimes, but who I didn't know how to talk to anymore.

So, without any of my friends, I spent the day with Cole. We went to a muddy sledding hill in the morning only to be driven out by heavy sleet. We spent the rest of the day playing board games and watching movies. Out of everyone, at least I still had my little brother. With him, nothing ever changed.

Twenty-One

IT WAS THE START of April when I stood outside Brayden's house with huge tears rolling down my cheeks. I refused to move off of his driveway, it couldn't be over and if I stayed on his property maybe it wouldn't be. High school relationships never lasted long and ours had lasted over a year.

After 20 long minutes of tears and sneezing, my face had become sticky and I could barely breathe. So, I pulled myself together and began to walk to my house. I wiped my face with the side of my arm, but I couldn't keep my head from spinning. I sat down on the sidewalk and allowed myself to cry even more. That day had been approaching for a long time, I had felt it for weeks, months even, but I still sat on the sidewalk, head between my knees, my throat aching from crying, feeling like an anvil had just fallen on my chest.

I pushed myself up from the curb and began to walk to my house again, when my feet turned me onto Quentin's block instead of mine. And instead of thinking and turning around, I let my feet carry me the few strides to his house and up the steps to knock on his door. I sat down on the steps and heard River barking at me, Leah yelled something that I couldn't make out and a few minutes later opened the door.

"Tori?" I heard her say from above me. She turned around and yelled into the house, "Quentin!"

"What!" I heard from inside.

"Come here!" Leah yelled back. Footsteps came shuffling to the front door and I heard Leah whisper, "Be nice," as she went back into the house and shut the door behind her.

Quentin sat beside me, as far away as he could. I didn't pick my head up from my hands, until I needed to sneeze again. I turned my head and looked him in the eyes. Seeing him for the first time out of the dim school hallway lighting for months made me realize I really had been inside my own head. His skin looked pale, paler than I had ever seen it, and deep groves ran below his eyes making them look sunken and dark. Brayden had told me he didn't join the track team that year, but I thought nothing of it and now I knew why.

I wiped the tears off my face. "Are you okay?" I asked him.

"I should be asking you that," he replied.

I frowned at him, "Quentin."

He shifted his sitting position uncomfortably. "What are you doing here, Tori?" he asked harshly.

Another tear rolled from my eye and I quickly wiped it off. I wanted to hug him and sit on the couch with him as we watched our favorite TV show. I just wanted him to be okay. I had been so lost in myself. I scooted closer to him. "It doesn't matter. Are you okay?"

He pushed himself up from the steps with a wince and stepped away from me. "Tori, what do you want from me?"

"I don't want anything. I just want you," I pleaded.

He crossed his arms over his chest, "What is it? Boyfriend broke up with you or something?"

I stared up at him, eyes wide.

He tilted his head at me, then the wave of realization hit him. "God, Tori! Am I your second choice? Is that what you are doing here? You don't have him anymore and now you realize how you want me in your life?" He waved his hands around his head as he spoke.

My chest felt clogged and I could barely get any breath in my lungs, my lip quivered and a tear escaped from my eye. I wiped the tear away from my cheek, smudging dirt across my face.

"This is what I am talking about, Tori! You need me but you don't let me need you. I give you everything and you give me nothing. I've tried to tell you this so many times, but you just don't listen. I tried to let it slide in eighth grade, because I knew you were going through something, but it just got worse. I tried to let you be, but I just can't do it anymore. You are so stubborn and selfish and stuck in your own world. It's like you can't even see me anymore. Have you ever heard of the book *The Giving Tree*? Or the song? That's what you're doing Tori and there is nothing left of me to give, nothing. Tori, I need a best friend who cares what I am going through, too. I am not going to just give you everything in exchange for nothing anymore!" He yelled, drumming his finger quickly on his leg. "I can't do this anymore, Tori," he cried tearlessly, pain streaked across his face.

I reached out to him, but he pushed me away and pushed himself into the corner of the porch. I backed away, unable to breathe. "Quentin," I managed to stammer. I clenched my hands in fists, resisting the urge to dig my fingernails into my arms. My head spun even more than before. I couldn't be losing him, too.

I looked up at him, but he had turned his face away from me. His whole body shrank back into the corner of the porch, stricken with the reality of what he had just said to me, but wouldn't look back at me. I choked up tears, letting them stream down my face and I sank back away from him again. His words ran through my veins like poison and I did all that I could not to let the poison rip through me and scream.

I hit my fist hard, over and over again against the wood of Quentin's house, until my arm throbbed with pain. "No, no, no," I whispered under my breath, trying to keep myself standing.

Quentin's eyes traveled down my arm and to my hand hitting the wall. "Tori, I'm sorry." He moved a little closer to me.

I backed away from him and backed down the steps of the front porch. My brain screamed with confusion. Each one of my thoughts lasted no more than a split second, making my head sound like chaos. I began to run away, stumbling over my feet as I went, but determined to leave Quentin behind me. To leave everything behind me. Brayden, Quentin, everything. I just needed to be rid of it all. I needed to be rid of thoughts, like intruders in my mind. I needed to get rid of the memories of us, good and bad. I needed it just to be over with. I needed the light in my life that disappeared. No, it hadn't disappeared, I pushed it away and now I was stuck in the dark without anyone or any reason to keep on going.

I stopped running and sat down on the sidewalk breathless. My heart pounded through my body and my chest squeezed. Each breath caught in my throat, I couldn't force them in or out, tears just streamed down my cheeks. I pulled out my phone and selected a contact. I hit the call button and turned it on speaker phone. I needed somebody. I just needed anyone to be by my side, anyone to care about me for just a little.

The phone rang once, the blaring sound echoing through the empty street. It rang twice. I looked up at the changing sky praying for something to happen. It rang three times. A cool wind blew towards me carrying pollen that blew into my face and made me sneeze. It rang four times. My finger hovered over the end call button.

Before I could hit it, "Victoria?" came echoing through the other side of the phone.

Twenty-Two

"CALLA?" I BREATHED a sigh of relief when I heard her rough voice come through the phone. Her voice had become so foreign in the year and a half I hadn't heard it. Memories of our goodbyes in the airport rang through my head, the tears that streamed down my cheeks and Quentin's arms wrapped around my shoulders. And now I didn't have him.

I burst into huge fits of tears, but not the silent kind that just rolled down my cheeks, big mucusy tears that ripped from my chest like an animal.

"Victoria? What's wrong?" Calla asked, concern filling her voice.

"I'm sorry for calling you like this," I sobbed into the phone.

"It's okay," she comforted. "What happened?"

"He broke up with me, and then he broke up with me." I blubbered, "Oh God! How did they both break up with me in one day! I knew... I knew it but I - wasn't ready. Holy shit." I slammed my fist into the sidewalk. "God damn it, Calla! What is wrong with me?"

"Woah there, slow down," she laughed.

I ran my hand through my hair again and again, then looked at my hand, which came back with hair weaved between its fingers. I rubbed it off and scratched my jeans instead. I took a shaky breath in, "Okay," I told Calla.

"Who broke up with you?"

"My boyfriend. And Quentin."

"And Quentin was not your boyfriend? They're separate people?"

I nodded, then realized she couldn't see me. "Yes," I replied.

"Wanna talk to me about it?"

"My boyfriend broke up with me because he doesn't like me anymore, although that's not how he worded it. Which is complete bull, I know he is into another girl at school and would just rather have her, because his parents don't like me and she is more popular. And because we thought— well, I'm sure he was gonna break up with me before that, it just prevented him from doing it. But I don't really give a shit about him anymore because all I want is Quentin." My breaths became uneven again and I let out a quiet sob.

"You're okay, Victoria. I'm here."

My bottom lip shook, "You aren't and I'm not."

"Just breathe," she hushed me.

I took a deep breath in and let a shaky one out, unable to keep my mind off of Quentin. "I don't know what happened, Calla. And I feel like I don't have anyone anymore."

I heard her words catch in her throat as she stopped herself from saying something. I held my breath waiting for her to respond. "You can talk to me if you want," she said as if she didn't know why I called her.

I wiped my wet cheeks again. "I never cry like this."

"It's alright, Victoria. Just tell me what happened."

"I don't know how, it's not the same as it was."

"Just start from the beginning."

"When he started dating his ex-girlfriend in ninth grade. I never liked her because she bullied him in elementary school and he didn't want to hear it."

"Victoria, both you and I know that is not true," she told me. "I remember when we were going into ninth grade, before he started dating that girl, things were already weird between you two."

She was right. "I don't know why. Hally is the only clear beginning."

"I don't think that is true. I think that you pushed him away."

"That's not fair."

"Why not?"

"We both know how depressed I was. It really isn't fair to just put this all on me, especially with everything. I didn't want to hurt him."

"There is a difference between protecting someone from your emotions and completely pushing them away. Your depression isn't an excuse. If that was your problem, don't you think it would've fixed itself by now?"

"That's exactly why I'm saying that's not the problem. It is him dating Hally and it always has been, and he is just always going to hold that over my head."

"You are going in circles Victoria," Calla told me in an even tone.

"This isn't my fault; it's Hally's!"

"Why are you being so defensive?"

"I'm not! I'm just telling the truth."

"Why did Quentin say that he didn't want to be friends with you anymore?"

"He told me that he gives me more than I give him. He also told me I am a bad friend," I scowled.

"You see, he knows it, too. You pulled away from him, that's what you need to fix," Calla urged.

"Why do you suddenly have an opinion now?" I snapped. "You never gave me your opinion before."

"Because you needed to fix your own problems, but clearly you can't fix this one on your own. You have had way too much time and you still can't see it," she snapped back at me. "You are your own problem, Victoria."

Her tone dug deep into my already aching heart and forced more tears down my cheeks. "No," I sobbed. I swiftly moved my finger to the bright red button on my phone screen and ended the call. My phone shut off and the silence of the empty street filled my ears again.

I stared off into the distance for a moment, the silence filling my mind. My brain became as silent as the streets for a moment and then it all came rushing to my head. I shakily pushed myself off the ground and stumbled home, my head turning in knots.

My hand opened the heavy wooden front door and let me into the house. The Oriental rug in the entrance way caught on my foot and sent me toppling to my knees. I frantically got back up and steadied my body. Cole stood in front of me with his mouth turned into a frown.

"Tori?" he burbled, or maybe my head was augmenting everything I heard.

I waved my hand at him and pushed my way to the stairs, which I managed to make it up. My breaths heavy, I found my way to the bathroom I shared with Cole. I slammed the door and locked it shut. Gripping the counter top, I stared at myself in the mirror.

The girl I saw had puffy eyes and red lips sore from biting them. Her hair covered her pale cheeks and sprawled down her back, exhausted. I touched my eye and the girl's hand went to her face and touched her eye. She swallowed all the words that were sitting there on her lips.

I reached out to her and touched her cheek, but didn't feel my gentle fingertips on my own skin. Instead, they trailed along the cool glass, leaving smudged fingerprints. The girl in the mirror was unfamiliar, not the person I knew myself to be for sixteen years. I finally saw who I was, an unaltered view of myself. Not the joyful eight-year-old or the depressed thirteen-year-old who still thought she was saving everyone but herself. I saw myself for what I had done.

Worthless.

I pulled my hand back from her cheek and felt a sharp sting across my own. I looked, astonished, at my palm and then back in the mirror at the crimson mark forming on my cheek.

I yanked open the medicine cabinet. Baby aspirin, bandages, iodine, ibuprofen. Useless. I desperately slammed open each drawer, hair products and make-up remover, extra toothpaste, soap, shampoo. All useless.

I cursed my fourteen-year-old self for the day I came back from Model UN and threw out the knife I kept hidden, taped to the underside toilet tank cap. I had done it on Calla's orders of course. I still could feel the imprint of Cole's initials on my palm as I imagined the dark wood of the swiss army knife in my hand. Cole had dutifully presented it to me after our dad gave it to him for Christmas. I treasured it for the longest time because my parents didn't know I had it. And then it became my only relief as I clutched it in the shower, blood streaming down my thighs.

And now I didn't have it or anything else to relieve my pain.

The orange of the pill bottle caught my eye, sitting there on the counter, just where I would miss it. *Of course*, Cole's anxiety medication. He had been on the meds for as long as I could remember, though we never talked about it. My mom always took him to his *appointments* but words about where they actually went were never spoken aloud. They were ashamed of him, just like I knew they would be ashamed of me if I went through with it. It wouldn't change how they saw me though, it would just confirm what they thought about their disappointment of a daughter.

I grabbed the bottle, walked backwards until I hit the wall and slid to the ground. I turned the bottle over and over in my palms, the tiny pills rolling back and forth. *Maybe you should just take the whole bottle, it surely won't be painful that way.*

You ruined your own life, it's your job to fix it.

Just get it over with! My head screamed.

I pressed down on the white cap and turned my hand. The bottle burst open with the pressure of my grip and the pills went rolling in all directions. I got onto my hands and knees and started collecting them as fast as I could. The lock in the bathroom door clicked and the door slammed wide open, hitting me in the side.

"Tori!" Cole gasped.

I looked up at him, eyes wide. The color had left his face, a single tear rolled down his cheek and he clutched a bobby pin in his right hand, used to pick the lock. "It's not what it looks like," I breathed. "I just dropped—"

"It's not?" he yelled.

I got to my feet and ushered him into a hug. He obliged and threw his arms tightly around me. I pressed my face into his hair and let out a tearless sob, a wave of disbelief consumed me.

"Don't leave me, Tori!" Cole cried into my chest. "You can't leave me."

"I'm sorry Cole." I breathed in the scent of his shampoo. His sweet smell was so familiar to me I only noticed it if I tried. He smelled like spring flowers and Halloween candy, smiles, and trying to wash the cat on a rainy summer day. It hadn't changed for years. No matter how much each of us changed, he was my constant. This was my home, my life. And Quentin was my home. "I'm here. I am staying here."

A surge of energy pushed my shoulders up and each breath filled a space that felt clear for once. I would fix this, no matter how long it took.

WEEKS WENT BY where I couldn't talk to him over fear of him not accepting my apology, weeks of approaching him and turning around, and unreciprocated smiles in the hallway, and awkward conversations in history class where he wouldn't even look at me. Weeks of me worrying when I didn't see him in the cafeteria, but helpless because I couldn't do anything about it. Those days where I would stare at Hally all of lunch forcing myself not to walk up to her and ask her if he was okay and instead forcing Oda to text him and always receiving an incomplete answer. One day I even took Oda's phone to text him myself. Moments later I saw his response: "Tori, I know it's you."

Even before then, despite the distance between us, something inside me told me I still had him as my best friend, but during those weeks I felt him pushing me away more than he already had. I tried and tried, spending my nights lying in bed, drafting speeches to give to him in my head, but every time I saw him my mouth locked shut and my throat dried up. So, I decided to write him a letter.

One day after school I approached him in the courtyard, letter clutched tightly in one of my hands. "Hi Quentin," I ventured. He didn't look up from his bike, fiddling with the already unlocked chord around it. "Can we talk somewhere, Quentin?" I asked, my throat catching on my words.

He looked up from his bike and nodded slowly. Without saying anything, he led us to the park by our school, walking carefully next to me and wheeling his bike along with him. He stopped at a bench in the park and leaned his bike against it, then sat down on the bench leaving room for me to sit beside him.

I didn't sit, just handed him my letter and stood back. "Read it," I told him.

Dear Q,

I'm so sorry for fucking things up. I really did fuck things up, didn't I? I am not writing this letter to you to make excuses for my mistakes, but I just want to let you know that I really was in a super dark place in middle school and I couldn't bear to let you feel it, even if you did anyway. I thought I was saving you and saving our friendship, but really, I was so selfish and so blind. I just wanted to fit in, to not be me and to get rid of everything wrong with me. Middle school does that to us doesn't it? It was so damn hard for me. I understand now how hard it is for so many people, that I wasn't alone. Now I know that all I need is you.

I can't apologize enough for everything that I've done. I am so sorry for pushing you away after I came out, even though you were always just there for me. I am sorry for not listening to you and for not being supportive. I am sorry for being stubborn and not understanding what I did wrong. I am so sorry. I am so sorry for blaming everything on Hally and influencing you to make decisions that you wouldn't have made otherwise. If you like her, I'm sure she is okay. I'm sorry for any mistakes I am forgetting and I'm sorry for even forgetting them. I am just so sorry for pushing you away. I have loved you just as much the entire way through, and I can understand if you can't forgive me. I am trying to change.

Quentin, you are my everything, I want you to know that and remember that. Nothing else should matter,

As he read, he squinted at my letter with a furrowed
brow, the side of his mouth turned down. After a minute
his face relaxed and the corner of his mouth turned up
a bit. When he had been reading for a while, he sighed
and his eyes smiled down at the paper. When he
finished, he looked up at me and grinned, then quickly
pulled the smile off his face. "I gotta go, Tori," he gave
me a half smile, watching me pacing in front of him with
his big green eyes.

I nodded, my heart racing with uncertainty. I
wanted to shake him until he told me what he was
thinking. I guess reading it was all I could ever ask from
him, and now I didn't have to live knowing that I hadn't
tried. At least I tried.

Quentin slung his backpack over one shoulder and
quickly hopped onto his bike. I watched as he rode away
and tried not to feel disappointed that my letter hadn't
worked. I tried to feel happy that he knew everything
and just maybe I would get to feel close to him again.

Then the next day, Quentin brushed by me in the
hallway and pressed a piece of paper into my hand.
Immediately knowing he had given my letter back, I
squeezed it tightly and resisted the urge to chase after
him. I shoved the piece of paper in my pocket and
trudged to my next class. I couldn't think of anything
else besides him for the rest of the day. I probably

retained no information in any of my classes, not that I do normally.

In history class Quentin actually looked at me and gave me a smile. I frowned back at him. Now he was just being cruel, riding away the day before without saying anything, giving me my letter back, and now smiling at me?

He furrowed his eyebrows at me and pretended to scribble on his hand. I pulled the crumpled piece of paper out of my pocket. It was folded neatly into quarters and on the front said, "*Tori*" in Quentin's handwriting. I looked back up at him and he grinned. I bit my top lip, trying not to shout, and shoved it back into my pocket.

After school I walked as fast as I could back to my house, wanting to read the letter in the privacy of my room. I ran up the stairs, slammed the door of my bedroom and threw my backpack on the ground. I settled into my bed and carefully opened the letter.

Dear Tori,

I was a jerk too. I'm sorry. Meet me, you know where.

> *Love (with all my heart),*
> *Quentin.*

A smile spread across my face as the words reached my eyes. I jumped up from my bed and danced around my room to the music I still had playing in my earbuds from my walk home, kicking my legs back and forth, and pumping my fists in the air. I had Quentin and that was good enough. I went to my garage and pulled my bike out from behind all the boxes that had piled up in front of it, then I rode as fast as I could to the clearing, beaming the entire way there.

When I arrived at the clearing, I saw Quentin sitting against the hemlock tree, bike propped up next to him. I threw down my bike and ran at him, breathing hard, my smile pressing at the edges of my face. "Took you long enough," he said nonchalantly.

I laughed and grabbed him under his arms, forcing him to stand up and then pulled him into a hug, squeezing him as tight as I could. "I missed you so much."

"I know," he said between strained breaths, "but I can't breathe."

I let go of him, then pulled him into a looser hug, "I'm sorry," I whispered into his shoulder.

"I know," he said casually.

I pulled away from him and smiled again, "shut up." I punched his arm.

He wrapped his hand around the spot I punched, "Hey, my bones are weak. You must be very careful. I am like Humpty Dumpty."

"Yes, King Quentin the egg, who fell off a wall and died. Pretty accurate," I joked.

He laughed, "What?"

I smiled at him and walked to the middle of the clearing. The sky seemed like it went on forever, pulling me into its expanses and making me wonder about the vastness of the world. Storm clouds approached in the distance, but I just spun around and listened to the birds chirping in the trees. I laid down in the middle of the clearing, not giving any thought to the damp soil that pressed into my white tank top and light-blue shorts. I took a breath in and closed my eyes, resting with the sun beating down on my face and taking in the perfection of the day. And in that moment, I wished for time to stop and keep me there forever. I had Quentin. He had me.

He lay down next to me, placing his head on my elbow. "I missed this," he whispered.

I turned to look at him, "Are you going to be okay?"

"You mean my health?"

I nodded.

He shrugged, "I guess we can't really know at this point, but I have always gotten better. And there is no use worrying about it."

I placed my arm over his chest and scooted down to rest my head on his shoulder, "Whatever you need. I am here for you." Then I moved off of him and placed my hands behind my head and stared up at the great blue sky. "Who knows if any of us are going to live past twenty anyways, right? The world might kill us by then."

"Exactly," he agreed. "Why can't we just be happy with the time we have."

"I'm sorry I wasted so much time," I told him.

"It's okay we have plenty left." He thought for a moment, "I will keep making my comics and I will become a famous comic book artist. I am going to live in some big city. I'm thinking San Francisco for most of the time and the rest of the time working on the movie adaptations for my comics and traveling around doing book tours. Eventually, I will find 'the one', and I will have made enough money for us to buy a house in San

Francisco and have kids. And I will visit you in Montana as much as I want to."

"Your mom would be so proud," I laughed, "San Francisco."

"And you will do the same with your writing. I think you have so much potential," he paused, "maybe not as much as me with my comics."

I bumped my shoulder into him, "Shut up, Q."

"And you will live in Montana to inspire you and your only joy all year round will be my visits to you. And you will be a great aunt to my children."

"That sounds good."

"Of course, all of this is if the earth doesn't explode before then."

I grinned at the sky, letting Quentin watch my face fill with joy, "I'd like things not to change. I would give anything to freeze this moment with you, Q. To just be able to have you here with me forever. I don't want to grow up; I just want us riding bikes at sunset and laying in the clearing talking and talking about the world and our dreams forever. We have so many memories here. I wish there was a way I could just keep them all in our box so I can hold them whenever I miss you in Montana."

He laid back beside me, "God, Tori. You even speak more poetically than I can write." He sighed and let out a little chuckle, "You could freeze us forever."

"How?" I asked.

"Write it all down. So, we can always remember all the moments we have had together. Like those papers, you always put in the friendship box but write it all out and we can always read it."

"I am not nearly a good enough writer to capture what we have. It would be impossible. I don't want that, Quentin; I just want us."

He sat back up on his elbow, "Hey. You know my birthday is on Friday. I am getting my driver's license."

I sat up as well and looked at him, "Really?"

"Yep, you wanna come with? Mom is taking me, she thinks this is her special moment, but I'd really like it if you would come," he rambled, "I mean and so would my mom. She is always talking about how much she misses you. We would really both like it if you would come." I put my hand on his forearm, feeling his very rare lack of confidence. "I'm in."

"I have an idea."

"What?"

"Let's ride that way." He lifted his finger and pointed in the opposite direction from town.

"Umm, there is no trail that way."

"So?" he shrugged his shoulders and got up off the ground. He ran over to his bike and swung his leg over the seat.

"Hey!" I yelled after him as he pedaled away.

"Catch me if you can!" He crowed, his voice echoing through the woods.

I hopped onto my bike and pedaled hard until I caught up behind him. "I wouldn't want to hurt my Humpty Dumpty," I joked and then pushed past him.

"If I'm Humpty Dumpty then who are you?"

"Queen Victoria, of course!" I yelled behind me.

I heard his laugh and the cracking of the sticks as he closed in on me. "You're dead," he told me, flaunting the double meaning of the sentence.

I picked my hand up from the handle bar and flipped him off. I quickly ducked out of the way of a branch that almost hit me in the head, but kept moving. Our pace in the woods certainly wasn't as fast as on the trail, we kept hitting roots and getting stuck in places where we couldn't get through the trees.

Eventually, out of breath and laughing, we stopped and sat down on a fallen tree. "This was one of your worst ideas," I breathed.

"I'll admit it, but we had never gone farther than the clearing. Curiosity killed the cat," he chuckled to himself.

I looked down at my hands, "I'm sorry."

"It's fine! I know it was a bad idea," he shrugged.

"No, I mean for being so awful."

"I forgave you, Tori. I told you that. All I wanted was for you to let me in."

"I can't. I love you too much." I rubbed my hands together and resisted looking into his eyes. "I want to, but I can't."

"Tori, that's so stupid."

I held out my hand and showed him the thin, white, jagged scar across my palm. "This is where it started isn't it?" I asked myself. "Don't you see I'm broken? I can't break you too."

He traced his finger along the scar on my hand, then reached up to my shoulder and gripped it firmly. "I'm not all that held together either, Tori. We're all broken in our own way, you just can't always tell."

"I know. I just still feel like it's my fault."

"It is and it isn't." He grinned, "That didn't come out the way I wanted it to. What I mean is: we didn't exist outside of each other! How were we supposed to be separate people when we never lived separate lives? Friendships are supposed to be simple, it's relationships that are supposed to be complicated."

"I guess it's just love that's complicated," I gazed up at him. For the first time I noticed how different his face had become. Different but the same. It had matured, his jawline and cheekbones were sharper and his hair even looked a shade darker, but his eyes were the same. His eyes were always the same.

We sat in silence for a moment, the trees above closing us in our own little bubble. I heard a noise in the distance, the quiet whooshing noise of a car speeding by. "Did you hear that?"

He nodded, "Thank God we don't have to ride back all that way."

I picked my bike up and walked it in the direction of the car. The confined woods opened up to the big empty road. I turned left, hopped on my bike and Quentin followed my lead. The road slanted into a hill at the next turn and I slowed, letting Quentin catch up to me, then lifted up from the seat and stood on my pedals, allowing gravity to carry me down the hill. I let out a loud "woohoo!" that echoed back and forth into the dimming sky of the afternoon. Quentin pedaled, the slant of the hill propelling his feet on the pedals as he zig-zagged back and forth across the hill next to me.

The wind blew through our hair and on our faces, pushing tears from our elated eyes and the warm golden light of the evening hit the bright hues of the late spring day. Everything inside me knew this moment would last forever, and somehow, I got my wish from the clearing. Infinity. In the clement air between us, connected by our bliss and wonder for the day that had just been, reminding us of the connection that we once had and knew was still there, hiding and holding on tightly. Most days we were both just people, innocent and out of control, full of longing and dark optimism, just trying to live each day at a time. But in our eternal time with one another, we became more. To each other we were not just people, we were the world.

Twenty-Three

"TORI," LEAH SMILED back at me from the passenger seat of the car, "it's so good to see you, hun."

"You too," I told her, my tone light. "And Quentin, as well. I thought when he didn't come to school yesterday. We wouldn't be able to do this."

"I couldn't be sick on my sweet sixteen. It wouldn't be very sweet." Quentin said, taking in a sharp breath.

"I swear this one was so determined to be here he just made himself better," Leah laughed.

Quentin forced a grin, "I'm stronger than you think." He stared intensely at the road in front of him.

"Well, you better pass this test so I can sit in the front seat," I said.

"Oh, I see, you are demoting me," Leah laughed.

"Well, only if this guy can pass his test."

"I'm gonna pass it alright, look at how perfectly I am driving," he told us, nodding at the dashboard.

"You better, because I still can't drive us anywhere," I laughed.

"It'll be nice, your father and I won't have to drive back and forth from the city so much," Leah added.

Quentin pulled into the parking lot of the DMV, parked the car, and unbuckled his seat belt, "Here goes nothing," he said.

After we dropped him and the car off at his appointment, Leah and I sat outside of the DMV chatting about school and my life. "Do you think Quentin is going to be okay?" I asked her after a while.

Her face dropped, "I don't know, but I am glad you are back in his life again. You certainly make him happier and he needs that right now."

"Do you think he should be going to school at all anymore?"

"I am more concerned that if I don't let him go to school, it is just going to make him more down on himself and alone. I just want him to be happy, that's all."

I agreed, "Yeah. It just feels so wrong, it's been years since he has been sick, it's just so surprising for it to happen all over again."

She looked at me confused, "He didn't tell you?"

I shook my head, "Tell me what?"

"He stopped taking his medications. I didn't notice for a while until it became really apparent and I found his full pill bottle in his room." My heart skipped a beat; he made himself sick. "He finally admitted to me what he'd done, but it's just impossible for the doctors to fix. They can't give him more blood than he was already getting, because it could make his organs shut down and they can't give him less because he would just get sicker. The meds were what kept it all under control."

I looked up at her shocked, "Did he tell you why?"

She sighed. "He was confused and angry, like teenagers are and he made a mistake like teenagers do, but I guess he didn't realize the scale of his mistake. He wanted control. You know, for most kids, mistakes like this don't have such large consequences."

I ran my hand through my hair until my fingers got stuck in my ponytail, "I can't believe I didn't see it." I wanted to ask what the "large consequences" were, but I didn't want to hear the answer.

"Don't beat yourself up, it's nobody's fault."

"I just hate that I didn't see this," I murmured, "I usually see everything, like when my brother is having anxiety I can feel it, or when Quentin is angry at me it gives me this buzzing sensation, even if sometimes I choose to ignore it. Or if Oda is acting even slightly off, I can tell. I have just always been able to read people well. I feel like I must have just chosen to ignore it in Quentin."

"It's not your fault Tori, it really isn't," Leah assured me.

"But what if something happens to him?"

"Then it still won't be your fault."

I rubbed circles around the button detail on my jeans pocket. "I just can't imagine—"

"Tori, just stop worrying about it." She held onto my wrist. "Today is a good day. And I have cake waiting for you two at home. Gary is actually a really great cook."

I relaxed my arm and leaned against her, "Thanks for always being so good to me, Leah."

"You are part of our family, Tori, no matter how much you fight with my son."

I turned and wrapped one of my arms around her, "You are the best not-actually-my-mom mom I could ever ask for."

"You are the best daughter I could ever ask for," she squeezed me. "If you ever need anything, I'm here."

I smiled, "So how are things with Gary?"

She chuckled, "They're great, we actually have some big news!"

"Really?" I grabbed her hand, "Oh my God, are you getting married?"

She shook her head, "Actually no, I'm pregnant! It's still early and I'm not twenty anymore, but we're really excited and so is Quentin. He's going to have so many little siblings he's not gonna know what hit him."

"Yeah," I said, releasing her hand from mine. My heart sank with the same heaviness I felt that winter.

She grabbed my hand again, "What's wrong sweetie?"

I looked up at her and felt tears start to well up in my eyes. I wiped fiercely at my face and turned my head away from her to conceal my wet cheeks. She nudged my face up to look at her. The world blurred with tears, distorting Leah's face and everything around her. I tried to take a deep breath in but it just turned into a soft sob. Leah wrapped her arms around my back and pulled me into her again. I wept into her shoulder until the tears stopped coming and relief washed over my body. I pulled away from her when I heard Quentin's chipper voice hovering over me, "Sorry to ruin the moment," he laughed, "but I passed the test!"

Leah and I both jumped up and Leah trapped him in a hug. "I'm so proud of you! My baby boy is so grown up." I stood back blinking hard so hopefully he wouldn't notice my red eyes.

He detangled himself from her arms, "Thanks, Mom."

I held up my hand for a high five, which he dutifully gave me, "Nice job, Q. Now you can be my chauffeur."

"I'm glad that's where you see my value," he joked, not mentioning my tearful face.

"Well clearly nothing else matters," I gave him a big sarcastic smile. "I call shotgun!"

"Driving!" Quentin laughed.

We ran to the car and I jumped into the front seat and slammed the door behind me. Quentin climbed into the driver's seat beside me. He scrunched his eyes together and breathed slowly. "You good?" I asked him. He shook his head up and down as if he could fling the dizziness out of it and then looked up at the windshield smiling.

"Yeah," he forced his lips into a pursed smile, "I'm good."

Leah got into the backseat of the car and buckled herself into the middle one. "Let's get this show on the road!"

Quentin put the key in the ignition and backed us out of the parking spot, then pulled out of the parking lot. I examined the front seat of the car, the old Subaru that Leah had driven for as long as I could remember and carried so many memories with it. I touched a bit of the dashboard that had faded and begun flaking with age. I settled back into the worn-down grey fabric of the seat. "How long have you had this car, Leah?"

"10 years maybe? I think I must have gotten it used when Quentin was in first grade." Leah patted the back of the seat I sat in, "She has been a good car, but is becoming more trouble than she's worth."

I looked over to Quentin who focused super hard on the road and didn't react to anything we said. He turned carefully onto the highway and blinked really hard to clear something out of his vision. I couldn't stop staring at his ghostly white face and, out of instinct, I held onto the side of the car with every tiny bump or jolt.

After a few minutes of driving smoothly on the highway, Quentin's face contorted, he shook his head and blinked hard again. "Mom..." he said slowly.

"What is it hun?" she asked.

"I don't feel good..." he said, still keeping all his concentration on the road, "Really light headed."

Leah sat forward in her seat and placed a calming hand on his shoulder, "Just pull over to the side and pull off the highway," she pointed to where she wanted him to go, "There is an exit right there."

We were in the center lane, going sixty miles per hour on a crowded freeway, which complicated the lane changes and exit for Quentin. I gripped tighter onto the side of the car, trying to stay calm, and not distract Quentin from the road. I concentrated on Quentin as he concentrated on driving.

His hands were as sweaty and clenched as tightly on the wheel as mine were to the side of the car. His eyes determined but pained and his whole face pale and cold, yet soaked with sweat. He made the turn onto the exit ramp and Leah sat back with a sigh of relief, but as I watched him, his eyes became distant and his arm didn't stop making the turn onto the ramp. His eyes closed and his body went limp at the wheel of the car.

Twenty-Four

I CAN STILL FEEL it in slow motion. First, the terror in Leah's eyes as we watched Quentin faint and both froze, not knowing what to do or how to stop what would happen next.

The car propelled itself forward and the weight of Quentin's body pulled the steering wheel right. The car rammed into the barrier of the exit ramp and broke through the railing that was supposed to protect us from falling the 10 feet between the off-ramp and the ground. My seat belt tightened around me and I felt the air bag slam into my chest, preventing me from flying up as the car's nose smashed into the road below us. The glass on the front windshield shattered and blew tiny pieces of glass all over me. I could only hear my heart beat pounding in my head. Each breath I took echoed throughout my body, each one thin and far apart. I could feel my hands shaking violently and I whipped my head around to take in my surroundings.

The car lay on its side. Quentin had been flung halfway out of his seatbelt and his body didn't so much as twitch. A crimson aureole pooled around his head on the asphalt, but I couldn't make out any wounds in my blurry vision. A piece of glass from his window had lodged itself in the side of his cheek and the rest of his window lay in scattered pieces around his head. I couldn't turn my head enough to see Leah behind me.

The bitter smells of blood and asphalt and gasoline filled my nose. I closed my eyes and prayed, for once in my life it was the only thing I could do. I clasped my trembling hands together in my lap, feeling the warmth of my own skin. I took a breath in. *God, you have to be there*, I thought, *please send help, and please let Quentin be okay.* The same words I repeated over and over again in my head. *Dear God, you have to be there, please send help, and please let Quentin be okay.* Over and over and over again, until the words screamed in my head. I couldn't breathe or move from my place in the car. My body was numb. I wasn't sure if it was out of fear or pain, probably both. *Dear God, you have to be there, please send help, and please let Quentin be okay.* I wailed it in my head and began to shake. "HELP!" I screamed.

I don't know how long we stayed there before I heard the distant sirens of the ambulances approaching. When I heard them, I tried to move for the first time. I shakily unbuckled my seat belt and struggled to push open the car door. I tried to climb out, but a shock shot down my arm and I had to let go. I tried again and again, until eventually I hoisted myself out the door.

A man who had been trying to get into the car to help ran over to me and brought me to the sidewalk. He sat me down and asked me if I was okay. I nodded slowly, not actually knowing the answer to his question.

"You have to get my friend, the one driving. And his mom, I didn't see her."

He put his hand on my shoulder and smiled, not saying anything, but helping me breathe for a moment. Two ambulances and a fire truck stopped on the road in front of me, people came running out of them and to the car. As they struggled to get Quentin and Leah out of the car, the man directed one of the paramedics to come talk to me.

She was a young woman, who couldn't have been working for very long. I remember being comforted by the kindness in her eyes as the touch of the man's hand had before. "Can you tell me about your friend and his mom in the car over there?" she asked me.

"Quentin, my friend, he has Thalassemia, it's pretty bad and that is why he fainted. He is sixteen," I stammered. "Today is his birthday." I held back a sob; I had complained just a few months earlier how terrible my birthday was. "Today is his birthday," I repeated.

"And his mom?" The paramedic coaxed.

"She is pretty healthy, I think. She is pregnant... and thirty-seven... I think." I tried to dredge up as much information as I could, but my spinning head made it impossible to think of anything else but the way Quentin had been so limp, blood surrounding his head like a halo. I wished I had helped him, but I got myself out of the car instead. "Please help them," I sobbed, without any tears coming from my eyes.

The paramedic put a soothing hand on my shoulder, "We are trying our best."

This made me even more upset; they were trying their best is what she had said, not that they would actually be able to do anything for them. Panicked thoughts played through my head; my arm that had been numb before began to throb with an unbearable pain. My skin stung in the places where the shattered glass had cut me and my lungs burned from not having any air in them. I let go of the breath I held in my lungs but couldn't force any more oxygen in them.

After that, I think I woke up in the ambulance. I remember being bumped around and looking up at the fluorescent lighting on the shiny metal ceiling, and hearing the noises of yelling around me. The face of a middle-aged male paramedic, white, and brown-eyed, looked over me, and asked me a question.

All that I remember after that is the hospital. I was conscious, but I can't quite remember what the doctor said to me. My mom hovered around me. They were putting my arm in a cast that hugged my skin all the way to my scar. Another doctor cleaned the glass out of the skin on my face and tried to ask me questions about what happened. I don't remember what I told her. The noise and fluorescent lighting made my ears ring until I couldn't concentrate on anything around me.

"We'd like to keep her overnight, to rule out any internal injuries, and for observation, to be safe," the doctor told my mom.

It felt like a fog lifted over my brain, I could think clearly for a moment. Quentin. I saw him lying on the asphalt, the glass from his window surrounding him. I saw his smile there too, detached. I snapped my head up at the doctor and she smiled, glad to see I was alert, "Quentin, is he okay?"

The doctor gave me an assuring smile, "We can get an update on your friend if you'd like."

I gulped air into my chest, "He's alive?"

"Your friend had a serious head injury and some internal injuries when he arrived at the hospital, they took him into surgery, and he has a great team of doctors working on him right now."

It felt easier to breathe for a moment, he was alive. He was alive. He was alive. I closed my eyes and prayed again. I prayed that the doctors working on him were actually great and that I would get to talk to him again and see him again and touch him again, that I would get to feel him breath again and hear his laugh again. I prayed that I would get to be with him again and that he would survive this, that we would all survive this. "And his mom?" I asked.

My mom frowned at me, "Honey, Ms. Flasch was just here. You were just talking to her."

The doctor turned to a nurse and said something to her, the nurse nodded and walked out of the room. The doctor gave me another assuring smile, "We're just going to give you another exam Victoria. Is that okay?"

I nodded, but turned to my mom, "Leah wasn't here. I haven't seen her since we were in the car." I remembered the terror in her eyes as we both watched ourselves being thrown off the highway. My mom tried to put her hand on my arm, but I swatted it off. "Where is she?" I pushed myself off of the bed and started to look for Leah.

"Victoria!"

I frantically looked around the room and then back at my mom, "Where is she? Is she okay?"

I felt the doctor's hand on my shoulder and she led me gently back to the bed. "Your friend's mom is just fine," she told me. "You can see her tomorrow, okay?"

I took a breath. "Okay," I agreed.

They did another exam on me, then decided to move me to a room where I spent the night and so did my mom, sitting in the chair next to my bed with her head resting at my feet.

I didn't sleep much, thoughts of the accident just kept running through my head. Over and over again I replayed it in my mind. There were so many things I could have done, telling Quentin not to drive in the first place, or I could have grabbed the steering wheel to reduce the damage. I could have tried to help Quentin after the crash, or at least found Leah. It drove me insane. I could hear the sound of the car crashing through the barrier, the barrier that was supposed to stop things like this from happening. That was supposed to stop sixteen-year-olds from getting into car accidents that put them in the hospital, under the knife of a surgeon, and stop their best friends and mothers from having to worry if they would live to see the next day, staying up all night, replaying it in their minds, and beating themselves up over every little detail.

IN THE MORNING the doctors took me to see Quentin, who lay barely awake in his bed. I walked into the room, my aching head dizzying me and my throbbing arm held up by a sling. Quentin had been propped up with a couple pillows. His head was wrapped in bandages, covering the incision made by the surgeons. Scattered across his face, deep cuts from glass had been stitched up and covered with tiny bandages. He gave me a weak smile. "You look great," he told me groggily.

I sat down in the chair next to his bed, "You don't look too hot yourself."

He gave me another weak smile. "I don't know what you are talking about. I look better than ever," he croaked.

I took his hand with my uncasted one and shushed him, "Just rest, Q. You need your strength." I laid my head on the bed next to his shoulder. "I'm here," I told him. "I'm not leaving."

We sat there in silence for as long as the hospital staff would allow. The beeping of the monitor told me his heart still beat beside me, that he still lived in my world. I remembered laying with my head on his chest in the clearing, listening to his heart beat, reminding me he was there. He was still with me. I needed that memory. I needed to be able to listen to his heart beat and feel the warmth of his hand in mine, the blood still flowing through his body. He was still alive, still next to me.

"Quentin," I said.

"Mhmm," he replied.

"Do you remember the day the summer before fifth grade when we went on a picnic with my family and my dad told the story about the bear?"

"Yeah," he gave me a knowing smile but then winced, the smile wiped off his face.

"Do you remember the fireflies?" I squeezed his hand, "I remember putting those fireflies in a jar so clearly. I used to call them lightning bugs, but you didn't like that very much, so you forced me to call them fireflies. We caught them and they were so beautiful. I was elated. They filled me with the strangest happiness; I don't even know, Q. Anyway, you really wanted to let them go, you didn't think they were happy in the jar anymore, you thought they wanted to be free. So I finally agreed even though I wanted to keep them forever, but instead we let them go. I remember watching them fly out of the jar, they filled the sky, lighting up the darkness, but they weren't mine anymore and what once brought me so much joy now just made me sad. I missed having them in the jar."

Quentin sighed and gave me a melancholy look that made a part of my heart twinge with sorrow. "I didn't have to say goodbye," he said.

"What?" I asked him.

He shook his head, "We don't have to say goodbye." I grasped his hand in mine, and nodded slowly, pretending that I knew what he meant. Something in me told me he wasn't telling me that we didn't have to say goodbye to the fireflies. Something in his voice made me think I missed an important detail or maybe it was just the pain meds messing with both of our minds.

He moved his mouth to say something else to me, to explain, but I shushed him and told him to get some rest.

I WAS RELEASED from the hospital the next day, but didn't go back to school. I had a pretty bad concussion and my doctor told me I basically wasn't to do so much as to think, but instead I spent most of the days with Quentin and trying to sneak around the visitation rules. My health started to get better rapidly, even my cuts were healing nicely and my arm stopped hurting as much, but Quentin's condition didn't improve. One day he would be sitting up in bed laughing and talking to me and things would seem like they might just be okay, but some days he could barely even keep down his food.

Even on the hard days, I still smiled at being able to sit with him as he slept. Every moment I spent with him I told my brain never to forget and every moment I spent away from him I prayed that he would be okay.

One day around four in the afternoon, I must have been getting something from the vending machine, when I saw Hally standing at the nurses' station. I walked over to her and tapped her on the shoulder, "Hally."

She turned around, "Victoria, thank God. I got lost. I cannot find my way around this place."

"What are you doing here, Hally?" I growled. Spencer and Oda had visited once, and Saul tried to visit every day, but that day wasn't a very good day for Quentin and I didn't really want anyone bothering him. My instinct to protect him was more active than ever and I wasn't willing to let Hally interfere with his health in any way.

"I'm here to visit my friend," she said back, her tone just as mean as mine.

"If you don't remember Hally, he broke up with you a long time ago."

"And that is exactly why I called him my friend," she scoffed. "I'm tired of you pushing me around, Victoria. I thought you had learned your lesson by now."

"Me pushing you around? You are the one who bullied Quentin in elementary school."

She shook her head at me, "Are you not aware how petty you sound." Her voice broke through her facade of toughness. "Quentin is my friend."

"Quentin is *my* friend."

Her voice broke again, "He is his own person." A tear fell onto her cheek, "I have never felt like I needed to explain myself to you, but now I know you just don't understand." Another tear fell from her eye, "It may seem like everyone likes me, but they don't and Quentin was the only one who actually ever cared about me. Except you kept trying to ruin that, because, although he would never say it to my face, I know Quentin cares so much more about you and your disapproval got in the way of us having any kind of relationship." More tears fell silently, "I've accepted that I'm always going to be second to you but he is the only one that cares. He is such a good guy. I just have to see him, Tori."

Before I even knew what I was doing, I had pulled her into a hug. I pushed away from her quickly, making sure that the moment didn't last too long. "Let's go see him."

I walked Hally over to Quentin's room and told her to wait outside.

"Can you just give me a second with him first?" I asked her.

"As long as you don't turn him against me again," she laughed nervously.

I gave her a soft chuckle, then walked into Quentin's room. "Hey," I said quietly. He squinted up at me, it seemed like he had dozed off while I was gone. "Hally is here to see you."

"What?" he exclaimed. "She didn't tell me she was coming!" He ran his fingers through the part of his hair that hadn't been shaved and covered with bandages, and tried to push himself up in bed further. He turned his head to me and raised one eyebrow, "You didn't scare her away, did you?"

I grinned, "No, she is standing outside."

He groaned, "I wish she would have come tomorrow. I look horrible."

I scrunched my face up, "Yeah, well she wants to see you."

He tugged on the oxygen tube in his nose, and flattened the bed sheets over his legs. "Okay," he grinned.

"Hey, Q," I whispered, "I'm sorry."

"I know."

"I know you really care about her," I told him. "I should have given her a chance."

"I love her. Not romantically," he added. "I don't think that was ever meant to be. You were right about that." He looked up at me, "Don't gloat." He paused for a moment, "But I think everyone seriously misunderstands her. Give her a chance."

"Okay, I will."

I went outside of the room and brought Hally back inside. She stood next to his bed with her arms crossed. He tilted his head towards the chair for her to sit down.

"School feels weird without you," she said. I backed out of the room and went to sit in the waiting room until Hally left.

About half an hour later, Hally came and sat down next to me. "Thank you," she said.

"Yeah, no problem, he wanted to see you."

"Did he ever tell you how we became friends?" she asked me.

"He told me that you talked to him on the first day of sixth grade."

She laughed, "No. I didn't talk to him."

"Really?"

"Yeah. On the first day of middle school, I sat alone in our gym class. Everyone else had friends from elementary school and they were all playing catch or something. Quentin and Spencer were racing each other across the field. I was just kind of sitting on the side and holding a ball. All my friends from elementary school stopped liking me when I told them they were all stupid and were going to grow up to be prostitutes. I got that one from my mom," she laughed. "Yeah, I am really good at screwing things up. I was about to cry when Quentin came over to me. He asked me if I wanted to play catch and then I burst into tears. I kept apologizing for everything I had done to him and he just kind of patted me on the back. You know how many times I have messed things up with him, but for some reason he always understands."

"He is too kind."

"Yeah, I didn't really deserve it," she sighed.

I cuffed her elbow with my knuckles, "Hey for what it's worth, I think if he thinks you deserved it, you did. I didn't deserve a second chance either, but he gave it to me."

"You know why we broke up the first time?"

I laughed, "Because I basically pressured him into thinking you were horrible."

"No! Because you were the only subject he knew existed. All the time we spent that summer it was: 'Tori' this and 'Tori' that and, 'you know what I would be doing with Tori right now?' You were all I ever heard about." She laughed, "I couldn't stand it. I basically told him if he didn't stop talking about you and spending all his time with you, we had to break up."

I laughed, "I'm sorry. I've stood in the way too many times."

"It's okay. He loves you. He and I will never have what you two do."

I laughed, "Probably all the kissing interfered."

"Oh c'mon, you know what I mean. Nothing can separate you two. I could tell how broken he was when you weren't talking. He would be just fine without me."

"He loves you, too."

"Yeah, I know," she shrugged.

I squeezed her forearm and smiled, "I guess we are going to have to learn to share."

TWO DAYS LATER Quentin sat up in bed again and laughed along with me.

"It's raining," I smiled and sat down on the edge of the bed.

He grinned back at me, "I love the rain."

"I think it is a good sign."

"I want to go outside," he told me.

I sighed, "I wish you could."

"I can!"

"Quentin, that's not a good idea."

"It's a great idea," he argued. "We always have fun in the rain."

"This is different, you can't even walk."

Quentin's nurse came into the room, "Is everything okay in here?" she asked. Most of the nurses had taken a liking to Quentin and checked in on us much more than they needed to.

"I have a question," Quentin said to her.

"What is it?" she asked sweetly.

"Can Tori take me in a wheelchair, just to get out of this bed for a bit?"

"Well, you have been doing well in your physical therapy. If you are feeling up for it, I don't see why not."

I gave Quentin a look, "Are you sure?" I asked the nurse.

"Yeah, I don't see a problem with it. He should be moving around more, to improve his recovery."

The nurse helped Quentin into a wheelchair and he gave me a huge smile as she did it. When he got in the wheelchair, he said he felt a little light headed, so we waited for it to pass. I wheeled him to the elevator and we got on.

"You're tricking the nurses," I told him.

"No, I'm just withholding my intentions."

"I'm still not sure if I am going to take you outside," I told him. "We're not allowed to leave the hospital."

"Are you going to deny the sick kid his only wish?" He faked a cough. "This could be my only chance to go outside ever again." He coughed again.

"Shut up!"

He raised his hands off his lap, "I'm just stating what we were all thinking."

My heart sank. He thought he might die. I couldn't let him think that. I couldn't even think of it myself, because it wasn't true. "Look how much you have recovered; you are going to be fine."

"I'm still sick, Tori. Let's just be realistic here, okay?"

The elevator stopped. I refused to think about what he was trying to tell me. He wanted me to be prepared for him to die, for him to be gone from my life forever. It was impossible, from day one we were going to be in each other's lives forever; we were going to die together. We had promised. "Let's just go to the rain." The rain would make everything better.

The sliding glass doors of the hospital opened for us and I stepped out into the cold. I took off my jacket and placed it over his shoulders. He took a deep breath in, smelling the earthy scent of the wet rain on the pavement and the mini gardens that lined the edge of the hospital. I didn't step out from the overhang that kept us from getting wet.

"Dance with me," he said quietly.

I looked at him skeptically, "What?"

"Dance with me," he repeated and stuck out his hand.

A song ran through my head, a song that reminded me of a day years ago, when Quentin was sick. I remembered standing in the rain with him and dancing him around, while singing the tune to that song. I took his hand and he started humming the same song that ran through my head. I smiled at him knowingly, neither of us saying aloud what we were both thinking.

I swayed along to Quentin's butchered version of the song, both his hands in mine, him swaying his head along with me. I pulled my phone out of my pocket and scrolled through it to find the song. I hit play and placed my phone on his lap. He grinned and looked up at me, his green eyes bright, the way they were supposed to be. I held onto his hands and danced around in front of him, squatting down low so I could duck under his arms and twirling myself around. He laughed and moved his shoulders slightly to the beat, holding onto my hands tightly and egging on my awkward dance moves.

By the end of the song my breaths were heavy from jumping around and I stood there laughing. The rain pounded on the ground around us, but thanks to the cover above us, we did not get wet. Quentin grinned and I shook my head at him.

The smile faded from Quentin's face and he sighed, the thoughts of why we were there, all coming back. I took a breath, having to come back to the reality that neither of us wanted to face. He let his hands slip out of mine and looked away from me. The rain couldn't wash away everything. I moved behind his wheelchair and grasped the plastic handles. Before I walked us back into the building, I gently placed my hand on his shoulder and gave it a loving squeeze. Given everything I felt, I couldn't imagine what he was having to endure.

THE NEXT DAY he got sicker, and even more the day after that. The date he was supposed to go home kept getting pushed back, until we couldn't see the light at the end of the tunnel anymore. He just kept getting worse and every part of me that believed the rain had helped the first time was diminished. I spent every day ignoring the pain because that's how you have to get through things that you don't want to get through in life. I just sat with him in silence most days and we didn't speak. The school year ended and we were officially done with our sophomore year of high school, yet neither of us had gone to school a single day in the month of June.

It was a Tuesday when I fell asleep with my head resting on his bed. "Tori," he woke me up with his groggy voice. "Tori, I'm scared."

I looked up at him and took his hand, "It's going to be alright."

His face contorted and tears in his eyes glinted against the bright sun shining through a crack in the blinds. "I can't breathe."

"Do you want me to get a nurse?" I panicked.

He shook his head, "I'm just scared."

I squeezed his sweaty hand that shook in mine. "Just take a slow breath." He closed his eyes and struggled to take a breath. "It's gonna be alright," I repeated, even though I could feel us both thinking that it wasn't. I should have gotten a nurse right then and there, but I didn't.

He attempted to smile at me and my chest ached seeing him like that, but I had to keep him as comfortable as possible. I swallowed down tears and forced a smile. I did exactly what I knew he needed me to do. I played "Down in the Valley" and I stayed with him. Quentin gave me a soft smile and looked my face over. His eyes didn't feel like his eyes anymore, there was no fire, they were covered with a foggy layer of pain that obscured the brightness that I always saw in him.

I swallowed my tears again and let the emotion of the song cover up my heartache. I remembered all the times we had listened to this song, the first time in the car, me watching him closely as the music drew him in, and for days after that, listening to the song over and over again. The number of times we had listened to that song was immeasurable. Each time it seemed to mean something to Quentin, which eventually made it mean everything to me. I don't know what first drew him to the song, but now it filled me with memories of us, happy and carefree, good days and bad ones, but that day, that Tuesday in June needed it more than any other day.

I felt Quentin give me a weak squeeze of his hand, and I looked up at his pale face. "You sure you don't want me to get a nurse?" I asked him.

In the moment before he responded I recognized the look in his eyes, the look I saw on the day we met. Except this time the desperation was fleeting, he resigned himself to the fear and hopelessness. He shook his head and closed his eyes to listen to the song again, leaving me deeply unsettled. I rested my head on his shoulder and held tightly onto his hand, praying. Praying to have us again. Praying that some force could bring me the Quentin I knew. Praying that he wouldn't slip away. Praying because it was the only thing I had left to do.

The song played over and over again and eventually, I began to doze off, letting the song keep him there for me. I hadn't been able to sleep those past few days unless I could feel him breathe next to me and hear his heart monitor telling me that he was still there.

I swear one second, I was awake with my head on his shoulder and the next there were alarms going off next to my ear and people were running into the room. I stood up frantically and looked around, Quentin was unconscious and there were people bringing in carts full of medical supplies. My heart thumped in my chest and I backed away from the bed, letting them get to him. I felt someone's hands on my shoulders, pulling me out of the room. Pulling me away from Quentin. I pulled back against them, struggling to stay in the room with him. Struggling to stay with him. I didn't want him to be alone. The world spun and all I could hear was the sound of the alarms going off. The hands pulled me out of the room and into the hallway. The door swept shut behind me.

I pulled back, and banged on the glass, pressing myself up against the window that led into his hospital room. I screamed for him. I told him I was still here and to hang on for me. The hands tried to pull me away from glass and lead me into a different hallway. I resisted, tears streaming down my face and screaming things that weren't even words.

Leah came walking down the hallway. She walked over to me and a look of pure anguish appeared in her hazel eyes. She shook her head, and looked in the glass window of his room. A sob tore its way out of her body, drawing her sorrow to the floor and tearing up her heart for the second time in just weeks. She was witnessing the unimaginable. I watched her, the tears falling from my eyes, silently.

The hands that had just tried to lead me away, made their way to Leah, to help pick her up off the floor and to lead her away from the unimaginable sight she had just seen. The door of his room burst open; the doctor's voices frantic. They wheeled him out, one doctor sitting on his body, and pressing urgently on his chest, up and down, up and down, pushing the blood through his body for him because he couldn't anymore.

I didn't run after him. I couldn't. I couldn't move for fear of changing the outcome of the situation in any way. I ached with regret. How could I have fallen asleep and not called the nurse for him? He told me he was just scared. He was scared of this and now it was happening. The hand was back, leading me away from his room, away from him. I let myself be led away and sat down next to Leah in the waiting room.

Time passed so slowly, every second felt like a century, every minute an eternity. All I could do was look up at the clock, 2:31, and look back down, fidget with the edge of my sweatshirt, then look back up at the clock, 2:31, over and over again, 2:43. My whole body was weak with fear. My hands wouldn't stop shaking. I looked up at the clock. 2:44. I stood up and sat back down. I looked at the clock. 2:44. I tapped my foot on the floor a couple of times. I looked up at the clock. 2:44. I stood up again. I looked at the clock. 2:44. I took a couple of steps. 2:44. I focused on my shoe laces for a moment, their frayed edges bothering me. 2:45. I walked back to my seat and sat down. 2:45. I played with the edge of my sweatshirt again. 2:45. I got up and sat in a different chair. 2:45. I scouted for a better chair, the one I sat in slanted to one side. 2:46. I went and sat in a different chair. 2:46. This one had a lump in the back rest. 2:46. I switched chairs again. 2:46. This one's arm rest jiggled when I touched it. 2:47. I stood up again. 2:47. Leah told me to just choose a chair. 2:47. I told her they were all uncomfortable. 2:48. I sat down next to Leah. 2:48. This chair had a screw that stuck out just the tiniest bit. 2:48. I tried to twist the screw back into place. 2:49. Leah took my hand. 2:49. A doctor asked for the family of Quentin Flasch. 3:34.

Leah jumped up from her chair and rushed towards the doctor. I followed closely behind her. The doctor was a middle-aged Black man, with salt and pepper hair tucked neatly under his scrub cap. He had smile lines engraved deeply into his worn-out face that didn't smile like I wished them to. I strained to read his emotionless expression, to find some hint of what he was going to tell us. My heartbeat sped up, such an emotionless expression on a face that had clearly felt so much emotion in its lifetime made unsteady. His emotionless face will forever be etched into my mind like the shadow of a smile in his skin.

"Can you two come with me?" he asked, leading the way to a small room. He motioned for us to sit in the chairs that were set up around a table in the middle of the cold room and let the heavy door slide into place and click shut behind us. I sat on my hands, trying to keep them from shaking, but instead my entire arms were just quaking with my fear.

The doctor sat down in the chair across from us. Leah gripped my leg with her sweaty hand. The thick walls of the room muted the buzz of the hospital around us. I stared closely into the doctor's face to see any hint of emotion, any hint of hope in his eyes. It wasn't there. His eyes remained blank; he wasn't allowed to feel the emotion of the news he was about to deliver us, and I knew exactly what he was about to say, even before the remorse spread across his face.

Organ failure. Heart failure. There was nothing else they could do.

My mind disappeared from my body, it became foggy and far away. I watched us from behind. The girl remained stiff and unmoving, her body and mind in shock from the news she denied would come. She refused to hear the words that fell out of the doctor's mouth. Not a single part of her moved, not even one of her long brown hairs, knotted with her anxiety, and pulled into a ponytail. The woman next to her, his mother, collapsed into herself, broken again, her heart torn out of her chest. She gripped onto the girl's shoulder, to hold herself up, the misery of the news beckoning her to give up. The girl still wouldn't move, couldn't move. She tried to take a breath, but the air clung to her throat, refusing to let her breathe, to let her live. She choked on her breath, her body willing her to live, but her mind refusing to obey. There was something missing from her, something she needed to survive, something as crucial as her heart. Something was gone.

I looked at Leah and back at the doctor, who had pushed a box of tissues across the table at us. All of a sudden, I felt my chest burning with a sensation like I was drowning. I gulped for air that wouldn't enter my body. I tried to breathe.

I stood up from my chair and backed away from the table, the world spinning around me, my heartbeat pounding in my head. In a moment, I could breathe again, but those breaths quickly became fast and weak and I choked on the air again. The most basic need for life, refusing to keep me alive. I backed up until I ran into the wall of the room and I slid down it, trying to slow down each of my breaths.

I lay my head between my knees. I took a deep breath in and let it out through my teeth. I longed to lay in the clearing one last time. I longed for the light in my life to be returned to my side. I slammed my fist against the ground, enraged at a world that took away all the memories we were meant to make, all the beautiful moments that he wouldn't experience. Moments that I had imagined for years, saying goodbye before we left to go to college, not wanting to let go of each other, but excited for the prospect of the future. I wanted to go see his first apartment and stand in the back of his first comic book signing with a smile across my face. There were too many moments that we were missing, and so much time that we had wasted arguing with each other instead of making more memories that I could cherish with him. There was so much I missed, so much I could have done. So much he gave me, that I never gave him. I planned to give him the world, because he deserved it. He deserved the world and now he is gone from it.

Quentin is dead. I hit myself on the head with the heel of my hand. *This isn't possible.*

I clapped my hands over my ears; they felt like their insides were leaking ice water, and I held onto a head that wasn't mine. The cheeks that pressed against my palms weren't there, it was just an unrecognizable weight in my hands. The only sensation I could feel in my head was the scorching cold of my ears.

How could I live anymore?

He promised me that we would die together, he promised he would not leave me alone in the world

without him. My soul had been torn in two, part of it
taken from me, leaving me broken in my own darkness.

Afterward

"It's so much darker when a light goes out than it would have been if it had never shown."

John Steinbeck

PEOPLE ALWAYS TALK about the seven stages of grief, how we all process differently. Quentin told me about the seven stages one winter day when my aunt died. People always talk about living our lives the way the people we lost would have wanted us to live. Quentin would have told me to be happy, I know that. The problem is when the impossible actually happens, none of that matters anymore. When the impossible happened, I couldn't even recognize my own feelings let alone try to deal with them in set stages. Quentin's wishes, whatever they were, didn't feel like enough to pull me out of the darkness, and certainly not enough to move on.

Yes, I know it's not helpful to wish things turned out differently. But that doesn't change the fact that sometimes all I can think about is how life would have been if he were here. Every moment he is missing. His voice singing "happy birthday" and his smile next to mine in pictures. In all the moments he should be there I can feel him.

There are times when I want to go back and yell at us as children for even considering that everything would fall into place the way it's meant to. But we were so young and so contently innocent that we couldn't comprehend the pain. And sometimes all I wish is to go back to before.

Because in the days after his death my mind became blank, the world turned dark and blurry and I could only hear my heart pounding. It was as if I had just woken up at 3am from the deepest sleep, and my body urged me to get out of bed. I was stumbling around in the darkness, barely able to stand up and trying to get where I knew I had to go. My hearing and sight almost completely impaired, I would stumble around the house until, moving on pure instinct, I would crawl back in bed and hardly remember it the next day.

Navigating the world without him seemed impossible.

I didn't sit shivah. I couldn't go back to that house after the day of the funeral. The funeral, which I can't remember, just the buzzing sensation that filled my head when I saw how bland it was. It didn't make sense to me that this thing meant to honor him was so unlike him. He wanted to have his ashes scattered in the clearing so we could be there together forever, not to be buried in the ground among hundreds of bodies, but truly alone. We wanted our deaths to be imperfect in the same way our relationship was not polished, exactly like everything else in this world.

After the funeral, we went to Leah's house for the wake. At the wake everyone seemed to be appropriately grieving, but my chest still clenched with anger until Leah hugged me.

She looked so frail in her black dress; her face looked 10 years older than it did before and her hair seemed to have greyed overnight. I tried to look down, to not look into her eyes full of loss, to not be reminded of him more deeply than I had allowed myself before. But she nudged my chin up with the side of her finger the way she had done many times before, a motherly gesture, not meant for me but for her son, and the child she was meant to have. In the crash, Leah had not only lost her son, but her unborn baby as well. I was all she had left, a daughter that wasn't even her own.

I couldn't take the forlorn look on her face and pulled her closely into me, embracing her thinning body in my arms. She relaxed into me and gripped my back with her flat palms. The room buzzed around us, but we held onto each other, both not wanting to let go, both feeling him in the other.

When I let go of her, I let go of the only person who felt his absence the way I did, she had a piece of him in her just like I had him in me. Neither of us cried like we were supposed to, but instead brought him alive again with the memories we had of him. We recounted numerous days that we had spent together, and the stupid jokes he always made. We laughed about the adventures we had, like when we got lost in the woods, or when Quentin forced us to go on every ride at the theme park, no matter how much Leah tried to chicken out. No one else bothered us, or tried to join our conversation, they all understood that we had to hold onto the pieces of him we still had.

"Tori, he cared about you so immensely."

"I know, and you, too. You are the best mom anyone could ever ask for."

Her voice shook with laughter before dissipating, "When you two were in seventh grade, he came to me, asking for advice. He asked me what to do if you came out to him. He didn't want to hurt your feelings and he wanted that moment to be perfect for you. I was so proud of him for knowing that it was okay that you were who you are and for caring about you enough to ask his mom for advice, being a teenager and all. I told him to just tell you that he loved you."

I laughed but tears rolled down my face. "You know what? He did exactly that." I smiled through my tears.

"Really? I didn't think he would execute our plan."

I nodded, "but then he kissed me." It felt so strange to share this piece of information with his mother, a piece of information that I had never told anyone, not Brayden, Oda, or even Calla.

A smile emerged on Leah's face. She placed her hand on her chest, "That boy, that boy had so much confidence."

"He had no fear."

"He had a sort of fire," Leah agreed.

I nodded, "He was my light."

At first, I convinced myself that I had to accept his death, move on, like I would any other bad thing in my life, but every day it felt as if I was losing him even more. Even though I spent most of the summer locked in my bedroom, each day that I didn't spend with him made me remember how much I didn't have him. Each event that he should have been at made it feel like the world had moved on without him, and I needed to stop that from happening somehow. I wanted to hit pause on the world and stop losing him.

I had to move on, is what my mom yelled at me when I wouldn't get out of bed one day in late August. She told me that there was no use in sitting and doing nothing and that it was time that I moved on. I had become lazy and gained weight. If I didn't live my life, this would be permanent and I would have no future.

For a while this seemed appealing. To let myself go. Why should I even have a future without him? He didn't get one and I didn't want one either. He promised me we would be in the afterlife together and that wasn't true. It brought me back to the darkest times, when death seems more appealing than life. I lost sight of survival, the most basic human instinct.

It seemed impossible to move on from that part of my life, a part of myself, to leave him behind, it wasn't right. I couldn't fathom living in the world without being reminded of him every time I see a comic or hear The Head and the Heart on the radio. I couldn't move on from him because he was a part of me and I was never going to let that go. But with every passing moment, pieces of him fell away.

Then, one fall day in late October, I walked into my house after school, when I had the sudden urge to go into the garage. I opened the door on the side of the house and went in. We only had one car in our two-car garage because my mom preferred to park her car on the street in front of the house, so we used the second half for storage. I pushed a couple of boxes out of the way, knowing exactly what I wanted.

I pulled it out, untouched since the day before the accident, when I had rode home from school on it, disappointed that Quentin hadn't been at school to ride with me. Frustrated about his disease, his constant absence from school and that our conflict hadn't felt completely resolved yet, I had shoved the bike back behind a bunch of my mom's boxes.

I wheeled the bike out of the garage and examined it in the front yard. It was a birthday present that my parents gave me for my twelfth birthday, the exact one I had told my mom to get for me, white with purple markings and a black seat. An emptiness hung beside me, Quentin's presence missing next to me. I started to pedal down my street, my brain running memory after memory of us through my mind, my chest aching, now even more than ever, with the palpable absence of him all I could see. As I got to the top of a hill, the hill where our first accident had happened, I could see the car coming and hear his voice yelling after me.

I pedaled even faster, trying to escape him as we had always done with our problems growing up, run off to the clearing. But we had done it together. I had let the loss manifest for so long, not wanting to even take a tiny step because I would lose him even more, because I wanted to hold onto all the little moments, like the times at lunch where he would have made a joke and I probably would have told him to shut up, but instead we just all stayed awkwardly silent. In the moments when I laid down in my bed to go to sleep and I had lived another day without him, I felt his loss the most. It was not his funeral, or even the day he died that made me truly feel like he was gone, like my world had been changed forever, but that day in October, riding my bike for the first time since he died, that made me understand I wasn't going to have those moments with him next to me ever again.

I took a huge breath and turned onto the street that led to the start of the path we had ridden so many times, that it almost felt like muscle memory to me when I arrived in the clearing. I threw my bike on the ground, lifted my hands up to the cloudy sky and let out a huge cry. I yelled and screamed. I couldn't tell if it was out of joy or pain or just pure inexplicable emotion. The wind blew my limp arms around above my head. I closed my eyes and despite the frigid air around me, I felt warm. I felt him. I felt him everywhere. I felt the opposite of what I felt on the bike, not the loss of him forever, but the realization that there were still parts of him everywhere.

The memories were as palpable as his absence. I could see us laying in the middle of the clearing, me with my head on his chest, matching my breaths with his. Or having a debate about God and the afterlife. Or wrestling on the ground and laughing about the moon. Or devouring squished watermelon out of a bag with our backs pressed against the hemlock tree.

I was never going to be able to lose him completely, because, like I have said so many times, he is a part of me. Our story is written all over, here in the clearing, in the park where we had a snowball fight the day my aunt died and I sat on a bench nervously trying to tell him that I was bisexual a few years later. Our story is written in the field where we caught fireflies in a jar one night the summer before fifth grade, where we sat in the middle of the field, our heads pressed together, admiring their beauty and then letting them go, observing their freedom and contemplating our own.

I lay down in the middle of the clearing and matched my breaths to the heart beat of the forest. As the afternoon turned to dusk, I started to ride home, but not before making one last stop.

I leaned my bike up against the railing of the front porch and pushed myself up the steps. I knocked on the door quickly, afraid I would chicken out, and just ride home. Voices from inside echoed through the door and I started to turn around when Leah opened it. "Tori?" she asked.

"Hi," I said timidly.

She didn't say anything for a moment, she looked exhausted, even more so than she had the last time I saw her, but I could feel her warmth. "Come in," she told me hesitantly.

I stepped into the house and saw Gary sitting on the couch watching TV. It felt wrong for him to be there, the house had changed so much. Leah's plants were all gone or dead, and the layout of the house changed; everything was in odd places and the decorations I knew had disappeared. It felt more masculine and bleak than it had before, less like a home. And the couch Gary sat on wasn't the same brown couch that was flattened from years of use, but one with thick blue cushions that looked fresh and put together.

"Can I find something? In his room?" I asked Leah.

She nodded and I headed into his room. The door was shut and when I turned the knob to open it, I realized that this was the only part of the house that had been left unchanged, untouched. My chest ached again, the room still waited for him to come home, trinkets in strange places, bed unmade with one pillow on the floor and clothes piled in one of the corners. The room had been waiting for him for months, and no one had told it to give up.

I placed the pillow back on top of his bed and pulled the sheets up so they were neatly in the right place. I walked over to his bookshelf to retrieve what I had come to get, our box. I reached up to the top of the shelf, where we had put it so we wouldn't be able to see inside, and pulled the box down. I placed it on his bed and sat down next to it. The box was a cardboard shipping box, still covered with the tape from when the box came in the mail so many years ago, but now flapped halfway open.

I sat on his bed and stared at it for a while, remembering the day we made it, the day of the first accident. I struggled to remember what he put into the box for me and longed to go back to that day. I lifted it up off the top shelf, much heavier than when we put it up there, its contents peaked out of the top of it. Neither of us had moved the box since the day we made it, we just had stood on chairs to place new items inside. I brought it over to the bed and tipped it over, breaking another promise we had made to each other.

The contents of the box were mostly trinkets and memories. I picked up the soccer ball keychain he put in for me the day we made it and held it to my chest. I pulled out a yellow piece of cardstock that had notes written to me, wishing me a speedy recovery after my accident. I found a small stone in the pile of trinkets and, next to it, a twig which had miraculously stayed intact for eight years. I picked up a stack of pictures and removed the rubber band off them. They were from the day we went dress shopping the summer before eighth grade. Leah must have printed them out for us.

In my pictures I made fake modeling poses and spun around in circles with the dresses that had flowy skirts. Underneath there were a few of Quentin in the dresses he allowed us to take pictures of, the best one with a horrified, yet amused look on his face as he emerged from the dressing room, the black, yellow, and red dress hanging loosely off his body where it was supposed to define a woman's shape, and the skirt weirdly tilted to one side, because he had no hips to hold it up. I snorted when I came to one of us wearing matching yellow jumpsuits that made us look like bananas.

I skipped through a pile of papers I knew were all from me, my recounts of days that we spent together. Funny memories and such that I wanted to keep together, so I would always know every detail. But mostly to help me win fights when we disputed past events.

At last, I found a letter Quentin had written to me. I pulled it out and opened it. It was written the day he told me we couldn't be friends anymore, the day I decided things had to change.

Dear Tori,

You are never going to read this so I'll be completely honest.

I can't believe what I just did. Actually, I can't believe I am writing this letter to you right now. I guess it is my only way to give myself a proper goodbye to you. What I said, it was all true. I don't want it to be true, but it is. I can't have you as my friend anymore when you refuse to try, but if I said that I would also be saying that I don't want any of what we had.

I have to admit that our friendship was everything I could ever ask for until it wasn't, all good things come to an end, I guess. I cannot be responsible for you anymore when you don't put any effort into being responsible for me. I am writing this to you, even though I know I will never give it to you, because I need this. I need closure. It seems like you don't understand why I broke off our friendship and I could explain to you all day, trying to justify myself and all, but I don't want to do that.

I just feel like I gave you everything I had and at a certain point you stopped giving it back. Since you are never going to see this, I'll just tell you that I need you. I don't know how I am doing this, because I need you. It feels like I've lost sight of everything good in my life. I'm sick again because I just felt so out of control and out of place and I stopped taking my meds. I've always been on them so I guess I never really saw the benefits. It was probably on purpose, but I just can't tell what's going on with my brain, Tori. I wanted to feel in control and like my actions mattered. I guess I am a proper teenager now. I feel so angry all the time.

My final gift to you, although I guess it is really to me, is to tell you what I loved about us, what I needed back in order to keep you in my life. I loved having you uncondi-tionally and the fact that you loved that about me too. When we were little, it felt like we were made *for each other, to be together forever, but somewhere we lost that. You lost that. I guess you seemed to have lost that with everyone. I feel bad for you in a lot of ways, even though I respect you enough not to pity you. I wish I could help you. I have tried. I don't think you just lost the ability to love me unconditionally, but to love yourself that way too. That is why this is so difficult, why I tried for so long to stay by your side.*

But Tori, now it feels like my love for you is giving me so much more pain than it is giving me joy, and I'd like to preserve that joy. Some part of me hopes that you will realize where you went wrong and come back to us, but even then, I am not sure if I will be able to accept your apology because I still don't know how we can make this right. I just know that I have to be happy now. I have to have hope, so I can fix the problem I created.

It's so stupid that I am even writing this, I am probably going to tear it up in the next few minutes. I am just going to write one last thing, I hope you understand.

Goodbye my firefly.

Love,
Quentin

I wiped a tear from my cheek, carefully folded the letter and placed it back in the box. A beat later, I scooped the letter back up and held it gently to my lips, clutching his words in my hands.

"Goodbye my firefly," I whispered back to the words on the page.

Acknowledgements

I first wrote this book for myself, like all my writing before. This story filled a void in my life halted by the lockdown that I desperately needed filled. But the story has grown from scattered scenes of a connection between two pieces of my soul to a saga illustrating two full and intertwined lives.

For my ability to form this story and transform it into the novel that it is, I have so many people to thank. For my amazing friends, I have so much gratitude. For Mia Collins, who showed me what friendship means. For Ruby Lauer, who has always appreciated the idiocy of my humor. For Sam Blattner and Michelle and Angela Seo, my first friends, my siblings, for always. (Extra points to Angela for creating the beautiful cover.) For Anika Venezia, who keeps my spark alive no matter how dark it is.

And to my support in creating this novel. To Christa Cassidy, who was enthusiastic about helping me, no matter how shy I was. To both my parents, who have done everything they can do to turn this dream into a reality. And to my dad, who is a significant part of the "self" when I say that I self-published this novel. And to all the family and friends who asked every step of the way when they could read my book: well, you are the reason I finally published.